They Had Searched the Area near the Mountains

where the plateau broke off abruptly, beginning again after a drop of some 400 feet.

Reluctantly, Scott peered down, careful of his own steps along the edge of the drop. Kirk searched a short distance away; the height was beginning to make him dizzy. . . .

He saw Scott stiffen and draw his head up quickly, and he knew with heartsickening certainty what the engineer saw. He ran to Scott's side, and, clutching his arm, was compelled to look down at what he could not bear to see.

"Dear God, Spock—"

Look for *Star Trek* fiction from Pocket Books

MINDSHADOW

J.M. DILLARD

A STAR TREK® NOVEL

PUBLISHED BY POCKET BOOKS NEW YORK

Another *Original* publication of POCKET BOOKS

POCKET BOOKS, a division of Simon & Schuster, Inc.
1230 Avenue of the Americas, New York, N.Y. 10020

This book is Published by Pocket Books, a Division of Simon & Schuster, Inc. Under exclusive License from Paramount Pictures Corporation, The Trademark Owner.

ISBN: 0-671-60756-1

First Pocket Books Science Fiction printing January, 1986

10 9 8 7 6 5 4 3 2 1

MINDSHADOW

Chapter One

IT WAS LATE afternoon. The sun slid below the mountain peaks that surrounded the mesas on all sides and the sky faded slowly to a dustier shade of blue. Kirk raised a hand to shield his eyes, not from the fiery glow of the setting sun, but from colors so vivid and intense that his optic nerves perceived them as almost painful, like dazzling light: the purple of the mountains, the brilliant blue of the sky, the incandescent golden-red of the vines, which crept up the sharp sides of the mountains and tumbled onto the plateaus below.

Kirk stood with his men on the tallest plateau in the valley, between the towering mountains and the terrain four hundred feet below, a tidy patchwork of fastidiously tilled fields and trellised vines stretching almost to the horizon.

Spock motioned silently with the tricorder, and the group crossed a thick blue-green carpet of vegetation, the humans with their heads tilted back to better drink in their surroundings, the Vulcan with his eyes on the tricorder. They had not gone far at all when Kirk stopped to fill his lungs with cool damp air. "Smell that, Doctor."

McCoy obeyed the order and turned to smile. "Well, I'll be . . . smells like the summer jasmine we had back home. . . ."

"When's the last time you had the chance to smell wildflowers, Bones?"

McCoy rolled his eyes even further heavenward. "I'd rather not think about it, if it's all the same to you. . . ."

"Too long," sighed Scott, his tone approaching reverence. He shook his head wistfully. "I can't believe that anybody would want to destroy this . . . ach, if this place inna a sight for sore eyes. . . ."

Spock looked up at last from the tricorder; he had been studying the readout with such a detached air that it seemed doubtful he was aware of the breathtaking landscape surrounding him. "Atmosphere oxygen-rich, Captain, slightly more than Terran standard." He hesitated for an instant. "Are your eyes troubling you, Mr. Scott?" he asked blandly.

Kirk grimaced. It was impossible to tell if his first officer was taking Scott's remark with typical Vulcan literalness, or merely enjoying some odd private joke.

McCoy responded with disgust before the groaning engineer could reply. "He's just trying to say that it's pretty here, Spock. Of course, I'm sure that's something you wouldn't understand. I'm sure you find that tricorder readout infinitely more exciting."

"I am not incapable of aesthetic appreciation, Doctor," Spock replied mildly, apparently not in the least bit insulted. "However, I must admit to finding certain data in the readout quite fascinating, particularly the concentration of mineral elements in the soil—"

"Later, Spock." Kirk silenced him with an absent-minded wave of his hand, afraid the spell cast by the planet's beauty might be broken. "How long has it been since I've been on solid land like this, near flower, animals . . ."

"Exactly four-point-seven months since our last shore leave," Spock volunteered.

"Too long," McCoy muttered to himself.

Scott's voice was plaintive. "We will be taking shore leave after we complete this mission, won't we, sir?"

"If Star Fleet can't come up with any more last minute distress calls." Kirk's weak smile was unconvincing. "Let's hope for the best, gentlemen."

As the light dimmed, the four came upon a small well-kept vineyard. Spock reactivated the tricorder. "Life form reading ahead, Captain. Humanoid."

Beyond the field of trellised golden vines stood a small hut, nothing more than a mound of dried gray twigs, homely and awkward compared to its glorious surroundings. But the lone being who stood in front of the hut was as striking and deeply colorful as her planet. Her skin was golden, her eyes as purple as the nearby mountains and her brows as sharply upswept. Silver hair spilled down her back onto a cloak the color of the sky. She was very, very old, and her demeanor was that of one whose age has brought her to expect a good deal of respect from her juniors.

As the aliens approached, she rose to her full height of four feet and studied them with hooded eyes. She spoke slowly, neither smiling nor making any form of obeisance. "I am Natahia, the representative of the growers of the Aritani."

Kirk inclined his head slightly in what he hoped suggested respect. "I am Captain Kirk, representative of the United Federation of Planets. First Officer,

Commander Spock. Chief Medical Officer, Dr. Leonard McCoy. Chief Engineer, Lieutenant Commander Montgomery Scott."

She did not acknowledge the polite nods directed toward her. "What protection does the Federation offer us? We do not welcome the intervention of outsiders, but too many of our people have died."

Kirk matched her directness. "We can show you how to shield your planet using a protective device that the raiders' ships cannot penetrate. Mr. Spock and Mr. Scott will install it for you and instruct you in its operation, and Dr. McCoy is here to help your wounded."

Natahia considered this information silently for a moment; when she spoke again, her eyes were full of pride and sorrow. "We are a people who revere the simplicity of life, Captain. We despise technology and its resultant complications, for our ancestors once worshipped it, as you do, and so destroyed themselves. We have learned to let the land provide all we need. But now we are forced to make use of your technology to save our people and our land in order to provide. Please understand that we welcome you with reluctance." She looked sternly at Kirk. "What price does the Federation demand for this service?"

"The Federation asks for nothing. If you wish, Aritani may ally itself with us."

She lifted an arched brow suspiciously. "What benefit is it to us to join you?"

"The Federation represents many planets, with no favor shown to its stronger members. All planets are given a voice. We have banded together because together we are strong. If Aritani joins, it would have a say in Federation matters and would receive the protection of the Federation."

"The affairs of the Federation are of little concern to

us," she said coldly. "What is the penalty if we accept your protection, but do not join the Federation?"

"There is no penalty. Our protection is freely offered, regardless of your decision."

"Aritani then accepts the protection of the Federation, Captain Kirk. Talk to us about the glories of your Federation when the attacks on my people have ceased."

Kirk privately congratulated himself for not matching her coldness. "Very well," he answered politely. "We'll beam down the necessary equipment for constructing the shields. Mr. Scott and Mr. Spock will stay here to assemble it for you and show you its operation."

"And if you can show me to your wounded, ma'am," McCoy suggested, stepping forward slightly.

"Only one still survives this morning's attack. The ships appear so quickly in the sky, as if from nowhere, that there is no time for those working in the fields to hide. Five died this morning, and their fields are scorched, useless." She lowered her eyes. "A terrible thing, to see land destroyed."

Kirk and McCoy exchanged dark glances. Spock, however, appeared not to notice her seemingly greater concern for her land than for her people.

"Cloaking devices, Captain," he said. "It would explain why we detected no vessels in the immediate area."

Kirk nodded. "Spock, can you compute the maximum amount of time that a small pirate vessel could operate a cloaking device without refueling?"

"Certainly, Captain. Of course, it requires an enormous amount of fuel to operate such a device. Depending on the type of ship, I would say no more than seven-point-four-two hours. That is, of course, a rough estimate, based on the types of vessels currently used for surface attacks and known to Star Fleet Intelligence—"

"Thank you," Kirk silenced him. "That is sufficient for our purposes."

"Sir . . . do you propose to trap some of the pirate vessels beneath the shield?"

Kirk smiled. "That is exactly what I propose to do, Mr. Spock."

"What exactly is this shield?" Natahia demanded.

Spock turned to her. "An electromagnetic force that repels any physical object coming in contact with it. The pirate ships will be unable to penetrate it and will therefore be unable to attack the populace on the planet surface. It will also prevent those remaining on the surface after the installation of the shield from escaping."

"And of course," Kirk added, "if we can succeed in capturing one of the pirates, we can locate their base. No doubt it's on a nearby planet or larger vessel."

"Natahia," asked Spock, "do you have any idea why the pirates have chosen to attack your people?"

She tilted her face up at him in a small gesture of uncertainty. "The land is full of many things which are not important to us. Perhaps the pirates value some of these things."

Spock's left eyebrow arched almost imperceptibly. "Perhaps."

Natahia looked with concern at the fading sun. "It will become dark quickly now. Soon it will be unsafe to be outside. Please come inside, gentlemen, while Dr. McCoy attends to the injured grower." She stretched a short arm toward the hut, the regal coldness in her voice melting slightly. "Accept my hospitality."

There was something about the woman Kirk liked in spite of himself. He smiled. "Thank you."

Spock turned to him before they crouched down to enter the low-ceilinged hut. "Captain, I wonder if I might examine the mountains for a moment before I join you. I have found some interesting indications that I would like to verify." His hand touched the tricorder.

Kirk turned to Natahia. "Is that permitted?"

"Provided he does not stay long. When the sun has set, the night animals come out—then it is extremely dangerous to be alone outside."

"My night vision and my hearing are well developed and will alert me to the presence of predators," Spock responded. "And I will not be long."

"Five minutes," Kirk said.

"That should be adequate, Captain." The Vulcan turned to leave.

"Don't stay out past your bedtime," McCoy remarked with exaggerated paternalism.

Kirk and Scott found themselves unable to repress grins. Spock frowned and began to reply, then stopped himself as though suddenly realizing that the doctor's statement fell under the context of what humans labeled humor and was therefore unworthy of recognition. "With your permission, Captain." He walked stiffly toward the now charcoal-colored mountains along the edge of the plateau.

The sky was indeed darkening rapidly and the brilliant colors had faded to shades of gray, but inside Natahia's hut a large fire fed off the abundant supply of oxygen and illuminated the interior with dancing orange-red light. Neat, orderly, primitive. The furnishings were handmade and crude. Natahia motioned Kirk and Scott to sit on the floor before the fire while she led McCoy behind a loosely woven tapestry to examine the wounded man.

Kirk relished the silence as one who never hears a

noise he has lived with all his life until one day it finally stops. The internal hum of the *Enterprise*'s engines, the whine of the turbolift, the flat mechanical voice of the computer . . . he'd never noticed how loud his technologically superior world was, until now, sitting in this very quiet place, listening to the crackle and hiss of Natahia's fire.

Perhaps her people had a point.

"A bloody shame," Scott said into the fire, his face glowing from the heat. He too seemed half hypnotized by the quiet inside the hut.

"What's that?"

"It's just a bloody shame for anyone to think of attackin' these people. They mean no one any harm, and it's such a lovely place."

"I can't remember when I was in a place that was more beautiful."

Scott sighed. "Bein' here almost makes up for shore leave."

"Almost," Kirk agreed. "Tell you what, Scotty. If you and Spock get those shields up and we can be sure we've cleaned up all the pirates caught under it, maybe I can convince Star Fleet to let us kill two birds with one stone and send our people down."

"I'd be all for that, Captain. I just hope that Natahia person wouldn't object. She doesn't seem to be too keen on outsiders—" He broke off as Natahia emerged from behind the curtain.

She gestured toward Kirk. "Your Doctor McCoy says that you may ask Grower Mahali some questions now if you like." She held the tapestry aside for Kirk and followed him into the room, where she watched silently from a corner.

Definitely not one to trust outsiders.

The only light in the room came from a torch that

flickered on the wall. The small form that McCoy hovered over was nearly obscured by the shadows; Kirk could hardly see its wounds, but he realized with horror the overpowering smell which filled the room came from burned flesh, not the wood from the fire.

"Burning phasers," McCoy hissed furiously.

"I thought those had been outlawed by just about everybody."

"They have. Renegades must have done this. I don't even think the Klingons would stoop so low." McCoy's hypospray hissed, and he straightened over the small figure stretched out on a blanket on the floor. "He's coming to now, Jim. He's badly burned and in shock, but he can answer a few easy questions. Natahia says his name is Mahali."

The golden man stirred painfully. Kirk knelt on the floor next to him, swallowing his revulsion as the smell of charred flesh intensified. "Mahali . . . when you were attacked this morning, what did you see?"

Mahali's thin high-pitched voice was cracked and tearful. "In the sky, silver triangles . . . light poured from them, and heat. It burned our crops."

"How many ships?"

"Two. No time to run . . ." His voice became a sob. "My sons . . . my sons . . ."

"Surface fighters," Kirk murmured.

"What are they?" Natahia spoke suddenly from the dark corner.

"A type of vessel used by certain of the Federation's enemies, and also by some renegade pirate groups."

Natahia turned to McCoy. "Can you help him, Doctor?"

"He'll live, Natahia. But it will be some time before he's completely recovered."

She nodded almost gratefully and led Kirk outside to Scott and the fire. He was relieved to get away from the smell of the Aritanian's burns.

"Grower Mahali had five sons this morning," she said softly. "Now he has none."

Scott stood up in his place in front of the fire. "It's a terrible thing that these raiders have done to your people, ma'am. This is a lovely place and I kinna understand why they would want to harm ye or your land. But you can believe Captain Kirk when he says that we'll put an end to it."

"I hope that you are right. I cannot understand them myself. They take nothing from us that I can see. They kill the growers, then destroy the crops and the land. They do not even eat the food. It is a horrible waste."

"Have you done anything to try to protect yourselves, such as banding together?"

"Growers do not band together, Captain, for battle or any other purpose. Each family takes care of its own needs; we value our autonomy. We have no weapons, and so we are helpless against the pirates."

"There is something here, Natahia, which is very valuable to the pirates, or they would not be attacking your people. Even renegades must have a reason for staying and killing in one area for so long. When Mr. Spock returns, perhaps he can tell us what the pirates are looking for."

She moved toward the door of the hut and peered out into what was now inky darkness. "He should have returned by now. It's very dangerous for one alone in the darkness near the mountains. The animals prowl, and one can easily lose one's step along the edge of the plateau."

Kirk looked beyond her at the moonless night, but could see nothing. "It's been more than five minutes, hasn't it? Spock is very punctual . . . maybe we'd better go look for him."

"You must wait until morning. It isn't safe—"

"We have weapons and light. I'm sure that Spock can protect himself, but he's been gone longer than he said he would, and that isn't like him. Scotty—"

"Coming, sir."

"Natahia, if we're not back in fifteen minutes, have Dr. McCoy call the ship."

Her expression was anxious. "I hope that you find your friend, Captain."

"We will," Kirk said confidently.

They found him.

They had searched the area near the mountains where the plateau broke off abruptly, beginning again after a drop of some four hundred feet. Scott put off suggesting that they turn the handlight on the plateau below until they had searched everywhere else. Reluctantly, Scott peered down, careful of his own steps along the edge of the drop. Kirk searched a short distance away; the height was beginning to make him dizzy, and his eyes were refusing to focus on the slender beam of light so far below.

He was calling the *Enterprise* to tell Chekhov to search with the scanners when he saw Scott stiffen and draw his head up quickly, and he knew with heartsickening certainty what the engineer saw. He ran to Scott's side, and, clutching his arm, was compelled to look down at what he could not bear to see. "Dear God, Spock—"

Spock lay on his left side on a bed of the tangling red vines.

McCoy's face was gray as he leaned against the wall in sick bay. "He'll make it, Jim."

17

Kirk closed his eyes and let his body go limp with relief. They had not expected Spock to survive.

"I've reconstructed the damaged part of his skull, set the broken bones. One lung was punctured, but that'll mend." McCoy paused.

"But?" Kirk stiffened. He knew that tone; it meant that the doctor was saving the worst for last.

"There's been a significant amount of damage to the left hemisphere of the brain."

Kirk drew a weary hand across his forehead and stared dully at McCoy. "What are you trying to tell me? What will that do to Spock?"

"There are a lot of variables involved, Jim. We won't know exactly for a little while yet. I'll have to do some testing."

Kirk's tone became indignant. "You can do something for him, can't you?"

McCoy sighed deeply, and when he spoke again there was a slightly sharp edge to his words. "I've done what I can for him, Captain. We're treating him with alpha-dextran for ischemia—those brain cells that survived but were cut off from the blood flow—but I can't reconstruct brain tissue that was completely obliterated, and it's too specialized to clone. It's likely that at least a few functions have been impaired—which ones permanently, I don't know yet. What we have to hope for is that Spock will retrain the undamaged brain cells to take over the functions of those that were lost.

"And some functions have definitely been affected. He hasn't gone into the Vulcan healing mode and he isn't controlling the pain. I've got him on medication for that. From the location of the damage, he probably has some speech impairment . . . but then, I'm guessing. You see, Vulcans don't have lateralization of function as we humans do—that is, the left side of the brain controlling certain functions and the right others. The Vulcan brain has an area controlling speech on each side of the brain. If one hemisphere is damaged, the other can take over. It's sort of an auxiliary backup system. They're also ambidextrous. Since neither hemisphere is dominant, neither side of the body is either."

"But Spock's right-handed," Kirk protested.

"That's right. Comes from his mother's side of the family. That indicates that certain functions are probably located on one side of his brain, just as they are in humans. And if he has experienced some damage to a function that is not lateralized in both hemispheres, he will need some type of therapy so that he can relearn the function. But he is a unique case. If he were all Vulcan *or* all human, I'd be able to use the standardized tests on him and I'd know a little bit more right now."

"Look, Bones . . . I didn't mean to sound hostile for a minute there . . ."

McCoy nodded, his lips curving slightly in something less than a tired smile. "It's all right, Jim. I'm just sorry I can't tell you more right now, but I'm going to have to watch and wait myself. I've already put in a request for a Vulcan neurologist."

"I wouldn't hold my breath," Kirk said. Star Fleet was notoriously slow about such matters.

"I won't. And Jim . . ." His face darkened again. "Don't hold yours, either. He'll pull through, but it'll be a long time before he's the old Spock again." He did not say, *if ever*.

Kirk looked beyond McCoy into the dimness of the intensive care unit in sick bay. The light of the life-function monitor softly illuminated the figure on the bed below. Spock lay on his back now, his face as peaceful as it had been when Jim and Scott had first found him; but this time his damaged left side was visible. Kirk repressed a shudder. He and McCoy had waited by Spock's side in the darkness for the transporter to beam them aboard, McCoy insisting that Spock not be moved except by the medical team waiting in the transporter room. The real horror came in the brightness of the transporter room, where Kirk could see the extent of Spock's injuries clearly, when McCoy and a medic gently turned Spock over to place him on the stretcher, revealing for the first time his crushed left side.

Kirk could not remember ever having been so terrified by the sight of anything before.

McCoy had done an excellent job of reconstructing the Vulcan's damaged left temple, but in spite of the surgery, Spock's pale face was mottled with dark green bruises. His left eye was nearly swollen shut.

"Jim," McCoy said softly, reading the pain in his friend's face. "I think you're overdue for some rest. When's the last time you got some sleep?"

Kirk murmured something unintelligible.

"Look, let me give you something to help you sleep—"

"No thanks, Doctor. I'd just as soon keep busy for a little while longer . . ." He looked at McCoy sharply. "One might ask you the same question."

"I . . . uh, I'm going to keep an eye on Spock for just a little while longer. . . ."

Kirk closed his eyes and pushed the image of Spock in the transporter room firmly from his mind. "Bones, call me when he comes to. I'll be on the bridge. I have some questions that need to be answered."

Kirk avoided all eyes on the bridge and headed straight for the con, his gaze fixed straight ahead on the viewscreen where Aritani rotated slowly on its axis.

"Captain, Mr. Scott is calling from the planet surface," Uhura said, but there was a hesitation, a kind of catch in her voice, as though she wanted to ask a question but did not dare. Kirk turned toward her in irritation, not understanding until he saw the concern in her eyes. He did not need to look behind him to know the others were watching him with the same expression. Of course they had heard what happened on Aritani below, and after seeing the grim expression on their captain's face, they probably expected the worst.

"Mr. Spock will be . . . will live," he said shortly. Uhura's shoulders relaxed visibly; Kirk could hear Chekhov release a sigh behind him.

"On audio, sir," she smiled.

Kirk sat in his chair. "How's it going, Mr. Scott?"

"The shield is up, Captain, and workin' just fine. I'd like to give Ensign Lanz some credit for the fine job she did helpin' me."

"Noted."

"How's Mr. Spock?"

"He'll live," Kirk repeated dully.

"Thank God, that was a horrible fall he took—"

"Did you get a complete tricorder readout yet on those mountains?"

"Aye, Captain, and Mr. Spock was right to suspect something. The land's full of uritanium and dilithium, not to mention other precious metals."

Kirk put a weary hand to his forehead. "Uritanium and dilithium—no wonder these people have visitors."

"Aye, sir, anyone with mining equipment could make more than a credit or two on this planet."

"Good work, Scotty. We'll start beaming personnel

down for shore leave in eight hours. In the meantime, we'll see if that shield of yours—"

"—and Ensign Lanz . . ."

"—and Ensign Lanz catches us some pirates."

"Well, sir, if you ask me, it seems terribly quiet and peaceful down here, nary a peep of trouble. Ensign Lanz and I could take a little shore leave right now . . ." Scott wheedled.

"I'm not asking you, Engineer. No one will be taking shore leave for another eight hours. Spock said their fuel could only keep them shielded for seven and a half hours at most, and I'm willing to give them a little leeway. In the meantime, I won't risk having crewmembers down there if any trapped pirates decide on another surprise attack."

Scott sighed tiredly. "Aye, Captain. We'll be beamin' up, then."

Captain's Log, Stardate 7003.4:

After being called to Aritani to investigate pirate attacks upon the population, we have discovered that the planet is a veritable storehouse of precious metals and fuel sources. My guess is that the attackers wish to subdue the population in order to set up some permanent mining operation.

Unfortunately, we have not yet located the pirate base nor any ships, and we assume they are using cloaking devices. Engineer Scott and Ensign Lanz have installed a protective shield around the planet, which will prevent other ships from entering Aritani's atmosphere and which will trap any ships in the atmosphere at the time the shield was erected. According to Mr. Spock, the fuel for the type of ship used by the pirates could last no more than seven and a half hours, assuming they are using a standard type of cloaking device. At that time, their shields will no longer be operable and our scanners will pick them up. I expect we will be able to capture and question at least one of the attackers.

Once the planet surface has been secured, we will begin beaming down our personnel for shore leave.

Commander Spock was seriously injured during the performance of his duty on the planet surface; I am hereby submitting his name for commendation.

Kirk yawned and ran a hand across his face as if to clear away the gathering cobwebs; it'd been some time since he'd last pulled a double shift, and his body was no longer accustomed to it. There was still no point in going to his quarters yet, however; he would be unable to slow his mind enough to sleep.

The bridge had been too quiet over the past several hours, the only disturbance being a shift change of personnel. On the viewscreen, Aritani still turned lazily, revealing no sign of the destruction that had occurred on its surface. But it was the silence from sick bay that Kirk found the most unbearable.

He snapped a toggle on the arm of the con decisively. "Kirk to sick bay."

McCoy's voice sounded as haggard as Kirk felt. "McCoy here. What is it, Jim?"

"How's Spock? Any change?"

"Not really . . ."

The hesitation in McCoy's voice made Kirk sit up straight in his chair. "Define 'not really,' Doctor. Is he conscious?"

"Well, uh, yes and no. He's very groggy from the medication—"

"He's conscious, and you didn't call me?" Kirk's

voice betrayed his anger. "That was an order, Doctor, whether you realized it or not."

It was McCoy's turn to sound insulted. "Wait just a minute, there, Captain—"

"No, you wait a minute, Doctor, because I'm on my way. Kirk out."

He cut off the communication before McCoy could protest.

McCoy was waiting outside the intensive care section of sick bay, his arms folded tightly against his chest and his chin jutting out in his best defiant pose. He began to speak before Kirk had a chance.

"I admit," he said, struggling to keep the irritability from his voice, "that neither one of us has had much sleep and we're walking around like a couple of exposed raw nerves. But I am not going to let you walk in there before you listen to what I have to say, not for the sake of my professional pride, but for the sake of that patient in there. In my medical judgment, there was no point in calling you. Spock is only semiconscious and unable to respond—"

"My order did not include any leeway for medical judgment," Kirk interrupted coldly. "Is he still awake?"

"Yes, dammit, but you won't be able to get any information from him right now—"

"We'll see." Kirk brushed past him; McCoy followed, seething.

At the sight of Spock, the coldness left Kirk's features instantly. The Vulcan lay in the shadows of the dimly lit room, his breathing irregular, labored as Kirk had never seen it, for Spock was in pain. His dark eyes fastened on Jim's face, but they were clouded, unseeing. Kirk felt a chill of fear.

"What happened down there, Spock?"

Spock closed his eyes slowly, but when he opened them again at Kirk, there was no recognition in them.

"He can't speak, Captain." McCoy's words stung. "And I doubt he even knows you. There's no point in agitating him."

Kirk ignored him. "Spock, can you hear me? Blink if you can hear me."

Spock hesitated for an awful moment, then lowered his eyelids and raised them again.

Kirk shot a triumphant I-told-you-so glance at McCoy. "Spock, blink if you know who I am."

There was a long silence filled only with the sound of tortured breathing as Spock fought the effects of his injuries and McCoy's painkillers and struggled to remember.

"Don't you know me, Spock?"

"Stop it, Jim! That's enough." McCoy moved toward Kirk as if to pull him from Spock's side, but the look on the captain's face stopped him.

You must know me, Kirk directed the thought toward the Vulcan desperately. *You know me better than anyone else; you've touched my mind a hundred times. How can I touch yours now?*

But it was useless; he was no telepath, and even if he could touch Spock's mind, he doubted that the Vulcan would be able to respond. He began to turn away.

And then Spock blinked once, slowly, and closed his eyes as though the effort had exhausted him. Kirk felt a sense of absolute victory.

"When he makes any improvement, or if he says anything, contact me," he said to McCoy, but his eyes were still on Spock. As he walked toward the door to leave, something made him turn and face McCoy. "And that's an order."

He left McCoy fuming behind him.

Kirk stepped off the turbolift to the sight of Aritani on the screen, a sight that was rapidly becoming more of an affront than a pleasure.

Sulu rose from the con. "Any change?" Kirk asked.

The helmsman watched as his captain attempted unsuccessfully to stifle a yawn. At present the captain had been on duty for close to twenty-four hours, and Sulu seriously doubted his ability to stay awake in the comfortable command chair. He toyed with the idea of suggesting that the captain repair to his quarters for some rest, but in light of Kirk's recent mood, decided it would be best not to mention it. Sulu did not need to call sick bay to find out Mr. Spock's condition; the look on Kirk's face when he'd first come back from sick bay had told Sulu just how serious the first officer's injuries were.

"No, sir," he replied simply. "All quiet. We haven't picked up the first sign of pirates, or any other vessels, for that matter. Apparently this is usually a very quiet neighborhood."

Kirk seemed keenly disappointed. *"No* pirate vessels?"

"Captain," Uhura called from her station, "Mr. Scott just called to let you know it's been eight hours."

"Eight hours . . ." Kirk was momentarily lost. "Oh, yes. Already? Let me talk to him."

"Yes, sir." Scott's voice came from the engineering deck.

"Scotty, what are the chances that one of the pirate vessels could go longer than eight hours with their cloaks up?"

"Impossible, sir. Of course, I'm not the expert.

Spock would be the one to ask—except I guess he's not up to answering questions right now."

Kirk did not answer.

"Of course, he did say seven-point-four-two hours, sir, and I'm sure his answer would be just the same now. You've allowed more than another half hour to be on the safe side. There's no ship I've ever heard of that could keep a cloakin' device operating that long."

Kirk sighed. "I'd hoped to catch at least one of the ships beneath our shield. It would have made it a lot easier to locate their base."

"Aye, that it would."

"Guess I'll have to tell the transporter room to start beaming down shore parties."

The sound of a muffled hoot came from the other end of the intercom. Kirk frowned.

"What was that, Engineer?"

"Nothing, sir," Scott replied meekly. "One of the men down here overheard you mentioning shore leave."

Kirk's expression softened. "It has been a long time, hasn't it? The crew has certainly earned a little R and R."

"You have, too, sir."

Kirk could not disagree with Scott's statement, but his reaction to being selected by the computer to be in the first shore party of one hundred to go down to the surface was something less than gleeful. He offered to let Scott take his place, a proposition that Scott accepted rather quickly, as Ensign Lanz happened to be in the first beamdown group.

The door to McCoy's cabin opened quickly in response to the buzzer; Kirk had guessed that the doctor, too, would not be sleeping. Instead, McCoy was sitting at his desk with a bottle of bourbon and a shot glass, pouring himself a drink—and not the first one, by the looks of things.

His bleary red-rimmed eyes did not look up from the glass. "I suppose you came here for an update on Spock."

Kirk stood uncertainly in the doorway. "I've already checked with sick bay. That's how I knew to find you here."

McCoy scowled. "I told them I was going on shore leave—"

"Christine said you'd probably be here . . . either sleeping or drinking."

"Remind me to have that woman fired. She's getting to know me too damn well. If you've been to sick bay, then you've also discovered that Spock is in the capable hands of Dr. M'Benga, who has sworn to me that he will contact you the instant Spock utters a peep."

"Bones," Kirk said suddenly. "Bones, I'm sorry."

McCoy tried at first to shrug off the apology, but he sighed and shook his head. "It's not your fault, Jim. Do you realize that neither of us has slept for more than two shifts now? It's no wonder we're a little temperamental. Especially after what happened to Spock—" He lowered his head for an instant; when he raised it again, his voice was tinged with exasperation. "But Jim, you've got to realize that there may be some things I just can't fix. I'm a surgeon, dammit, not a magician . . ."

"I know," Kirk soothed. "And I was out of line today. I'm sorry. You did a fine job on Spock. Thank you for saving his life."

"Well," McCoy said, more than mollified. "You're under a little stress, Captain. Apology accepted." He nodded at the bottle tucked under Kirk's arm. "I can see you're using the same prescription I am. Have a seat and I'll get you a glass."

Kirk sat gratefully. "Now, Doctor, tell me how I can get some sleep."

"What's that you brought—some of that Saurian stuff? Drink a sizable portion of that, Jim boy, and your old country doctor promises you'll get to sleep tonight. In fact, why don't you try some of my brand? Kentucky bourbon, aged in the cask and twelve years old if it's a day—"

"I'll stick with my usual poison, thanks."

"It's your liver." McCoy handed the glass to him. "Look, Jim, when *was* the last time you took shore leave?"

"I dunno. Same time you did."

"Then it's definitely been too damn long. And with everything else that's been happening around here lately, it's no wonder you've felt like blowing off some steam. So cheers. Doctor's orders." McCoy raised his glass.

"Thanks." Kirk lifted the glass to his lips and stopped. "I'm not sure I *can* remember my last shore leave."

McCoy grinned devilishly and leaned across the desk in his best dirty old man imitation. "I can. Regla Kanete, remember? That little bar where they do the most outrageous form of dancing. The kind that could knock your eyes right out of your head . . ."

Kirk snickered, "I remember, of course . . . a native dance, based on an ancient religion—"

McCoy rolled his eyes. "They don't make religious dances like that back home. Seems to me you almost succeeded in getting rather friendly with their best dancer, too—what was her name?"

Kirk's teeth were showing. "Lolama. Lolama . . . I can't remember her last name."

"Wasn't important anyway. You were doing just fine I recall, until that boyfriend of hers showed up."

"Thank God for transporters." Kirk swallowed more of the brandy and was almost beginning to feel good. "I'm afraid though, that this time I'll be spending my shore leave here."

"As your personal physician, I'd advise you to reconsider. You said it yourself—you need to be someplace where you can be near animals, trees, birds . . . After a while, the insides of this ship can begin to get to you."

Kirk's lips tightened. "I'd rather stay here. Come to think of it, I don't see you rushing off to enjoy your liberty."

McCoy's lascivious grin faded entirely. "I thought I might be needed here."

"You mean you don't want to leave Spock. Maybe he's why I don't particularly feel like taking shore leave down there."

"Because he was injured down there?" McCoy asked quietly.

Kirk didn't answer.

"That's why we're so angry," McCoy continued. "Because it was such a stupid accident . . . so unfair, especially to someone like Spock."

"Explain." Kirk felt the knot in his stomach beginning to tighten again.

"To have such an incredibly logical mind . . . and to receive damage to the left hemisphere."

Kirk looked at him vacantly.

"You do remember from your academy days which functions are controlled by the left hemisphere of the brain?"

Anatomy had not been Kirk's favorite subject. "Language?"

"Yes, and some memory, mathematics, analysis . . . and logic."

Kirk sat forward quickly. "What exactly are you trying to say, Doctor? That he's lost all of that?"

"I'm saying that he could experience some degree of impairment in any one of those areas. The left hemisphere sustained a significant trauma. The alpha-dextran can only restore those brain cells that were not physically destroyed and only starved from lack of oxygen. Spock will probably recover certain functions, but it'll be another day or so before we know the extent of the permanent damage."

"Then you're telling me that you don't know yet."

"That's one reason I sent for a specialist."

"God knows how long that could take. What do we do in the meantime?"

"Wait," said McCoy.

Pain. Helpless pain along his entire left side, a hideous nonpain in his head and a dizzying nausea that seemed to snatch the bed from under him and send him falling into the dark void. . . . They must have given him something for the pain, something so strong that he could not think clearly, could not summon the mind rules to silence the fierce ache in his side. But why? Surely they knew how nauseous the medication made him. . . .

Again he struggled to retrieve the mind rules, looking deep into his clouded consciousness, searching, concentrating, and for a moment he felt he might find them; but they eluded him again, like a cruel parent who teases a child with a toy, pulling it farther and farther away as the child moves closer. He sighed with frustration and turned his head to one side; it was a mistake. He held onto the bed with his right hand as another wave of dizziness clutched at him.

And the mind rules were not all that was lost to him;

there were other things hidden in him which he could not retrieve, words of great consequence which must be spoken, and quickly, but he could not remember what he should say it nor to whom he should say it.

Someone bent over him, fuzzy, out of focus. He closed his eyes gingerly, to avoid offending his swollen left eye, and opened them again. It was a man, wearing a blue tunic, a man that Spock knew, but he could not remember his name.

"Feeling any better?" the man asked soothingly. "Sorry that we had to medicate you; you won't be able to control the pain yourself for a while. Try to rest."

Spock saw no other alternative at the moment. He studied the man in the muted light; dark-skinned, humanoid. Probably Terran, by the accent. The blue tunic had significance—it reminded him of the other, the one who had been with him earlier: a doctor. Then this one was also a doctor. His urgent message was not for them, but for another man—the man in the gold tunic, the man who had asked the questions. He grimaced with the strain of remembering, determined to speak the man's name or to die.

When the name at last came forth, Spock was flooded with a sense of relief and accomplishment stronger than any he had ever known.

"Jim," he whispered.

M'Benga was as good as his word. Within minutes, Kirk and McCoy had arrived in sick bay.

"Sorry to have to wake you both," M'Benga apologized. "He's still heavily sedated, but he's fighting it. Apparently he feels it's quite urgent that he speak with you, Captain."

Kirk felt as though he were fighting the effects of

heavy sedation himself, after being roused from the few hours' dreamless sleep induced by the brandy. "You did the right thing, Doctor, thank you."

Spock appeared to be sleeping, but when the Captain entered, his eyes opened and fastened on Kirk with clear recognition.

"Spock, what did you want to tell me?"

Spock shuddered with the effort to speak, his voice no more than a halting whisper. "I . . . must tell what I . . . saw—" He stopped abruptly, his face clouded with confusion.

"Take your time," Kirk soothed. "Try to remember."

Spock gritted his teeth with frustration. "I . . . can't."

The three humans looked over Spock's head at each other. "We've given you some strong painkillers," McCoy said. "You're going to have a little trouble remembering things for a while."

"Important." Spock grimaced in a sudden spasm of pain. Kirk was forced to look away.

"It's all right, Spock. We know what you saw: uritanium, dilithium, just for starters. We completed the tricorder analysis. So you see, everything's taken care of. You can rest now."

Spock stared at the captain dully, considering if that was indeed what he had wanted to tell him. But the effort of speaking had exhausted him; he closed his eyes.

Kirk followed McCoy outside and leaned wearily against the bulkhead. "He doesn't remember, Bones. Is it really the medication?"

McCoy studied the tops of his boots for a moment before squaring his shoulders and looking his friend directly in the eye. "No. No, Jim, it isn't."

The intercom on the bulkhead next to Kirk whistled. He answered it without taking his eyes off McCoy. "Kirk here."

Uhura sounded unusually agitated. "An urgent message from Mr. Scott on the surface, Captain. The pirates have gotten through the shields—they're attacking our people!"

Chapter Two

"MY GOD! CRIED McCoy. "There's over a hundred crewmen down there!"

Kirk did not answer him, but his eyes showed how well aware he was of the fact. "On my way."

A casual observer on the bridge might not have guessed that an emergency situation existed; bridge personnel were too well trained not to function smoothly under pressure. But Kirk could tell by the subtle tautness of their movements, by the way all eyes fastened on his, awaiting orders, the moment he stepped from the turbolift.

Sulu vacated the con and seated himself at the helm with graceful swiftness as Kirk approached. "Uhura, see if you can raise Mr. Scott for me again. Mr. Chekhov, status on the protective shield."

Chekhov moved to Spock's station and peered down into the viewer, his solemn face bathed in the pale blue glow. "No change, sir."

Kirk turned his head toward him sharply. "They're still up?"

Chekhov made no attempt to hide his surprise. "Yes, sir. Completely functional. There is no indication of any malfunction. We'll have to lower them if we want to beam our personnel aboard."

"That's what I intend to do, Ensign. In the meantime, I want you to scan the surface and get a fix on a pirate vessel. They always lower their cloaks before the attack. Sulu, stand by with the tractor beam."

Uhura interrupted. "I have Mr. Scott for you, Captain. On audio."

McCoy blessed her silently for having the tact not to put Scott on the screen; the sounds of screams and blasts of flame that filled the bridge were terrifying enough without the picture.

Scott spoke in a hoarse shout. "Scott here, Captain. The pirates are right nearby—I'm afraid this inna very safe place at the moment."

"Scotty, can you get to the controls for the shield? We have to lower it to get you out of there."

"Aye, Captain, I'm not far from the hut. I think I can make it."

"Is there any way the shields might have been lowered, even for an instant?"

"Sir, do ye think I'm completely daft? I'd never let a thing like that happen. I checked 'em myself not half an hour ago—I dinna ken how those divvils got past 'em." The sound of the flame blasts grew closer, drowning out Scott's voice. Kirk could hear the crackle of the fire.

"Speak up, Scotty, I'm having trouble reading you."

"Captain, I'd best go now. I doubt as it'll be safe to stay here much longer. I'll get to the controls."

A thundering roar caused Kirk to put his hands over

his ears; when the noise cleared, there was silence.

"Scott?" Kirk's voice rose. "Are you there? Can you read me?"

For a moment, no one on the bridge dared breathe.

"Aye, Captain, but tell McCoy to have some medics waitin' in the transporter room. We've got some casualties here."

Kirk was numb. "I'll tell him. Good luck, Scotty."

The muscles in Chekhov's back tensed as he looked up from the viewer. "Keptin, I've got one of the ships!"

"Tractor beam, Mr. Sulu . . ."

Sulu was apologetic. "The shield isn't down yet, Captain. I can't hold onto him."

"Stay with him, Mr. Chekhov . . ."

"With him, sir."

"Shield still up, Captain," Sulu reported.

Chekhov swore softly under his breath. "Lost him, sir. He has his cloak up again. It's almost as if he knew we were trying to get a tractor on him . . ."

"Shield down, Captain," Sulu said.

Kirk's jaw twitched. "Don't leave that spot, Ensign. I want you to stay there until you get another fix on one of those ships. Sulu, stand by with the tractor beam and make sure whoever is in it gets beamed up to this ship. We are going to catch a pirate. Do I make myself clear?"

"Aye, sir," the two replied meekly.

"Sulu, you have the con. Get someone up here to mind the helm. I'll be in sick bay if you need me."

Chekhov waited for the turbolift doors to close over the captain's stern visage.

"I am so stupid," he said sorrowfully. "I could have computed his trajectory. I shouldn't have lost him like that."

Sulu comforted him. "You did what you could. We'll get one next time, Pavel. You'll see."

The evacuation had proceeded in a calm and orderly fashion. One hundred and three crew members had been beamed in groups with no one panicking, the most critically wounded coming up first, the dead last. Miraculously, only six had been killed and thirty-eight wounded.

To Kirk it felt like something less than a miracle. The area from the transporter room to sick bay was a chamber of horrors; he could smell the burns the moment the doors to the turbolift opened. Those who could still stand were crowded together outside sick bay while medics administered first aid. McCoy and M'Benga were already in surgery with the critical cases.

Scott was one of the lucky ones waiting for a medic. He held up his arms like an old-time surgeon awaiting sterile gloves; the sleeves of his tunic had been almost completely seared away from pulling the red-hot switch that neutralized the protective shield—underneath, the skin was mottled red and gray. Kirk forced himself to watch as the medic dressed Scott's wounds, first with a coolant spray to stop more cells from dying, then with a temporary sealant to provide air-permeable protection until McCoy had the time to make more skin synthetic. Kirk looked at the faces of the crewmen around them, some of them dazed and unable to grasp the horror of what had happened to them on what was supposed to have been a relaxing interlude, a brief vacation. . . .

"Did you get a good look at them, Scotty?"

The pain on Scott's face eased as the medic's hypospray hissed. "Aye, Captain—Romulan surface fighters, all right. Maybe six or seven of 'em, but none of us cared to get close enough to see who was inside. Did you manage to get hold of one?"

"No. Chekhov's still scanning. And we still haven't located their base."

"It can't be too far, sir. They don't have much fuel storage capacity."

"Agreed. But what I want to know is what the hell they were doing under our shield."

"Like I said, a fighter doesn't have the fuel capacity to sit under the shields that long, especially not with a cloakin' device in operation. If you ask me, the only thing that accounts for it is a shield neutralizer."

"Come on, Scotty, the Romulans have been trying to develop one for years, but they've never been successful."

"Can you be so sure, sir?" Scott seemed to be swaying slightly.

"It's just as likely they developed a cloaking device which doesn't require as much fuel." Kirk frowned at him; the Scot was definitely turning paler. "You know, you're still officially on leave, Mr. Scott. I suggest you go take it easy in your quarters."

Scott began to speak, but Kirk cut him off. "That's an order. We'll talk more about this later."

"Then, sir . . . could you do me a wee favor?"

"Name it."

"Could you find out about Ensign Lanz for me?" He nodded toward sick bay. "She's in there, and they tell me she was pretty badly hurt. She's an awfully young lass . . . this is her first assignment."

Kirk smiled in spite of the sinking feeling Scott's words caused. "I'll find out, Scotty. I'm sure McCoy's taking good care of her. Go on."

"I'll just wait out here for a minute—"

"No, I'll come tell you. Now *go*." He shooed Scott with a playful gesture, but the moment the engineer turned to shuffle off to his quarters, the smile fled from Kirk's face.

The smell inside sick bay was as bad as he had imagined; Kirk tried not to look at the wounded lying on the makeshift cots that lined the walls. He was waiting until he was sure he could no longer bear the stench when the door to surgery opened.

McCoy sank shakily into the nearest chair and wiped the perspiration from his brow. "I'd like to give those responsible for this a taste of their own medicine. What kind of being could do this to innocent people? I bet you can smell it all the way up to the bridge." He slumped lower in the chair and closed his eyes. "I haven't even had time to have a hangover."

"How many did we lose, Bones?"

"Eight. Six on the planet, two in surgery. The burns were so severe, their bodies just shut down in spite of everything we could do. Damn those bastards . . . ."

A muscle in Kirk's jaw twitched. "I shouldn't have let them go down there."

McCoy opened one eye. "Don't do it to yourself, Jim. And if I had gotten to those two in time, maybe they wouldn't have died. . . . There's nothing to be gained by playing the if-I-had-only game. You couldn't have known."

"I could have at least waited longer—at least a few more hours, before I started risking my people—"

"Please explain to me how you could have anticipated the impossible? Because it *was* impossible for any ships to be down there. Scotty told you that—hell, even Spock told you that. How could you have known?"

"I don't know," Kirk said darkly, but his eyes did not surrender their guilt. "Let's change the subject.

I'm supposed to ask about Ensign Lanz for Scotty. How is she?"

The change in McCoy's expression was so quick and subtle that anyone else might have missed its meaning, but Kirk had seen the look on the doctor's face enough times to know what McCoy was going to say.

"I'm sorry, Jim. She was one of the two who didn't make it."

Scott did not respond to the buzzer, but the door was unlocked. It was pitch-black inside the engineer's quarters.

"Scotty?"

Kirk heard someone move heavily.

"Captain?" Scott's voice was thick. "I musta fallen asleep. They gave me a hypo for the pain . . ." Kirk heard the Scot struggle to a sitting position on the bed. "Ye've come about Ensign Lanz, haven't ye, sir?"

"Yes," Kirk said softly.

There was a silence. "Is she dead, Captain?"

Kirk was grateful for the darkness. "Yes. I'm sorry, Scotty."

For a moment the only sound was Scott's labored breathing. When at last he spoke, his voice was rich with sorrow. "She was a damn good engineer. She was barely twenty-five years old." He made a choking noise. "If I get my hands on one of those pirates . . . sir, I swear I'll kill 'em! I'll kill 'em!"

"It won't change things," Kirk said in a low voice.

"Why would anyone want to hurt her? How can such people exist?"

"I don't know," Kirk said, "but we're going to stop them."

He left Scott alone in the darkness.

*　　*　　*

A slight smell of scorched skin clung to the bulk-heads in the corridors outside sick bay and refused to be deodorized completely by the ship's air filtration system. Many of the personnel who had had occasion to walk through the corridors by sick bay had complained about the nauseating odor, but thanks to the concentrated efforts of the maintenance crew, it was now almost completely gone—almost—but its lingering trace was still enough to disconcert anyone visiting sick bay.

Anyone, that is, except Lt. Nyota Uhura. A person of strong will, once she set her mind to do something it was as good as accomplished. She squared her shoulders as she entered sick bay, and although the smell grew stronger, she had already predetermined that it would not bother her in the slightest.

The sight of the wounded, however, was another matter altogether. It was the first time she had actually seen the cruel burns inflicted by the pirates' phasers, and she lowered her eyes so that her revulsion would not be seen.

But Leonard McCoy must have seen it, for he pounced on her with an exaggerated cheerfulness she was certain could not be genuine. McCoy looked worse than Uhura had ever seen him, and she was tempted to tell him he belonged in one of the beds himself.

"Well, Miss Uhura," he called in his best Southern gentleman's drawl, "have you come to cast a ray of sunshine in our den of gloom?"

"How *did* you know, Doctor?" she replied sweetly.

"Who's the lucky devil you've come to visit? Me, I hope."

"Well, I was coming to see one of the patients, but you look like you could use a visitor far worse."

"Someone noticed," McCoy beamed wryly. "Someone cares."

"Actually, I've come to say hello to everyone, and to one person in particular. That man over there."

Mohamed Jahma grinned as widely as the injury to the side of his face and neck would permit; the dark olive skin was speckled shiny pink and red under a thick coat of clear, glossy sealant. Uhura sat on the side where his burns were less visible.

"Some people get all the breaks," McCoy pouted. He went back to his rounds.

"*Kef'halik?* How are you?" Uhura asked in Arabic. She and Moh were just friends, but their relationship was marked by a light, teasing humor with more than a hint of flirtation. She was unsure if Mohamed meant for it to evolve into something more serious, but she enjoyed his friendship too much to worry about it. They shared the same continent as their birthplace— Moh was North African—and they were beginning to share their respective languages with each other. Uhura had always felt slightly embarrassed that she had never learned Arabic, the second most important language in the United States of Africa, and Moh had never bothered to learn Swahili, since Arabic was widely spoken in the north.

"Not too bad, beautiful," he responded in Swahili, then switched to English. "Better than most. I'm just waiting my turn for a little cosmetic touch-up and I'll be good as new. I'm afraid we've really overworked these doctors."

"When will you be getting out?"

"Tomorrow, if I stay on good behavior."

"That should be just about impossible for you." She turned her head for a moment to survey the main ward, and some acquaintances who were not too weak or sedated smiled in her direction; she waved back. "It's terrible," she said in a low voice. "I must know half the people in this room."

"There's two more in intensive care—really critical cases."

"Worse than this?" Uhura was aghast; she could not imagine wounds more terrible than the ones she saw now.

"I wish my injury was the worst one." Mohamed's expression darkened. "We lost two from engineering—Giorgo Mikahlis and Rachel Lanz."

"Oh, Moh, not Rachel. She was so young. . . ."

They were silent for a moment until Moh nodded toward intensive care. "They say Commander Spock's still in there, too."

"How is he? The captain doesn't say anything about it."

"No one says much here either. M'Benga and McCoy go in there all the time, and they always look pretty grim when they come out. It doesn't sound too good."

"I wonder if he's able to have visitors."

"I doubt it. I haven't seen anyone go in there except the doctors and the captain."

"Well, I'm going to ask Dr. McCoy about it. After all, even Mr. Spock needs cheering up when he's sick." She paused. "But first, since I came to see you, tell me what I can do for you. Within reason, of course."

Mohamed smiled again. "Sing me a song. I've been dreaming about your singing the whole time I've been in sick bay."

"Moh, I can't sing here—it'll disturb the others."

"Doctor," Mohamed called, "can Uhura sing us a song?"

McCoy, two beds down, looked up from the knee he

was patching together with skin synthetic. "As long as she sings loud enough for the rest of us to hear it. A song is exactly what these people need. Not to mention the medical staff. What's good for growing flowers has got to be good for mending people, in my medical opinion."

"At least he didn't call us his vegetable garden," said Moh.

Uhura grimaced. "Any special requests?"

"Something African, of course."

Uhura thought for a moment, then began to sing a lullaby she'd learned as a child.

Christine Chapel was checking on Spock when Uhura began to sing. Spock's broken bones were mending rapidly, but otherwise, his condition remained essentially unchanged; he had not spoken a word since he first talked to the captain. Christine leaned over to check the monitor, then paused to gaze down at his face, which still bore the mottled dark green marks on the left side. Impulsively, she reached a hand toward his face and let it hover above the bruises as though she longed to smooth them away with a touch.

His eyes snapped open so quickly that she gasped as she pulled her hand away, embarrassed. "Hello, Mr. Spock," she said, recovering quickly. "How are you feeling?"

It was a rhetorical question. Even if a patient could not respond, Chapel knew it was good therapy to assume he understood and to speak to him accordingly. She did not expect a reply.

"Uhura," he said clearly.

She hesitated for an instant, at first thinking that he had mistaken her for the communications officer. The door to intensive care was shut, but it was not soundproofed so that a doctor outside could hear the monitor panel signal a patient in trouble; Christine could faintly hear Uhura's voice floating in the strains of an ancient melody.

"Why yes," she said, "that *is* Uhura singing. She's out in the main ward. Would you like her to come in here?"

Spock blinked once.

"I'll get her." Chapel fought to contain her excitement.

Unlike the main ward, intensive care was quiet and dark. Of the three crew members who lay inside, two had been badly burned and were molded together with so much skin synthetic that Uhura did not recognize them. The third, Spock, was the only one conscious.

Externally, his wounds were not nearly as terrible as his roommates', but there was a look of such searching loss in his dark eyes that Uhura thought they must belong to someone else, not to the Spock she knew.

"Hello, sir," she said, uncertain whether he understood her. "We've all missed you on the bridge."

"Where my heart is," Spock said suddenly.

Chapel seemed embarrassed for him at the maudlin sentiment. "Of course you want to get back to the bridge, Mr. Spock—"

Uhura almost giggled. "No, Christine . . . I understand. He's asking for a song."

" 'Beyond Antares,' " said Spock.

"Oh," Chapel said stiffly. "Of course."

"It's a song we used to do together. Would you like me to sing it for you, Mr. Spock?"

Spock blinked once.

"That means 'yes,' " said Christine.

Spock's eyes closed as Uhura began the haunting tune; McCoy heard it out in the main ward and came inside to enjoy. "It's a lovely song, Uhura."

"Thank you. Spock and I used to play it together—he played the harp and I sang. Right, Spock?"

The Vulcan did not answer; he appeared to be sleeping.

"We have him on medication," McCoy said. "Of course, you could soothe anyone to sleep with that beautiful voice of yours. . . ."

"I appreciate the compliment, Doctor, but I don't understand why Spock could say some of the song lyrics, but had to blink instead of saying 'yes.'"

"The left side of his brain, which controls speech, was damaged. It's the right side that controls memory of music, poetry, and so on."

"Yes, Doctor," Chapel said, "but he also asked for Uhura by name when he heard her singing out in the main ward. His speech was very clear, not at all garbled, the way it was before."

McCoy sighed. "Well, thank God for small improvements. Maybe the alpha-dextran's beginning to take effect."

"Will he get his speech back?" Uhura asked.

"We hope so, Uhura." Even in the dim light, McCoy looked painfully haggard. "Just keep singing those pretty songs for him. It'll encourage him."

Uhura smiled. "I think I just thought of something even better."

Kirk lay on his bunk in the semidarkness. The reading lamp in the outer office was still lit, but he'd been unable to read and now, fidgeting uncomfortably on his bed, was unable to sleep. The one thing he had been able to do with any success was think, and his thoughts now were anything but restful: Ensign Lanz and seven others . . . Spock . . . the charred fields on the planet below. . . .

And the ships, the ships below the protective shield where they could not possibly be. Kirk's mind rolled over the only two possible explanations for the millionth time that night and rejected both of them. Not even the Vulcans or the Romulans, for all of their superlative skill and inventiveness in the field of electromagnetic physics, had yet developed Scotty's theorized shield neutralizer; and if they had, Star Fleet Intelligence would know about it, just as they would know of any design improvements in the cloaking device.

Kirk sighed and threw an arm across his open eyes. Try as he might, he could not shake the conviction that Spock knew something, something locked away within his damaged memory, that could explain the appearance of the ships. Of course, Spock's urgent but forgotten message could easily be explained: the tricorder had shown the uritanium and dilithium deposits in the mountains, and Spock had realized that Aritani was politically valuable real estate.

Kirk could not make himself believe that was all there was to it.

He had just gotten up to do some unproductive pacing when the intercom whistled. Lt. Krelidze appeared, fair-haired and moon-faced, on the screen.

"Communication from Admiral Komack in response to your message, sir." Her watery blue eyes widened slightly. "In code."

"Relay it here, Lieutenant."

Coded. It meant that Star Fleet suspected that more than a group of renegades were involved in the attacks on Aritani. Kirk wondered if he should kick himself for not coding his own message.

The content of Komack's response, however, was less than enlightening:

* * *

Intelligence reports no information available on shield neutralizer. Romulans using improved cloaking device, but fuel uptake relatively unchanged.

Enterprise hereby ordered to remain in area and offer Aritani all possible protection. Situation currently under intelligence investigation. You will be updated as facts are uncovered.

James H. Komack, Admiral.

Kirk's expression hardened as he read the decoded message. All possible protection—in other words, next to none! He signaled Krelidze on the bridge.

"Get me the Aritanian representative."

Natahia's face, once stern and regal, was now forbidding and cold with anger. Kirk recognized the scene behind her: what had been her fields, her warm quiet home, was now a gaping black wound in the midst of Aritani's colorful splendor. The cool breezes no longer carried the perfume of wildflowers, but the stench of things burned that were not meant to burn—huts, trellised vines, clothing, hair, and flesh . . . .

She glared at him, her golden face pale, her violet eyes rimmed with red, and Kirk thought she trembled; whether with rage or grief, he could not tell.

"Natahia, I wish to express my sorrow at what has happened."

Her words were spoken with icy politeness, and Kirk knew at once that he had lost her. "We regret that your people were also harmed, Captain."

"Representative, you must know how impossible it was for the pirates to have penetrated the shield—"

"It is obvious that you felt so, else you would not have sent your people down."

"Up to now, the technology has not existed for such an attack to be possible. Star Fleet is investigating. In

49

the meantime, the *Enterprise* will stay in orbit around your planet and attempt to capture one of the pirates for questioning. They can't remain cloaked forever, and when they lower their shields, we will catch them."

"No, Captain. There is nothing to be gained by further intervention from the Federation. There is no point in your people dying as well."

"If we can capture one of the pirates, we can find their base. We can find out who's attacking you, and why. Don't you want that, Natahia?"

"You will use your devices to try to capture one of them. Who can say that you will be successful? Can you be sure that more of your people will not die?

"We are a people of strong beliefs, Captain. Technology almost destroyed our race; we have chosen a simpler life. In spite of your weapons and devices, you have not saved a single life, and you and the pirates are engaged in a battle of wits to see what new mechanisms of war you can develop. Who is to say who is the more civilized?

"It was our decision that brought you here, Captain Kirk, and on behalf of the growers, I thank you for your services. We are sorry it resulted in the loss of life. We cannot let you stay and further risk yourselves. Your technology has failed us. It is time for us to return to the old beliefs. We will protect ourselves as best we can without depending on the devices of others."

"And if all of your people are killed and your planet becomes unfit to support life?" Desperation made Kirk blunt.

She looked at him sharply. "It seems that the same might happen if your ship remains. It is the will of the growers . . . it will be as I have said. I will no longer communicate with you on this device."

The sad, proud image shimmered for a moment before the screen went black.

Kirk watched for a moment before he called the bridge. Scott answered.

"Scotty, what the devil are you doing there?"

"Well, sir, seein' as how I'm the senior command officer on duty, I—"

"Why aren't you resting in your quarters?"

He could almost hear the indignant look Scott gave him over the intercom. "Captain—sir—I'm feelin' just fine, thank you. I've been by sick bay and they've put some skin on my hands so they're good as new. Dr. McCoy has certified me fit for duty. Sir."

"All right, Scotty," Kirk relented gently. "Let me talk to Chekhov."

"He's not here, sir."

"Not there . . . !" Kirk's voice rose half an octave. "I told him not to leave his station."

"He went off shift hours ago, sir. But Ensign O'Connor took his place, Captain. Mr. Chekhov explained to her that she mustn't leave her station. She knows what to do, sir."

"Yes, of course," Kirk said quickly. "Just be sure that when she goes off duty, she's replaced instantly. I don't want that station uncovered for even a second."

"Understood, sir. And believe me," a strange, dangerous undercurrent crept into Scott's tone, "I want to get my hands on those pirates as much as you do. We'll get one, Captain, if it's the last thing I do. Scott out."

Kirk sat down at his desk and laid his head on his arms; he wondered what the first officer's reaction would be to his decision to stay.

"Captain, you are failing to respect the decision of the growers. Are you forgetting the right of a culture to self-determination?"

Yes, he thought, he was failing to respect the growers' decision. He couldn't bring himself to respect the decision to commit cultural suicide. Once the Aritanians no longer existed as a race, their right to self-determination would be a moot question. If anyone was guilty of interference, it was the pirates, not he, and he would not let them destroy that beautiful planet, will of the growers be damned.

Kirk lifted his head. Sleep would not come of its own accord again tonight, and he needed it before he lost his wits completely. He was beginning to lose all sense of time, and could not afford to slip up with another crew member.

Nor could he afford to let the pirates win again.

He rose and went to find McCoy.

Uhura looked furtively about her; the lights in sick bay were dimmed to simulate night, and the patients in the main ward all appeared to be sleeping. There was a light on in the lab, but no one came out to see who had entered. She walked stealthily toward the intensive care ward.

The door slid open to reveal Commander Spock, awake and propped up in a half-sitting position on his bed. Apparently he was not in sync with sick bay's circadian rhythm. Uhura pulled back, startled and a little embarrassed that he should be awake now to see her; she had wanted this to be an anonymous visit. But it was too late; his unsettled eyes had focused on her and then on the instrument in her arms. She smiled apologetically and held it out to him.

"Forgive me for taking the liberty, sir," she whispered, "but your quarters were unlocked and I thought you might like to have this."

He took the harp from her with his right hand and propped it against his stomach. He looked up from the instrument and the unsettled look had been replaced by one of gratefulness.

Haltingly, he said, "There is no need to apologize, Lieutenant. I appreciate your thoughtfulness."

Slowly, softly, so as not to disturb the others, he sounded each string with the fingers of his right hand.

He was merely testing to see if the harp was still in tune, but to the two of them it was beautiful music.

McCoy's eyes closed. On the computer screen before him was a list of articles that pertained to left-hemisphere brain damage in humans, and in Vulcans; but nowhere had he been able to find any medical studies done on Vulcan-human hybrids. Given the rarity of romantic relations between the two races, it was not surprising that no one had been able to collect a large enough sample for a study. You could probably count the number of Vulcan-human hybrids in the universe on your fingers, and of those there was probably only one suffering from brain damage.

His eyes snapped open with the happy realization that he'd almost fallen asleep. No doubt the aridity of the reading matter had been responsible; at times, an article from one of the medical journals worked better than a pill. It was time to take advantage of the soporific effects of the reading matter; he hated taking a pill, although insomnia had sorely tempted him to do so. Too many people in his profession found it too easy to prescribe for themselves . . . and keep on prescribing.

He stood up and was just about to turn off the reading lamp when the door buzzed—Jim, no doubt, desperate at the prospect of another near-sleepless night. "Looking for a good night's sleep, eh?" McCoy said as the door opened.

"Maybe," said the girl . . . or was she a woman? Her

small frame was at first glance misleading as to her age; she was scarcely five feet tall.

"Dr. McCoy? Emma Saenz." She extended a warm delicate hand to him. Somewhat taken aback, he took it. Her grip was surprisingly strong.

"Yes?" he asked. Her voice was startling too, bold and arresting, not at all congruous with her physical appearance. It was a far better indicator of her age than her stature.

"Star Fleet sent me," she said, as though it completely explained her appearance at his door at this late hour.

"That is obvious," said McCoy, looking at her blue medical uniform. She had to be newly assigned personnel, but he'd received no notification and the name was completely unfamiliar. Although he had to admit that she certainly filled out the uniform well; he wondered how he'd ever mistaken her for a young girl.

She cleared her throat, and he looked up with such a guilty expression that the luminous black eyes danced. She tried again. "*Doctor* Emma Saenz, the neuropsychologist? You sent in a request." The eyes narrowed slightly. "They *did* inform you I was coming, didn't they?"

"Can't say that they did."

She sighed. "Typical."

"Actually," McCoy said gently, certain that personnel had made a mistake, "I requested a *Vulcan* neurologist."

"Yes?" Her eyes widened, making her look like a child again.

"Well, uh . . . how shall I put this tactfully? I'm afraid your ears are all wrong for the job."

She laughed so delightfully that McCoy laughed with her, a little uneasily. "Dr. McCoy, what was your request for? A neurologist *for* Vulcans or a neurologist who *is* a Vulcan?"

"The first, of course," he said, feeling very foolish as he realized what she was going to tell him. "I guess I just assumed they'd be one and the same."

"I see. Well, I am a Vulcan neurologist of the first sort, even if my ears are wrong."

"I guess you got me on that one. Is there anything I can do to make it up to you? Help you find your quarters or show you to sick bay?"

"No thanks. I'm sorry, I didn't realize what schedule you were operating on here; I can see it's late for you, so I'll take a look at the patient tomorrow. But you could tell me where I could find a drink."

"You can get beer or wine in the rec lounge."

She wrinkled her nose. "Nothing better?"

He thought for a moment. "Do you drink bourbon?"

McCoy sat with Emma Saenz in the rec lounge and poured shots for the two of them. He knew that he would regret the loss of sleep the next day, but there was something so intriguing about this woman that he resigned himself to enjoy the situation and catch up on his sleep another time.

The universe was in some ways infinitely vast but at times could seem amazingly small. McCoy had just discovered that Emma had attended the same medical school as his daughter.

"I was in the class two years ahead of Joanna. I can't really say that I knew her very well, but I did meet her. Of course," she said with exaggerated seriousness, "I was *much* older than she."

"Very tactful." McCoy smiled and refilled Emma's glass. "And are you still much older than Jo?"

Emma grinned and took a sip. "I guess that's the way it works. What did she specialize in?"

"Same thing I did—general surgery."

"You must have had a great influence on her."

"Not as much as I would have liked to." McCoy looked down at his glass, his pride tinged with guilt. "Her mother and I were divorced when she was still quite young. Then I went into the service and I was unable to share custody. Oh, we visited from time to time, but these days we're both so busy we don't get much of a chance to see each other. Last time was three years ago."

"Even so, you were obviously a very important part of her life. You must be very proud."

"I am."

"And you never remarried?" Her voice seemed more concerned than prying.

McCoy drained his glass. "I've heard that there are some people who have successfully mixed Star Fleet careers with marriage, but I'll be damned if I know how they do it."

"I know what you mean," Emma said darkly.

"Not to try to change a depressing subject, but, would you like to know anything about your patient?"

Emma brightened. "Yes. I've never worked with a Vulcan-human hybrid before. I find the opportunity to study the lateralization of Spock's brain fascinating."

"Funny you should put it that way," McCoy muttered under his breath, but continued before she could ask him to repeat what he had said. "After the accident on the planet surface, there was obvious severe trauma to the left hemisphere of the brain. I treated it immediately with alpha-dextran, but the patient still showed signs of severe aphasia and retrograde amnesia. Earlier this evening, I got a report that the patient spoke clearly—a couple of sentences with his usual choice of vocabulary. The aphasia seems to be improving, but the improvement seems to come and go. I questioned him and he spoke very little. I'm not sure what that indicates.''

Emma seemed encouraged. "Actually, that's a fairly good sign that the aphasia will improve rapidly. And the amnesia?"

"No improvement."

"Any other sign of functional impairment?"

"I've done some brain scans, but it's very difficult to know if the scanner is properly calibrated for him; I'm not even certain what the readings are telling me. He may have some impairment of mathematical ability."

The slight constant smile that Emma had worn throughout the evening swiftly metamorphosed into a frown. "I've never really trusted those things. Of course, I realize that having the proper equipment is extremely valuable in testing for damage to brain function, but I don't like depending on them entirely for my diagnosis. God knows they're not infallible. The slightest loss of calibration can cause an incorrect reading."

"Amen," McCoy agreed fervently. "It's happened to me more than once. I need them, I admit, but I don't trust 'em. And with Spock—"

"I can help you calibrate it for Spock, and I've brought a Vulcan scanner that can help us map his brain function. But to be perfectly honest with you, I'll put just as much stock in my own physical examination of the patient. I have a pretty wicked medical intuition."

McCoy was beginning to feel relaxed and slightly

tipsy, more from exhaustion than from the bourbon; the thought made him chuckle. "Just don't tell Spock, will you? He wouldn't be able to stand it if he thought his diagnosis rested on human intuition."

She smiled at him and pushed the hair from her face carelessly. It was coal-colored, the same as her eyes, and cut sensibly short. She clearly did not have the inclination to bother with it, just as she did not bother with other cosmetic enhancements. She didn't need them, McCoy decided, not with those eyes and that fearless manner of hers. Perhaps at first glance some would not consider her beautiful, but anyone who took the time to look again would be able to see how attractive she really was.

And McCoy was definitely taking the time.

"Then we won't tell him, Leonard," she said. "Of course, I don't mean to say that the tests aren't important. Some of them are critical—especially those which let us know what kind of personality changes to expect."

Now it was McCoy's turn to frown. "Personality changes? But we're talking about a Vulcan here—"

She became totally serious. "Funny how the old prejudices still exist. The fact that Spock considers himself a Vulcan and has received emotional training does not exempt him from the possibility of a personality disorder. Changes in the chemical neurotransmitters or damage to certain receptors can cause personality changes, or emotional illness, or whatever you want to call it. It's chemical. It has nothing whatsoever to do with one's emotional control. Even the Vulcans, as logical a people as they are, find it hard to admit that mental disease exists among their own people."

"What kind of changes are you talking about?"

"In the case of traumatic injury to the brain, in both

humans and Vulcans, we must be alert to the possibility of tendencies toward depression, irritability—in extreme cases, violent psychosis. Look, I'm upsetting you. I'm just talking about possibilities, Leonard. I haven't even seen Spock yet—"

"You haven't upset me. I appreciate being informed." He forced a weak smile. "You know, you must have driven the Vulcans crazy, with your talk of emotional illnesses and your intuition . . . ."

She took it as a compliment. "I must admit I . . . how shall I put it? . . . perplexed them a little. They never seemed to appreciate my frankness."

"I'll bet they didn't. But it's something we certainly appreciate around here." He smiled warmly and leaned closer, but Emma was not listening. Something had distracted her, and she stared at it intently. McCoy followed her gaze.

She was watching James Kirk.

McCoy had been right in assuming that Jim was having another one of his sleepless nights, but you wouldn't know it from his charming demeanor as he approached the table.

"Mind if I join you?" he asked.

McCoy felt a surge of irritation. If Emma hadn't been here, McCoy would have received little more than a grunt for a greeting. Sometimes Kirk's overly unctuous manners around women got on McCoy's nerves, and he had half a mind to tell Jim about it. Later, of course.

"We haven't met, have we?" Kirk asked Emma with a disarming smile. He almost succeeded in masking his exhaustion. "I'm Captain James Kirk."

"Emma Saenz," she said, offering her hand in the Terran manner.

"*Doctor* Saenz is here on temporary assignment

with us," McCoy said coolly. "She's here to give us her expert assistance with Mr. Spock. She's a neuro-psychologist."

"Sit down and have a drink with us, Captain." Emma returned Jim's smile.

"You mean Star Fleet actually filled your request? This soon?" Jim sat next to Emma and fastened his hazel eyes on her in a way that made McCoy fidget. "I'll sit for just a minute, but I'll skip the drink if that's all right. Doctor, we appreciate anything you can do for Mr. Spock. Perhaps Dr. McCoy has told you how important he is to us."

"Actually, I can probably do very little for Mr. Spock," said Emma.

"What do you mean?" Kirk's charming smile faded.

"I can diagnose him. Dr. McCoy helped him more than anyone else by administering the alpha-dextran in time—but the rest is up to Spock. He'll have to do ninety percent of the work. Motivation is the key to recovery in cases like this, and will be the deciding factor in how complete Spock's recovery will be. But there is something you can do to help, Captain."

Kirk's expression was intent. "Name it."

"Be his friend. Do everything possible to encourage him in his recovery. Let him know you need him. Of course, Leonard tells me he seems to have some trauma-related amnesia. It would be very frustrating for him to be questioned about events which he has difficulty remembering."

"I see." Kirk studiously ignored McCoy's dark glance. "Have you ever worked with Vulcans before?"

"I spent a year doing research and treating neuro-logical and psychological disorders on Vulcan. Before that, I worked in the same field for six years on Earth. I imagine that's why Star Fleet sent me here."

"Well," said Kirk, "I'm glad Spock is in such capable hands." The charming smile crept back. "We need him on the bridge and I sorely miss him as an exercise partner."

"Captain," McCoy lectured, "if you would just learn to enjoy some individual sports—jogging, swimming, gymnastics . . ."

"I know. I wouldn't have to worry about someone else's schedule and losing weight." Kirk grimaced. "Thanks, Doctor, but I prefer the martial arts."

Emma sat forward eagerly. "Do you need a partner?"

Kirk hesitated. She was petite, fine-boned . . . .

"I know what you're thinking, Captain," she said with a sly half-smile. "Let me work out with you tomorrow. I need the exercise and you need to change your opinion of my capabilities."

"All right." Kirk sounded totally unconvinced. "What time, then?"

"Oh-seven-hundred?"

"Fine. But before I leave, I'd like some idea of when I can expect my first officer back."

She turned sideways in order to face Kirk directly. "You have requested a replacement, haven't you, Captain?" She looked from the surprise on the captain's face to McCoy, whose eyes were downcast. "Perhaps you haven't been told the true extent of Spock's injuries."

"Are you telling me that Spock will not return to duty?" Kirk's jaw had tightened so much that it ached.

Her eyes were sympathetic but unyielding in their honesty. "That's one possibility. The best we can hope for is that it will be months before Spock is able to return to duty again."

Chapter Three

EMMA TURNED SHARPLY to McCoy. "You *did* tell him that, didn't you, Leonard?"

McCoy shifted uncomfortably in his chair. "I told him Spock's recovery might take some time."

Kirk had already regained his composure. "I wasn't aware . . . that it would be months, that's all."

"That's if he recovers well enough, Captain. However, since I haven't seen Spock yet, I can only speculate. But I am experienced in treating this type of injury, and recovery is usually quite protracted. For the smooth functioning of your crew, I recommend getting at least a temporary replacement."

"Yes, of course." Kirk was still expressionless. "It's the logical thing to do."

Emma leaned back in her chair and took another sip of bourbon. "Look, I don't mean to be insensitive. I'm just used to speaking my mind freely and I feel an obligation to be honest with you about Spock's condition. I see no point in trying to soften the truth."

Kirk had found Emma attractive enough at first

glance, but he certainly wouldn't have termed her pretty . . . until she spoke. There was something striking about her directness, her honesty, that was indeed beautiful.

"I appreciate that very much, Doctor," he said.

"I promise I'll take a look at Spock first thing tomorrow and let you know as soon as I've made my diagnosis."

"I trust that will be after the oh-seven-hundred workout."

"Well, yes."

Kirk rose. "If you'll excuse me, I think I'll be retiring to my quarters now if I have to be in the gym that early." He did not ask McCoy for a sleeping pill; not here, in front of a crew member.

"I'll be there." She smiled warmly at him, and they exchanged a look that left McCoy feeling distinctly uncomfortable.

Emma watched the captain leave. "He's very worried about his first officer, isn't he?"

"Yes. They're very close friends."

She turned and raised an eyebrow at McCoy. "Close friends? A human and a Vulcan?"

"Does that seem so strange to you after living for a year on Vulcan?"

"Especially after living for a year on Vulcan."

The pained look on her face made McCoy laugh. "I take it you don't much care for Vulcans."

"It's not that I don't care for them, but that they found me too exasperating. I decided that it would be kinder to them to relocate elsewhere."

"In that case, you're definitely my kind of person," McCoy said warmly. "But it is true—Jim and Spock are close, in their own special sort of way. Spock isn't the type given to emotional display, and I can't say that Jim is the type to broadcast his deepest feelings, but each has risked his life for the other dozens of times. There's a deep sense of loyalty between them. And while I can't tolerate any of Spock's insufferable logic, I like to think of him as my friend.''

"I see.'' Emma drained her glass. "I certainly can't afford to mess up on this one, can I?''

The gym was large and airy, and the overhead lighting simulated a skylight, giving the impression of filtered sunlight. To one side was an Olympic-sized lap pool, and over on the well-padded deck, a few crew-members were already working out, using the graceful defense moves taught each cadet at the Academy. Martial arts was the old Earth term used to refer to them, but over the years the intricate moves had become a combination of many ancient defense disciplines from many different cultures.

Emma was waiting on a far corner of the padded deck, already dressed in a stiff white toga and loose-fitting pants. Her uniform seemed one size too large for her, as though the computer had synthesized it with the idea that she would grow into it. The sash that circled her waist was black.

She looked so small and vulnerable waiting there that Kirk immediately regretted accepting her invitation. While he did not mind an occasional workout with a partner of lesser strength, today he needed a challenge, a match that demanded his total concentration and made it impossible for his mind to return to the worries awaiting him on the bridge. He felt some resentment at having to worry about hurting her.

She began stretching on the padded floor while he went into one of the cubicles to change. He came out wearing a similar uniform, down to the color of the belt around his waist.

"Did you sleep well, Captain?" Emma asked cheerfully. She could not have had more sleep than he'd had last night—three or four hours at most—but she seemed quite animated.

"Yes, thank you," he replied without thinking.

"You're a rather bad liar, Captain. You seem quite tired."

He made a face. "You really believe in telling the truth, don't you?"

"I do. I'm not fond of deceit, even in little things."

"Then I'll attempt to be perfectly frank with you in the future, Doctor," he replied good-naturedly. "And did you sleep well?"

"Not really. New assignments can be unsettling, but I intend to wear myself out so I'll sleep well tonight. I suggest you do the same."

Kirk did not ask her how in the hell she intended to wear him out.

"Any particular reason you haven't been getting much sleep lately?" she continued casually.

"Ah," said Kirk. "The psychologist part of the neuropsychologist."

"I don't mean to pry, Captain. It's just that I thought you might have a lot of things on your mind. Dr. McCoy told me that you are good friends with Spock, and I also know that the situation on Aritani is critical."

"I appreciate your concern, but there's not much I have to say about Spock. And as far as Aritani's concerned, the situation is under investigation by Star Fleet. I'm afraid I can't discuss it with you until I know your security clearance." He intended this last as a joke.

"It might be higher than you think, Captain," she teased. "We'd better start the workout then, if you don't feel like talking. I have to be on duty in an hour."

"We both do," he said, and they bowed to each other in the traditional manner.

As they began warming up, pacing around each other slowly, carefully, Kirk knew that he was indeed the stronger. But something strange was happening. True, he threw her twice, easily, and let her throw him once out of politeness; but then she threw him again, and then a third time, without his cooperation. The second time she threw him, he realized that he was not in as complete control of the situation as he had thought—far from it. She had let him see that he was in fact stronger than she was, and then began to trick him into making incorrect guesses about what her next move would be; more often than not, he wound up on the deck.

The third time she threw him, he felt a sense of relief; he no longer had to be polite and hold back. He lashed out with the anger that had consumed him for the past several days. As he reacted with more of his strength, so she reacted with more of hers, which Kirk guessed was twice that for a female her size. She was small, but she used it to her advantage, throwing him again with no more effort than one might exert doing a lively dance step. Kirk fell on one shoulder and rolled to his feet.

"You didn't learn those moves in medical school," he gasped and they sat, sweating, on the deck. "You're definitely anything but an amateur. You've been studying for years."

"Everyone needs an outlet." She shrugged away his compliment.

"Well, you have quite an outlet there, Doctor. You tricked me into quite a few stupid moves."

"I prefer to call it strategy."

"Call it whatever you like. And you're really quite strong."

"For a woman my size," she finished for him good-naturedly.

"Yes, if you insist on total honesty. Strength like that is another thing you didn't acquire in medical school."

"I lived on Vulcan for a year, Captain. The heavier gravity begins to affect muscular size and strength after a relatively short time. After I left, I took care not to lose my newfound strength."

"You've maintained it very well. Look, I'd like to work out with you again sometime, and learn some of those tricks. . . ."

"Strategies," she corrected him. "It's basically just the art of luring people into false assumptions and then surprising them."

"You're very good at it."

Her lips curved up slyly at the ends. "Thank you."

They were dressed in their uniforms and leaving the gym when Emma asked again about the Aritanians.

"The pirates are still attacking the populace. They've either found a way to get around the shields we installed or they've developed a new cloaking device."

"What will happen to the Aritanians?"

"That's one of the reasons I haven't gotten much sleep lately. They've asked us not to interfere."

Her eyes widened with horror. "Just let the pirates wipe them out? You aren't going to leave it at that, are you?"

Kirk was relieved to see that someone shared his reaction. "No, I'm not. The *Enterprise* will stay in the area and do what we can."

"Which is?"

"We'll try to catch one of the pirates. It's a long shot, but there's not much else we can do to help."

"Do you think you'll catch any fallout from Star Fleet about staying against the Aritanians' wishes?"

"Star Fleet ordered me to do what I can to protect the Aritanians. The way I see it, I'm just following orders." He lowered his voice. "I can't just leave them. . . ."

Emma's expression darkened, and something in the black eyes burned. "For the sake of the Aritanians, Captain, I hope you capture a pirate . . . after what the pirates have done to them, and to your people."

She leaned forward out of conviction for what she was saying; her black brows were knitted together over wide eyes whose intensity nearly overpowered her delicate features. Kirk made up his mind that she was beautiful, all the more so because of her complete unselfconsciousness.

They both realized at the same time that he was staring at her, and they lowered their eyes. Kirk cleared his throat. "Give me a call when your diagnosis is ready, Doctor, and I'll come to sick bay. I prefer to discuss it with you in person, if that's all right."

"Certainly, Captain," she replied, her eyes shyly fastened on a point just beyond his left shoulder. "I'll call you as soon as I've discussed the results with L— with Dr. McCoy."

"Thank you, Dr. Saenz," he said formally. "I'll be waiting."

The testing was completed, and Emma Saenz dimmed the lights in the intensive care ward again. A brightly colored printout of Spock's brain scan covered with scribbled notes lay on the empty bed next to Spock's; both of the critically burned crewmembers had improved and had been moved into the outer ward. The temperature of the room had been raised twenty degrees to accommodate Spock; most humans would have found it oppressive, but Emma was not even perspiring. Out in the main ward, Christine Chapel was making rounds; McCoy hadn't come on duty yet.

Emma Saenz was alone with Spock.

He sat on the bed, propped up, watching wearily while she sat on the empty bed to scribble more notes on the printout in the dim light. This one was not like the other humans who had been taking care of him; he dreaded the others' touch, for he had lost the ability to shield himself from the minds of others, and found himself being invaded by their thoughts and emotions.

This woman was different. She seemed to sense his difficulty, for her touch brought nothing, no chaotic thoughts, no swirling emotions. Perfect mental shields, unheard of in humans.

Emma put the printout carefully aside and stood up. Even in the shadows, her eyes shone with a strange light; they sought out Spock's. She moved toward the side of his bed with slow, measured steps.

"I ask you to trust me, Spock," she said in a voice so low it could be discerned only by Vulcan ears.

Spock did not reply, but met her gaze; he could not have looked away had he wanted to.

She was closer now, bent over the bed with her pale olive face close to his. He watched in fascination, and did not flinch; her nearness did not irritate him, as other humans' did, for her mental shields were still up.

Then with a slow, steady hand she reached for his temple. "You must trust me, Spock." Her voice was soothing, hypnotic.

His eyes filled suddenly with horror, and he raised a weak hand to stop her. But it was too late, for she had both hands fastened on his temples now, and her strength was greater than his.

"No," she ordered sternly, as Spock fought to pull himself from her grasp. "Don't fight it. It will be worse if you fight me."

He shuddered as he felt her mind reaching for his. She was free to take what she wished, for he had lost the power to hide his thoughts from her. But what she was doing was hideously obscene, an unpardonable breach of the most basic decency . . . those who learned the discipline of the mind meld on Vulcan were required to take an oath that they would die before violating the privacy of another's consciousness against his will.

He could see nothing but her face above him, now, and huge black eyes fierce with concentration as they looked deeply into his; opaque eyes, unreadable and so black Spock could not distinguish pupil from iris.

"My mind to yours, Spock . . ."

She had to lower her own shields to go deeply, and as she did so, Spock gasped and tried to pull away.

"No," she said quickly. "Don't think about me. It's not important. Think about Aritani. What do you remember, Spock? You can fool our instruments, if you are clever, but you cannot fool me. I must know what you remember."

The furrows in her forehead smoothed as she found what she wanted, but she did not relax her grip on Spock.

"You know who I am now," she said as he struggled weakly in her grasp. "But you will forget that as well."

As she spoke, Spock's eyes dulled and went blank like a light suddenly extinguished.

The sound of the door opening made her pull away from him abruptly.

"Sorry if I startled you. Whew, it's hotter than

Hades in here. Don't know how you stood it all this time. And how can you take notes in this dim light?" McCoy turned up the lights. "You haven't finished yet, have you?"

"I'm afraid you're out of luck, Leonard." She smiled and picked up the printout. "I just completed the last test."

"Oh." He did not hide his disappointment. "I was sort of hoping to learn a thing or two." An odd expression came over his face as his eye caught Spock. The Vulcan was leaning heavily against the pillows, breathing rapidly, his eyes glazed as if he were in shock. "What in blazes has happened to Spock? Is he all right?"

"He's fine. But the verbal tests can be physically and emotionally exhausting. I think that the kindest thing we can do for him right now is let him rest in privacy."

McCoy looked uncertainly at Spock for a moment. "Yes, of course, Doctor."

The lab was empty; McCoy closed the door behind them. Emma sat at the counter and spread Spock's brain scan out in front of her.

"All right—diagnosis first, Leonard. Take a look— right hemisphere, left hemisphere. You can see the damage to the left cerebrum. The result is as you said—retrograde amnesia and nominal aphasia. The intellect is unimpaired, with the exception of a slight loss of mathematical ability, which should respond to tutoring. The aphasia is improving, no doubt because of your prompt treatment with the alpha-dextran. However, there seems to be no improvement of the amnesia. And there is an interesting result of the amnesia—he has lost the Vulcan mind rules."

"All of them?"

"As far as I can tell."

"How permanent is the damage?"

"Amnesia of this type often improves, but there is no way to predict how long recovery will take."

"It could be months?"

"Or years." Emma looked up at him. "Or it might never improve."

McCoy digested this for a moment, then said quietly, "So what is your recommendation, Doctor?"

"Keep him here for a while until he improves, at least physically. The aphasia will clear up rapidly. We can monitor him to see if the amnesia improves. Even if it doesn't, we can get him a tutor to reteach him the mind rules."

McCoy nodded. "Even if he doesn't ever remember what happened to him on Aritani, he'll still be able to function."

She started to say something and stopped.

"Won't he?" asked McCoy. "There's something else, isn't there?"

"Yes," she said. "The damage also affected certain loci—neuroreceptors—here," she pointed, "and here. When these are damaged in a Vulcan, they may trigger violent psychotic behavior. He is a hybrid and it might be that he won't react in that manner, but the possibility exists and you should be aware of it. I recommend someone keep a constant watch on him. You may want to keep him under restraint."

"I'd rather not do that to Spock until absolutely necessary," McCoy said with sudden vehemence.

"Of course, Leonard, I understand. But you should also be aware that as a result of losing the mind rules, his psionic rating has increased. In humans and in Spock, telepathy is a right-brain function and his is unimpaired. But without the mind rules, Spock is unable to shield his own thoughts from other telepaths, or to block out the thoughts and emotions of those around him.''

"You mean—he can feel the emotions of whoever's around him? And read their thoughts?"

"Without wanting to or trying. It's a very unpleasant experience for a Vulcan. You should take that into account."

"If Spock—if he does experience behavioral changes, is there anything we can do to help?"

"There is a medication we could try, but it's still experimental. I prefer to wait and see if we need it." She leaned forward and rested a hand lightly on his arm. "You know, Leonard, I've seen some very bad cases and considering what could have happened to Spock, the prognosis is very hopeful. But there is one more problem."

He tensed. "What else?"

"I don't know how to make the chief medical officer feel better about the situation."

"I do," he answered, surprised at his own response. "Have dinner with me tonight."

"To discuss the prognosis?" she teased softly.

"Definitely not."

Kirk had almost stepped onto the turbolift in response to Saenz's call when Chekhov called to him excitedly from Spock's station.

"Keptin! Two uncloaked pirate wessels—on the surface below!"

Kirk raced back to the con, heart pounding, but he did not sit down.

"They're hovering, sir." The Russian bent over the hooded computer screen. "Near the same area we beamed you up from."

The area where Spock fell. "Mr. Chekhov, compute

73

the trajectory of those ships if we 'borrow' their pilots for a while.''

"The wessels should crash—into the mountains, sir." He straightened and looked at Kirk. "It should present no danger to the population.''

Kirk walked toward the helm. "Get a tractor beam on those vessels, Mr. Sulu." He leaned over the helmsman's shoulder anxiously as though his presence might somehow help to keep them from getting away this time.

"Tractor beam on, sir."

Kirk had to force himself to sit in his chair to call the transporter room.

"Lyle here, sir."

"Two to beam up from the planet surface, Mr. Lyle. Chekhov will feed you the coordinates."

"Captain," said Sulu. "One of the ships is tearing up."

"Did you adjust the beam for the size of the vessel?" Kirk was immediately embarrassed at his own question; Sulu was one of the most competent helmsmen in the Fleet.

"Yes, sir. He's trying to move the ship off course."

Kirk punched a toggle on the console. "Kirk to Security."

"Tomson here."

"Lieutenant, I need a security team of four to the transporter room on the double. We have two prisoners to escort to the brig."

"Right away, Captain."

Kirk called Lyle back. "Bring them aboard, Mr. Lyle."

He could hear the whine of the transporter, and the sound of Lyle drawing in his breath sharply. "What's wrong, Lyle? Are the prisoners aboard?"

"Yes, Captain." Lyle sounded shaken. "I'm afraid

I'll need to have some medics to pick up one of them. He was only half-caught by the beam.''

"The other?"

"They're taking him to the brig now, sir."

"Keptin," Chekhov interrupted. "The ships have crash-landed near the mountains. One was completely torn apart by the tractor beam; the other is damaged but salvageable."

Kirk almost laughed with exhilaration. They had done it at last—they had a pirate, and now his ship. He called Scott.

"Scotty, I've got a pirate ship on the surface we need someone to disassemble and beam up here. Think you can find some volunteers who'll risk it?"

"Aye, that we can," Scott said exuberantly. "Did we catch a pirate, Captain?"

"That we did, Scotty."

Scott emitted a low rumble in his throat. "I'm not responsible for what I might do to him, sir. What kind is he?"

"I'll know soon, Scotty. I'm on my way down to the brig now. How soon can you get some people down there?"

"Yesterday, sir."

The Vulcanoid behind the force field was tall, lean and aristocratic of bearing, but there the similarity ended; the expression of open hatred on his face negated the possibility of his being a native of Vulcan. Romulan, then; but he did not fit Kirk's idea of what a Romulan should look like, for he did not wear his hair in the Romulan style. Thick and wavy, it was brushed straight back from the widow's peak on his forehead and curled onto his shoulders. Nor did he wear the sedate Romulan military uniform; his bright red tunic fit snugly underneath a long, loose-fitting vest.

He had apparently not been blessed with the discipline and courtesy of the Romulan culture, for as Kirk approached the brig he spat at him. The spittle hit the force field and slid to the floor of the brig without hitting its target.

It did not surprise Kirk to see a Romulan dressed as a pirate. The Praetor's Empire placed heavy demands on its subjects; nothing less than excellence was accepted, whether one served the Praetor in the military or as a civilian, and dropouts were not tolerated within the society. Those who did not fit into the spartan way of life were dispatched, or they escaped to become outcasts . . . or pirates.

"Murderous whelp!" The pirate cursed Kirk.

Kirk answered coolly in his best imitation of his first officer. "I've murdered no one. The death of your cohort was an accident. You, on the other hand, have no doubt killed a number of Aritanians and quite possibly some of my people as well. What were you doing under our protective shield?"

The Romulan eyed Kirk as though he were insane. "Shield? I encountered no shield."

"Perhaps you used a shield neutralizer." Kirk watched carefully for a reaction. "Are you working for the Praetor?"

The Romulan laughed scathingly. "Shield neutralizer! You *are* a stupid human. I work for no one but myself."

"What were you doing on Aritani?"

"My friend and I were merely flying over the planet surface when you attacked us—"

"We beamed you aboard," Kirk said calmly.

"Yes, and in your incompetence, you killed my friend! And you accuse me of killing people—"

Kirk leaned forward, his voice so soft the Romulan had to strain to hear it. "I regret that. I would like to have two of you, so you could try to corroborate each other's story. Why wasn't your cloaking device on?"

The Romulan's eyes widened. "Such accusations! I don't know what you're talking about."

"We'll see. We have your ship."

"I don't believe you." The Romulan's sneer faded slightly.

"It really doesn't matter," Kirk continued in the same low voice; he clenched his fist as a wave of irrational hatred swept over him. The Romulan seemed to sense it and pulled back slightly from the force field. "Why don't you relax now? Our medical officer will be down later to talk to you and give you a little something to help relax you."

"You Federation types are pathetic. What makes you think you have anything that could make a Romulan talk? We are impervious to your interrogation methods."

Kirk smiled tightly. "You meant to say, the trained and disciplined members of the Romulan military are impervious . . . to almost anything. But you aren't Vulcans. We can get information out of you."

"I have nothing to hide." The pirate turned his face away.

"We'll see," said Kirk. He left while he could still control his impulse to put his hands around the Romulan's neck.

Emma and McCoy were in the laboratory looking at another brain scan; Emma sat at the counter with the printout spread out in front of her while McCoy leaned over her shoulder—a little too closely, Kirk thought, even for colleagues. They were laughing when he came in, but when they saw his face, they stopped abruptly.

"What's happened, Jim?" McCoy asked. The captain was no longer weighed down with fatigue and concern; his movements were electric, purposeful.

"We got one, Bones," Kirk gloated.

McCoy's face broke into a broad grin.

"What did you catch?" Emma searched Kirk's face and then McCoy's until she understood. "A pirate?"

Kirk nodded. "Romulan."

"Is he really a pirate," asked McCoy, "or one of the Praetor's boys?"

"That's what I want to find out. I'm going to need you later, Bones. We're bringing up the wreckage from one of the ships, and I want to examine it before we question him, but after that—"

"You'd like me to concoct a little potion to loosen his tongue."

"Exactly."

Emma looked surprised. "Do you really have a truth serum effective against Romulans?"

McCoy shrugged. "It sometimes is. A lot depends on the individual. With a little perseverance, we can usually find out what we need to know."

"Would you like to come along with McCoy during the questioning?" Kirk asked. "Your knowledge of Vulcan psychology might be useful."

She wheeled on him with such angry indignance that Kirk drew back, surprised. "Vulcans and Romulans are hardly similar when it comes to psychology, Captain, although I suppose most humans assume they are the same since they share a few minor racial characteristics. Their cultures and philosophies are completely different—"

Kirk held up his hands. "Sorry, Doctor. I didn't mean to overgeneralize. It was stupid of me. Still, you have more experience in psychology than either of us—"

"What time?" she said, suddenly cool. "Leonard and I were going to have dinner later."

McCoy did not need to look in a mirror to know his cheeks were flaming; and he was even more embarrassed that such a perfectly normal statement would embarrass him. Everyone else had a love life; it was perfectly normal. What did he have to blush about? He waited for the captain to make some taunting remark, to say, "Excuse me, *Leonard,* I didn't know" . . . but he did not.

"I don't wish to interfere in Dr. McCoy's social life," Kirk said in clipped tones, "but I am unable to predict when we'll be finished searching the ship. I'll call the minute I know something. But first, Dr. Saenz, I'd like to talk to you about those test results on Spock . . ."

The door to Engineering opened to reveal total chaos. Pieces of metal had been strewn all over the deck; Kirk could recognize pieces of the debris as parts from a surface fighter. One of the pieces was a small, streamlined cloaking device, and he picked it up, marveling at its size—the one he had stolen from the Romulans scarcely three years ago had been twenty times the size.

Scott wriggled out from under a large piece of bulkhead on the floor; nearby, a small engine had been completely dismantled. Kirk smiled to himself; at least part of Scott's thoroughness was not motivated by his desire to find the shield neutralizer as much as by the chance to tinker with someone else's engines. Scott brushed dust and ash from his rumpled tunic and walked over to Kirk, who knew the moment he saw the engineer's expression that they had not found anything yet.

"I dinna understand, Captain." Scott shook his

head. "Ye kin see the little cloakin' device there, but that thing's designed to consume a goodly amount of fuel. They couldna stayed cloaked more than seven hours with it. They weren't under the shields to begin with."

"So Spock was right." Kirk turned the device over in his hands. "Scotty, there's got to be something else here to explain it."

"But sir, we've just about finished checkin' everything, and there's not one piece of equipment here to explain either how they got past the shield or how they stayed cloaked more than seven hours."

"Just about finished." Kirk looked up at Scott. "That isn't the same as completely finished, is it, Engineer?"

"Well, no, sir, I suppose not, but the only thing that remains is to tear apart every bulkhead and see if the device is concealed somewhere—but I can't believe it could be small enough for that and still work."

"Keep looking, Scotty. I've got to know something before I go in to question the prisoner."

Scott's expression was dangerous. "I wish I could go with ye, Captain. I have a few things I'd like to clear up with that murderous divvil—"

"I know," Kirk said softly. "But I need you here. Keep up the good work, Mr. Scott. Give me a call when you've found something."

"We will, sir."

The instant the door to Engineering closed behind the captain, Scott muttered, "But I guarantee ye we won't find a bloody thing." He eyed the wreckage on the floor and suddenly gave a piece of it a disgusted kick.

Emma was waiting for McCoy in front of his quarters; he'd stayed on duty a half-hour longer to make up for being late that morning. "Hi," he smiled.

"Hello yourself." She leaned against the wall and smiled up at him with an expression that could hardly be called professional.

"Look, I'm going to be a little late for dinner tonight. Why don't you go ahead and we'll take a raincheck."

"No thanks, I thought I might go along when the Romulan is questioned. It sounds fascinating."

McCoy winced. "Did I ever mention that you remind me of someone sometimes—no, never mind. I haven't heard from the captain yet today. It seems he has Scotty and half of Engineering going over that pirate ship with a fine-toothed comb, and he wants to wait until they're finished before we question the prisoner."

"Have they found anything?" Her eyes glistened with interest.

"Oh, just the usual Romulan pirate paraphernalia—cloaking devices and whatnot. I take it dinner's after the interrogation, then? Let me give Jim a call and see how it's going."

McCoy knew that something was urgently wrong the instant he heard Kirk's voice on the intercom. "What is it, Jim?"

"I just got a call from Security, Bones. It looks like I won't be needing your help with that prisoner after all. He's dead."

Chapter Four

WHEN MCCOY AND Emma arrived at the brig, the force field which had contained the prisoner was dark; inside, security personnel were searching for evidence. Kirk stood where he had once faced the Romulan, but this time he confronted Security Chief Tomson.

Lieutenant Ingrit Tomson was a colorless, lanky woman who stood a good half a head taller than Kirk in spite of her tendency to slump. She came from an icy colony planet that rarely saw the sun, and her skin and hair were so pale that she seemed lashless and browless; when she blushed, the capillaries were clearly outlined in red on her white cheeks. Normally serene of manner and countenance almost to the point of apathy, she spoke to Kirk now with what was for her an alarming degree of agitation. Her security team had just made one of the most serious mistakes a security team can make: they had lost a prisoner.

Tomson had not been on the *Enterprise* long, and she was keenly aware that her promotion to security chief was recent enough for any miscalculation on her part to be interpreted as greenhorn incompetence rather than simple bad luck. She spoke slowly, choosing her words with care so that the captain would understand that the situation had been handled with complete professionalism. The fact that the captain stood listening silently, jaw clenched, with a look of barely controlled fury on his face, did not bolster Tomson's confidence any.

"The facts are, sir, that Ensign al-Baslama was guarding the entrance to the brig when he was stunned by a phaser blast coming from someplace outside the brig. When he came to, he discovered that the force field was down and the prisoner and his own phaser were missing. At first he assumed that the prisoner had escaped, and he contacted me. We did an internal scan of the ship, but we couldn't locate a Vulcanoid on board, other than Mr. Spock in sick bay."

"Any idea how long al-Baslama was unconscious?"

"By his condition, I would say the phaser was fired on light stun. He was probably out three or four minutes at most. Then we found his phaser on the deck of the brig." Tomson handed it to Kirk for inspection. "It has the Romulan's fingerprints on it, sir. I'm taking it to forensics to see if it was fired.

"After al-Baslama notified me, I immediately checked with the transporter room and the shuttle deck. No one has left this ship, Captain. So right now we're checking the air in the room to see if we can pick up any random molecules."

Kirk's scowl deepened. "Of what?"

"Of someone who was recently vaporized."

"The pirate," Kirk said, understanding.

"Yes, sir."

"But how did the prisoner get the phaser in the first place?"

83

"I had trouble figuring that one out myself, sir. My best guess is that someone brought it to him."

"Someone on my ship brought it to him," Kirk's irritability was increasing, "so that he could kill himself? It doesn't make any sense. If someone was in collusion with him, why wouldn't they help him escape?"

"I don't know, sir. But there was no way he could have gotten past the force field to take it from Ensign al-Baslama himself. This brig was absolutely secure."

Up to this time Emma and McCoy had been standing silently nearby; when Emma spoke, Kirk and Tomson turned quickly to look at her. "If the pirates could get through the protective shield on Aritani, why should it be impossible for one of them to get past a small force field?"

"A good question," said Kirk. "But we didn't find anything resembling a shield neutralizer on their ship."

Tomson took the question as an insult to her professional competence. "The prisoner didn't have any type of device on him when we put him in the brig, ma'am. My people are very thorough when it comes to searching prisoners." Tall and pale, she stared coldly down at small, dark Emma; McCoy thought they looked for all the worlds like two exact opposites.

Emma persisted. "But you just said there weren't any other fingerprints on the phaser except the guard's and the prisoner's."

"I don't have to explain to you how easy it is to avoid getting fingerprints on something, do I, ma'am?" Tomson's tone was less than charitable.

Emma almost seemed to enjoy Tomson's disgruntlement. "Maybe the prisoner did escape, and planted the phaser to throw us off."

Tomson's cheeks slowly turned pink. "First off,

Ensign al-Baslama swears that he was fired at from the corridor, not from the brig. Secondly, we've already searched this ship, and there aren't any Romulans aboard. Thirdly, the prisoner didn't leave via the transporter or a hijacked shuttlecraft. Would you like to suggest just how he managed to get off this ship?"

Emma raised an eyebrow but remained silent.

One of the security men walked over and displayed a tricorder reading to Tomson. "That confirms it," she said, pleased. "Someone was recently vaporized in this room. Unless you're missing any crewmen, Captain, we'll assume it was the prisoner." She smiled coldly down at Emma. "I'm afraid your Romulan didn't escape, ma'am."

"*My* Romulan?" Emma muttered so that only McCoy could hear. "I didn't realize I owned one."

"I'm aware that suicide is a favorite pastime of captured Romulans," McCoy said aloud, "but who on this ship would attack a security guard to bring the prisoner a suicide weapon?"

"Maybe not to bring a suicide weapon," Tomson answered.

"Murder," Kirk said softly.

Tomson nodded. "It's the only good explanation I can come up with to fit the facts. Of course, I'll know more when I get the results of all the tests."

"But who—" Kirk began, and stopped abruptly.

McCoy finished for him. "Who on this ship would have a motive?"

Tomson looked down at him grimly. "Are you forgetting, Doctor, how many of the crew have suffered at the hands of the pirates? They all have a motive."

More than enough, Kirk thought, remembering Ensign Lanz. "I'll be in my quarters," he told Tomson. "Notify me when you get the results."

* * *

"Come on," said Uhura, "see if you can play along." She had just finished singing a song from the heartland of Africa. Her forehead glistened with perspiration, and she thoughtlessly ran the back of her hand across it. Spock was sorry that he had not properly adjusted the temperature in his cabin to accommodate her; he had thought it should be tolerable for humans, since it felt chilly to him.

"Come on," she urged, and Spock joined in with his harp, the instrument blending with Uhura's voice in an eerily beautiful harmony.

Uhura nodded, smiling, and Spock nodded back. His physical injuries were now almost unnoticeable except for a slight limp. At Saenz's urging, he had moved back into his quarters. His speech had improved as well, although at times he found himself at a humiliating loss for a word, a situation that caused great awkwardness for himself and his visitor. Even worse was his almost total loss of recent memory; he was unable to converse about anything save the present and the far-distant past. Kirk, who had at first come the most often, now visited him hardly at all, for there was little else on Kirk's mind these days besides Aritani, a word which held no significance for Spock.

Dr. Saenz, on the other hand, came to see him almost every day, and her visits did not trouble him much, but they always left him with a vague sense of uneasiness and he could never recall the sessions clearly afterwards. Even so, her controlled thoughts were a relief after being bombarded with the emotions of the others.

Especially those of Christine Chapel; her visits were most distressing. She came to give him physical therapy for his left arm and leg and to encourage him to speak. The physical contact between them during the therapy session was almost unbearable for Spock, a touch-telepath. Her emotions were violent and disconcerting; the overwhelming one was pity for him, which shamed him. Her pathetic struggle to hide her emotional attachment for him made Spock in turn feel pity for her. It also reminded him pointedly of his own pathetic efforts to deal with his own surging emotions: frustration, anger, self-pity.

Ironically, it was his human side that now struggled to control his emotions, guarding them until his Vulcan control could be restored; but it was a tenuous control, one which could break easily at the first critical moment.

The only visitor he did not dread was Uhura, for he did not have to speak and be reminded of the words and incidents he could not remember; instead, he could let the music flow from him and forget for a moment that things were not as they had always been.

"That was great, Spock," Uhura said. The beads of sweat on her brow had become small rivulets and she tried again to inconspicuously wipe them away. Spock laid his harp aside and walked stiffly to the temperature control. He'd lowered it already to a temperature he thought a human should find comfortable, but his memory was not reliable these days; he turned it down another ten degrees.

Uhura sighed gratefully. "Bless you."

At the same time as her sigh, Spock heard a shuffling sound outside the door to his cabin.

"What's wrong?" Uhura asked. "I didn't hear anything. Come on, let me teach you another song."

The sound of Leonard McCoy emitting a monstrous sneeze just outside the door was unmistakable.

Spock rose.

"Someone just passing by," Uhura said quickly, her soft brown eyes wide.

If someone had told Spock that his expression was

one of affectionate exasperation, he would have denied it. "Uhura," he said disapprovingly. He could never seem to remember her rank.

She giggled. "Oh, what the hell," she said, and went to open the door.

"Surprise," the crowd in the doorway chorused weakly.

"Not much of a surprise," Uhura said. "Really, Doctor."

"I think I may be coming down with something," McCoy snuffled. "They can transport a man's molecules across space, but they can't prevent the common cold." Standing beside him was the captain, Dr. Saenz, M'Benga, and Christine Chapel.

Spock regarded them with curiosity as they trooped into his cabin. The conflicting thoughts were reeling; he couldn't sort them out to interpret the reason for the mass visit. They stood nervously around the captain, who was holding a small square object in his hand.

He smiled at Spock. "I have a little something for you from Star Fleet Command, Mr. Spock." He held out the small dark box and opened it.

Neatly arranged within the box, the shiny silver medallion hung from a dark blue ribbon. Spock held it up to the light; it was inscribed on the back with his name and the date of his injury in Vulcan script; on the front was the Federation logo, the Roman letters *UFP* enclosed in a shield.

He did not remember what the captain said to him afterwards; nor did he remember thanking the captain or watching everyone leave. But after they were gone, Spock sat in the traditional posture before the stone meditation statue in his room. He could remember the posture, and the purpose and symbolism of the small stone statue with the throbbing flame in its belly, for his earlier memories, especially those of Vulcan, had not been lost—if anything, they had become stronger. Yet he was unable to summon the discipline of meditation; a part of him was gone, a part without which he could not function as Spock.

He drew the silver medal from the box—the Award of Valor, the Federation's highest decoration for the wounded—and turned it over in his hand. The date meant nothing to him; he could not even vaguely remember the incident for which he had been decorated. His hand closed over the medal.

For a long time, he sat before the statue, his eyes wide and unseeing, and in his mind one word pulsed like the flame: Remember.

Kirk was back on the bridge when Tomson called with the report from forensics.

She sounded quite pleased with herself. "I think you'll find this interesting, Captain. Ensign al-Baslama's phaser was fired twice—once on stun and once to kill."

"That's what you expected, isn't it? Al-Baslama was stunned, then the prisoner—"

"Remember, sir, al-Baslama was not stunned with his own phaser. He was wearing it at the time he was stunned."

"Of course. So it means—"

"It means that al-Baslama was stunned with someone else's phaser, of course; then that person took al-Baslama's phaser and stunned the prisoner with it, then put the prisoner's fingerprints on it, then—"

"Then murdered him." It was not what Kirk had hoped to hear. "A very good attempt to make it look like suicide. Now what?"

"I'm afraid we're going to have to start an investigation of our own personnel, sir. I suggest we start with those who were wounded down on the planet surface. Do you have any idea who might have had a particularly strong motive for killing the Romulan?"

"No," Kirk lied.

"Well, sir, I'm afraid that leaves me with the very unpleasant task of finding out which of our crewmen is a murderer."

It was Christine Chapel who found Spock unconscious on his bed; his wrists had been slashed with the ceremonial dagger taken from his wall.

Emma and McCoy hovered over Spock in sick bay, but there was nothing more they could do except wait for Spock's body to heal itself. Slender green tubing ran from the crook in Spock's right elbow to a packet above his bed; to one side lay Spock's harp—McCoy could not remember who had thought to bring it in all the confusion.

Emma spoke barely above a whisper. "He seemed to be doing so well. I should have noticed the warning symptoms . . ."

"No one can believe it." McCoy's eyes were fixed on the life monitor. Spock, as always, would survive. That Vulcan had the toughest hide . . . "I just don't understand what prompted him to do it."

"We shouldn't have left him alone in his quarters. It's my fault. I've seen enough of these cases to know better. Rational one moment, psychotic the next. I should have insisted he be under constant watch."

McCoy looked at her tenderly. "I thought you were a psychologist, Doctor. Are you really going to try to take all the blame?"

She smiled at him, a small, unhappy smile.

"Maybe instead of trying to figure out what we did wrong," McCoy said, "we should try to figure out what to do right."

"Okay." She straightened and squared her shoulders. "Let's put him on that neurotransmitter and see if it helps."

"Sounds like a step in the right direction. What's the name of the medication?"

"Neodopazine."

His eyebrows flew upwards. "Neodopazine? That's very experimental stuff."

"I know. I was one of the first to work with it. I've used it very successfully with the violent."

"It's never been tested on Vulcans, has it?"

Emma gazed back down at Spock; the Vulcan's breathing was slow and regular. Her voice sounded very far away.

"Would you prefer Spock try to kill himself again?"

"Of course not, Emma, but I want to know what other alternatives we have."

"We can send him away. To a star base hospital if they'd take him—if he becomes more violent, to Ebla Two."

Ebla II was a maximum security sanitorium for the violently insane. McCoy closed his eyes briefly and shuddered.

"Let's start the medication, then."

McCoy had not expected to sleep well that night, but the last thing he had counted on was a call from sick bay rousing him from deep slumber. Spock had torn the transfusion tubes from his arms. The medic had replaced them at once, noting that they had not been out long, and gone about his rounds. Now they were out again. Did McCoy want the patient restrained?

Reluctantly, McCoy ordered the restraints. But he could not return to sleep after that, and when the Vulcan finally awoke, McCoy was watching by his bedside as he had been for the past several hours. The confusion in Spock's eyes cleared gradually as he came to realize where he was, and turned to irritation at the sight of the tube in his arm and the restraint.

"Spock?" McCoy spoke gently. "Do you remember what happened?"

Spock frowned.

"Nurse Chapel found you in your quarters. Spock . . . it seems you tried to kill yourself."

Spock tried to sit up, but the restraints held him back. "No," he said. "That's impossible."

It was the answer McCoy most wanted to hear; it was the answer he wanted desperately to believe. "Then suppose you tell me what happened."

"I don't remember," Spock said vehemently. "But it was not I . . . it was someone else."

"I want to believe, Spock, God knows, but—"

"Then believe," said Spock, with such conviction and so much like the old Spock that McCoy believed.

He leaned over to loosen the Vulcan's restraints out of pity. "But who would try to kill you, Spock?"

"Someone's out to get you, Spock?"

McCoy could not recognize the voice—cold, skeptical, ugly—and turned around to see who spoke.

Emma Saenz stood in the doorway. "He's generalizing his paranoia, Doctor," she said loudly. "He's managed to convince himself that someone else has done this to him."

McCoy could not believe that Emma was saying these things, nor could he keep from losing his temper. "For God's sake, if you have something to say, say it to him. Don't talk about him as if he can't understand you!"

Her anger matched his. "I know he understands me. And I won't let him deny the truth." She moved to the side of Spock's bed. "You attempted suicide, Spock.

Face it. You're depressed and it must be dealt with if you are to get better. Lying about it won't help."

Spock's eyes flamed. "No," he said explosively. "I do not lie."

Emma leaned toward him fiercely. "If you didn't do it, Spock, then tell us who did."

"I . . . don't remember." Spock turned away from her.

"I thought so." Her manner became calm. "Spock, if you're going to deny the truth, I can't do anything to help you. I suggest you think about that, because your captain and this ship need you to get better." She turned abruptly to leave, but paused in the doorway without turning around. "I suggest you put the restraints back on him, Doctor."

The door closed behind her a split second before the harp struck it with an angry twang. Spock slumped back in the bed, breathing rapidly.

McCoy picked up the instrument gently and examined it. One of the strings had snapped, and there was a small crack in the body. He returned it to Spock's bedside without comment, but the Vulcan did not look at it—Spock was fighting an internal battle now, and the enemy was his own rage: rage at Emma Saenz because she did not believe, rage at himself because he could not remember, rage at the unspeakably irrational, destructive act he had just committed.

A moment passed before Spock replaced his anger with the cool expression McCoy knew so well, an expression the vehemence of his words belied.

"I can no longer remain here. I must go to Vulcan."

McCoy could not pretend that he did not understand; Spock, of course, feared the loss of emotional control far worse than the other infirmities he faced. Still, McCoy tried to soothe him.

"Let me discuss it with Dr. Saenz, Spock."

For a moment he thought Spock's anger might erupt again, but the Vulcan contained himself and faced the doctor calmly. *Vulcans do not beg,* McCoy had to remind himself, but the look in Spock's eyes was the closest thing to a plea that McCoy had ever seen.

"I must go *now.*" Hoarse with desperation, Spock resorted to a word McCoy could not remember hearing him use before. "Please."

McCoy closed the lab door behind him. He was furious with Emma, so furious that he shouted.

"You'd better have a damn good excuse for what you did in there. You just called a Vulcan a liar, and you, of all people, should know what an insult that is!"

"I know," Emma said quietly. She sat with her elbows on the lab counter, her chin resting on one fist; the ugliness that she had shown to Spock was gone, and the anger, too, as though it had been a role she'd assumed for a few moments and discarded the instant she left intensive care.

She was once again the person with whom McCoy was falling in love.

He scarcely heard her, though, and went back to venting his anger while she sat patiently and waited for it to subside.

"And how dare you treat him as though he doesn't exist, talking about him in the third person! Dammit, how can you be so insensitive to all he's gone through?"

"Do you believe it?" Emma asked, watching intently. "Do you honestly believe that someone tried to kill Spock?"

McCoy faltered, losing some of his steam. "Well . . ."

"If you had believed it, Leonard, you would have called Security, and reported it. But you didn't."

"Well, I believe him when he says he doesn't remember doing it."

Emma sighed. "I do, too. But that wasn't all he said—he's trying to blame someone else for it, and I refuse to coddle him by pretending I believe it."

"Coddle him—" McCoy sputtered. "You were downright insulting! You called him a liar, the worst thing you could call a—"

She lifted up her chin and sat up straight on the stool. "Leonard, you are too emotionally involved with this patient to do either one of you any good."

"Yes, of *course* I'm emotionally involved!" McCoy exploded. "But that doesn't mean I'm incapable of helping Spock. You, on the other hand, seem to be totally insensitive to his situation. If you ask me, you have something against Vulcans!"

Emma gasped and stood up so quickly that the stool almost tipped over. "That's the most irrational thing I've ever heard you say—"

McCoy thrust out his jaw. "Maybe you'd better send me to Ebla Two with Spock."

She drew a quick breath as if to reply heatedly, then suddenly stopped and sat back down on the stool. She closed her eyes and seemed to gather herself; when she finally spoke, her tone was infinitely patient.

"Please, Leonard, I can't bear to fight with you on this. We're both trying to help Spock. It's just that we have different ideas of how to go about it. Let's not argue."

"Fine." He stood, arms folded tightly, his eyes still flashing with anger. He was not about to capitulate. "Let's discuss it calmly, then."

Emma did not let herself hear the sarcasm in his voice, but leaned heavily against the polished black countertop and sighed. God, she looked lovely, McCoy thought in spite of his anger, and so very sad.

She spoke in such a soft murmur that he had to lean very close to hear her. "I truly wish that I could believe Spock's story. I know you feel the same way. Spock's subconscious has invented a way out of accepting responsibility for his desperate action. If we go along with it, he'll begin to truly believe it, and Spock will never deal with the problem. I've always believed that you don't solve problems by pretending they don't exist. I was trying to shock him, Leonard—by being cruel, I was trying to show him that he can't run away from what he has done."

McCoy did not pull his hand away when she reached for it; her touch was strangely hot, as though she burned with fever. His anger melted.

"I'm sorry I upset you," Emma continued, leaning still closer. "But I've never been very diplomatic. I want to help Spock, but I will not encourage his fantasies."

"I'm sorry I yelled . . . but I'm very worried about him. I still think you were too hard on him."

She smiled up at him, still holding his hand. "Maybe I was."

McCoy was close enough for the first time to notice her perfume, a strangely familiar sweetness that he could not place, until he remembered the wildflowers on the planet below.

Clearly, the only logical thing to do was to bend down and kiss her.

Some time later, Kirk stood indecisively in front of McCoy's quarters in the dimly lit corridor. As much as he hated resorting to McCoy's concoctions, he hadn't had much sleep in the last forty-eight hours and had long ago finished the last of his brandy supply. These days he was becoming too tired even for his workouts in the gym, and they were his only release of tension.

And he was looking forward to seeing Emma Saenz again.

Kirk pressed the buzzer with reluctance. It took such an uncomfortably long time for McCoy to respond that he was convinced the doctor was sleeping too soundly to hear, and he turned to leave.

He stopped as the door slid open. McCoy wore a short robe, and Kirk managed to repress a sarcastic whistle as he studied McCoy's pitifully pale legs ending in two bare bony feet. He'd never known the prudish doctor to sleep in the nude before; perhaps he'd been in the sonic shower. But the room behind McCoy was dark.

"Sorry to wake you," Kirk apologized, but McCoy's face was not sodden with sleep, nor was his voice groggy. If anything, he seemed alert—perhaps even a little anxious.

"No problem," he said quickly. "What can I do for you, Captain?"

"No sleep in two days. I give up, Doctor. Give me something."

"Okay, Jim—just give me a second. I'll call sick bay and tell whoever's on duty what to give you." He disappeared into the darkened room, and Kirk began to follow, but the door slid shut in his face. He pulled back, surprised and a little insulted.

He excused the doctor's rude behavior by deciding that McCoy was probably suffering from the cumulative effects of exhaustion himself when McCoy appeared in the doorway again.

"M'Benga's there. He'll give you what you need, Jim."

Kirk smiled wanly. "I really appreciate this, Bones. You'll never know—"

A sound emerged from the darkness behind McCoy, a sound that Kirk recognized as a feminine yawn. His first reaction was amusement; his second, as he placed the owner of the voice, was a far darker emotion.

It must have shown on his face, for McCoy faced him with glittering eyes. *You have no right*, they said.

They were right; Kirk cast his eyes downward. "Thanks again, Doctor."

"Don't mention it," said McCoy.

Christine Chapel was on duty in the main ward the next day when McCoy entered, whistling loudly and tunelessly.

"Whoever told you you could whistle?"

Mercifully, he stopped, but her affectionate sarcasm did not dampen his decidedly good spirits. "How are you this morning, beautiful?" McCoy inspected her with paternal solicitousness. "You're looking a little tired."

"I *am* tired," she answered, immediately suspicious at his unusually complimentary appellation for her. *Beautiful* was somewhat less than accurate; she'd just finished an eight-hour shift and knew with bedrock certainty that she resembled something the cat dragged in. "More than a little. I was just on my way out—"

"Have a good rest," McCoy said warmly. "God knows you deserve it after all the double shifts you've pulled these past few weeks."

"We've *all* pulled double shifts the past few weeks." Her suspicion deepened; she folded her arms and assumed a no-nonsense stance. "All right, Doctor, what gives?"

McCoy's watery blue eyes regarded her innocently. "Whatever do you mean?"

"Ever since Spock's injury and then the pirate attack, you've been coming in here with a sour expression on your face, complaining to the heavens like Job about the unfairness of it all. Not to mention being so dead on your feet that you hardly knew which end of the patient you were working on. Now, today, suddenly, you are filled with a limitless abundance of *joie de vivre*—"

"We released the last burn victim yesterday, and I got a good night's sleep," he protested, but he could not keep from grinning. Chris knew him too well. They were comfortable around each other after so many years, and had built up a trust—enough for her to tell him about her feelings for Spock, enough for him to scold her into admitting the hopelessness of them, and enough for her to scold him for the protective barrier he had kept between himself and the female sex since his divorce.

He decided to keep her guessing at least a little while longer. That is, if she hadn't figured it all out already.

"Who is she?" Chris asked.

McCoy attempted and failed to keep his grin from growing ever wider and stupider. "I really don't know what you're talking about, Chris." He tried to sound briskly professional. "Is Dr. Saenz on duty yet?"

Chapel smirked. She knew, all right. "In there." She directed a thumb at the door of the lab.

McCoy started toward it, muttering loudly so that Chris could hear. "Man gets a good night's sleep, and suddenly his staff starts accusing him of all sorts of things . . ."

Chris called to him on her way out without turning around. "Whatever you may have gotten last night, Doctor, it wasn't a good night's sleep."

She disappeared through the door and he laughed softly, feeling lighter and younger than he had in years.

He walked into the lab just in time to see Emma put two capsules in her mouth and swallow. His grin faded instantly. "What's that you're taking?"

She turned around, startled. Her hand moved instinctively toward the lone bottle on the counter as if to hide it. "It's nothing, Leonard. How are you this morning?" Her eyes were very bright.

McCoy picked up the bottle and read it. "Levirol! My God, do you have any idea what this stuff does to you?"

"Do you think I'd take it if I didn't?"

"This stuff can dangerously elevate your blood pressure, Emma—"

Her voice was that of a mother's calming an excitable child. "Leonard. I have chronic pathologically low blood pressure, and I have been taking Levirol for years. I monitor my blood pressure every day, but you're free to check it, if you're concerned."

"I *am* concerned," he said in a way that made her smile. "You'd better be taking good care of yourself."

"I am. Now what is it you've come to see me about?"

"Spock."

"It's still too early to judge his response to the neodopazine—"

"That's not what I need to talk to you about." McCoy hesitated, looking for the right words. "Spock has asked me to send him to Vulcan."

"Eventually, perhaps—"

"He wants to go immediately. I can tell he feels very strongly about it."

"I hope you told him it was impossible."

"I promised to send him."

"You didn't!" Emma confronted him, hands on narrow hips, suddenly all sharp angles. McCoy was not surprised at the quick display of temper: he had recently come to appreciate the fact that this woman possessed a passionately volatile, aggressive nature, which her outwardly constant good humor belied.

"You can't send him away now, in this condition. I don't even know his reaction to the medication yet—"

"They'll take good care of him on Vulcan," McCoy countered evenly.

"Good care!" Emma's laugh was bitter. "Have you ever been in a Vulcan hospital, attended by Vulcan physicians? If you think I'm unsympathetic . . . they'll have no sympathy for what Spock's going through emotionally. He'll be reduced to a series of numbers on a diagnostic screen."

"I'm not sending him to a hospital," McCoy said quietly. "I'm sending him home."

Emma quieted and listened.

"Physically, Spock doesn't need to be in sick bay. His parents will keep us informed about his progress on the neodopazine, and they'll take excellent care of him. His mother is human. I've met her, and I know that emotionally, she'll be a great source of encouragement to him."

"Leonard, you know they can't monitor him constantly the way we can here—"

"Maybe so. But he's ashamed, Emma, because he's lost the Vulcan mind rules. He can relearn them on Vulcan. I think they'll be the greatest help to his recovery."

"You talk about shame—you said I shamed Spock by calling him a liar—but that's nothing compared to the shame that Spock will experience on Vulcan because he is unable to shield his thoughts from other telepaths."

"How else will he learn to do that? Besides, he'll be with his mother most of the time, and she's not a telepath." McCoy looked at Emma quizzically. "Why are you fighting me so hard on this?"

She sighed silently and dropped her hands from her hips in a conscious attempt to eradicate the outward signs of her anger. "I'm angry, because I can't help thinking—how will I sleep nights if Spock hurts himself, or worse, a member of his family?"

McCoy didn't have a convincing answer for that one, only a gut feeling that Emma could not seem to share. "I just don't think he'll try to hurt himself again. I know he would never hurt his family."

"I don't buy that, Leonard. If you send Spock home without me to monitor his behavior, then you'd better make sure that someone sees that he takes his medication. Damn sure."

"I will."

Emma stood on tiptoe, trying to put the Levirol back on the shelf; McCoy took it from her and replaced it easily. She pulled away from him, her movements tight with contained anger.

She turned to face him at the lab door. "I can't take responsibility for sending Spock home, Doctor. I won't sanction it. If anything happens—"

"I take all responsibility," McCoy said.

He hoped like hell that he was right.

Chapter Five

EMMA SAENZ SAT pensively at the desk in Spock's cabin and watched intently as the Vulcan gathered the few things needed for his journey: a desert softsuit, boots, cassettes to study and, perhaps, to understand. His blue science officer's uniform was already carefully packed away, and he now wore a camel-colored tunic of a lightweight material better suited for Vulcan's oppressive heat. It occurred to Emma that he looked far more like a professor on sabbatical from the Vulcan Science Academy than a Star Fleet officer on leave. She forced her mind quickly to other thoughts, but it was too late: the painful wave of homesickness was too strong to completely eradicate.

Spock picked it up immediately, of course, and straightened from his packing to stare at her with gentle eyes, unable to comprehend what he had sensed her feel. Emma's eyes were wet, glistening black. She looked away.

He returned silently to his packing, and was still

attempting to interpret the sensation when the buzzer rang. "Come," he said, before Emma could rise to answer it.

James Kirk entered, and stopped abruptly when he saw her, making no attempt to hide his disappointment. "Oh. Dr. Saenz. I didn't realize you would be here . . ."

"Hello, Captain," she said smoothly. Surely he must realize that Spock could no longer be permitted to remain alone in his quarters after the suicide attempt—perhaps he'd expected to find McCoy here, under the circumstances. But McCoy was on the hangar deck, fussing over the shuttlecraft interior to make certain that his patient's journey would be a comfortable one.

Kirk had wanted to avoid the hangar deck altogether. "I was hoping to talk to Mr. Spock," he said to Emma. He did not say *alone*.

Emma knew it would be cruel to pretend she did not understand; she pushed herself away from the desk and stood up. "I'll be outside if anyone needs me."

"Thank you," Kirk said gratefully.

When the door closed behind Dr. Saenz, Spock closed the dresser drawer and faced his captain. It was not a moment to which either of them had looked forward, but one that both knew could not be avoided.

Jim smiled, but his eyes were full of misery. Spock permitted himself a small sigh; he had mind-linked with the captain many times before, and such a telepathic bond was not easily broken, especially with this man, to whom he was closer than any other living soul. He steadied himself as Jim's despair washed over him with an almost physical force; he felt Jim struggle with the fear that his first officer would not return.

Spock knew the feeling well; he also knew it was a fear that might very well be realized. It was a possibility he regretted, for he knew the captain needed him, needed the solid Vulcan logic to temper Jim's bursts of intuitive insight—logic that Spock could no longer provide. It was at the same time both reassuring and distinctly painful.

Spock had already decided that there was no sense in prolonging the pain by trying to say anything; each knew the other's thoughts too well for speech to be necessary now. Wordlessly, he offered Jim the Vulcan salute, fingers parting and uniting again.

The captain returned it awkwardly. Suddenly, Spock perceived an impulse Jim had stifled, aware of the Vulcan's distaste for physical contact. Spock decided it would cause no harm to indulge the wish of his friend; he extended his hand to the captain.

Jim took the hand, aware that Spock was now forced to feel what he felt himself; he no longer tried to smile.

The whistle of the intercom ensured that the contact would be brief; Lyle in the transporter room was looking for the captain.

"Glad I found you, sir. I thought you'd like to know that Lieutenant Commander Varth has come aboard."

"Varth . . ." Kirk tried to remember the significance of the name.

"The new first officer, sir."

"Yes, of course," Kirk said shortly. "Kirk out." He hit the intercom with more force than was necessary to terminate the conversation; when he turned back to Spock, the look on his face was almost more than his friend could bear.

"Go," the Vulcan said.

Emma Saenz was waiting outside the door when Kirk came out. He tried to pass her without speaking, but she stepped in front of him, an unreadable expression on her face.

"He's that important to you," she said slowly. Her tone was hesitant, rising, almost a question.

Kirk did not understand what she was talking about; he could not have answered her even if he had. Angry at the intrusion, he pulled blindly away.

She stood outside in the corridor for a moment, looking after him.

They were about an hour from Star Base 12 when Mr. Scott first mentioned the slight malfunction in the control panel.

He shook his head. "I checked this vessel out completely before we boarded her. I know for a fact I dinna miss anythin'. She was in perfect shape."

"What's wrong?" Chapel asked. She was sitting behind and to the right of Scott, in the passenger's seat next to Spock. She hadn't wanted to come along, considering the awkwardness of the situation, but McCoy had insisted. She was the one person he trusted to see that Spock made it to Vulcan in one piece.

"We're three hours out now," Scott answered, "and the indicator says we haven't used any fuel."

Spock's eyebrow rose sharply. The temptation to ask the engineer how he had failed to notice the problem much earlier was almost too great; Chapel, however, had no such compunctions.

"Why didn't you tell us sooner? You must have noticed it before—"

"I dinna want to worry ye," Scott shrugged. "I thought the indicator might just be stuck temporarily."

"Stuck?" Spock's monosyllable managed to convey volumes of insinuation.

Scott became indignant. "Aye, *stuck*. It happens. All of the sudden, ye'll see half your fuel gone where it indicated full charge not a second before. Or do ye think I don't know what I'm talkin' about?"

Spock deemed it wisest not to reply.

"Will it cause any problems?" Chapel asked.

"Ach, no, it shouldn't . . ." Scott began in a soothing tone, swiveling around in his chair to look at her.

". . . unless, of course, we run out of fuel." Spock qualified the engineer's statement.

Aghast, Christine looked at Scott.

"Don't worry, lass," he said in the same soothing tone, "I'll notify Star Base Twelve of our predicament, and we'll have it fixed when we land."

"You mean *if* we land," Christine said coldly. "What if we run out of fuel *before* we reach Star Base Twelve?"

Scott remained determinedly cheerful. "Then we'll drift, but we can always radio for help."

"Assuming," Spock began, "we aren't close enough to the star base to be affected by its gravitational pull, in which case—"

"You don't have to finish," Chapel said firmly. "I took physics." She turned away from Scott, who looked very much as though he regretted the rapid improvement in the Vulcan's speech, and pulled the medikit from under her seat. "Here, Mr. Spock. Even if we *are* doomed, I don't want it said that I forgot your medication." She held out a cupped hand to Spock.

The capsules resembled small violet ovals of polished porcelain. Once in the mouth, they would dissolve without need of liquid; however, Spock could not help thinking they looked more like something to be aesthetically appreciated rather than digested. He picked them from Chapel's hand, careful to avoid physical contact.

While Spock was greatly relieved that McCoy had

prevented Emma Saenz from accompanying him, he had been less than comfortable with the knowledge that Christine Chapel would be at his side throughout the entire journey—although he had to admit that thus far she had comported herself admirably, exhibiting a degree of control of which he had not thought her capable; perhaps Dr. Saenz had warned her of his increased telepathic vulnerability.

They traveled in silence for a time, the only sound the soft, hypnotic drone of the *Galileo*'s engines. Spock began to feel drowsy, but tried to stay awake by focusing his attention on the control panel. If he were going to be incinerated in Star Base 12's atmosphere, he would prefer to remain conscious for the last hour of his life.

He started at the sound of Scott radioing for landing instructions—he had been sleeping, a fact he found highly embarrassing; sleep had previously always been a conscious act over which he'd had complete control. He glanced up to see Chapel studiously not looking at him.

Star Base 12 radioed permission for descent.

"How about that." Scott directed a triumphant grin at Christine. "Looks like we'll get there in one piece after all."

"Why, Mr. Scott," she replied with mock surprise, "don't tell me you had any doubts."

"Nooo . . . of course not."

The planet designated as Star Base 12 was not particularly scenic or suitable for shore leave, although some Star Fleet unfortunates were compelled to use it for such. The Federation had claimed the uninhabited world—since no one else wanted it, as it consisted of little more than sterile desert and a hostile atmosphere—and built airdomes that contained hangars, restaurants, and bars, none of which were particularly enjoyable places to be, but which were always crowded to capacity with bleary-eyed space travelers. Star Base 12's popularity was due not to the quality of its eating and drinking establishments, but rather to the fact that it was the one spaceport in this rather remote sector that offered connecting shuttles to more civilized parts of the galaxy: Rigel IV, Earth, Vulcan.

The *Galileo*'s descent into the atmosphere was rapid. Relaxed by Scott's good-humored confidence, Christine leaned forward to watch the viewscreen: sleek white edifices covered by transparent domes rose gracefully from the lifeless yellow soil. From the rapidity with which the size of the buildings was increasing, Christine guessed that the craft was gaining velocity, and turned to Scott to ask if they shouldn't be slowing.

She never asked the question. The engineer's eyes were fixed on the instrument panel; the red warning light was flashing, despite the fact that the fuel indicator blithely insisted that the *Galileo*'s reserves were full.

"That's it, then," Scott pronounced quietly.

"Oh, God," Christine said in a very small voice. She crouched low in her seat, no longer wanting to watch as the city loomed toward them ominously.

Spock was not sitting that close to her, but he could feel the depth of her terror, although she sat quietly with her arms clasped about her knees. As for himself, he felt nothing other than a mild sensation of relief. Death could not have come at a more convenient time. He was no longer useful to his shipmates, the Service, or his family, but a burden to them all.

The loss of Scott and Chapel, on the other hand, was something to regret. Spock tried to decide on the most logical course of action as he watched Scott desperately try to maneuver the *Galileo* as she approached the hangar. Incineration was no longer a danger—they were already too far down in the atmosphere—but impact would be a problem.

The solution came to Spock in a flash, but in images, not words, and the power of speech chose that particularly inopportune moment to desert him once again. He struggled agonizingly to find the words, to tell Scott . . .

But the words did not come in time.

Kirk and Emma Saenz stood arguing outside sick bay, still barefoot and wearing their white togas.

"I don't see why you won't let me take a look at it," Emma said, her hands on her hips. "It could very well be separated."

Kirk winced as he touched his right shoulder. He had no doubt that it was, but was just as determined as Emma about the proper procedure. "It could be just a strain. I'll be just fine if I get some rest. There's no need to make such a fuss, Doctor."

"I'm not making a fuss. And if I get to beat you up off duty, the least you could do is call me Emma."

"Fine, Emma. I'll just be going to my quarters now." He turned gingerly and began moving away.

"You're really something," she flared behind him. The sudden heat in her voice made him stop and face her. "Quit being so ridiculous. We both know the shoulder hurts like hell and it's going to keep you up all night. It's my fault it happened and I refuse to let you lose any sleep because of it."

"It's not your fault," he protested quickly; perhaps *too* quickly, because her anger was replaced by a grin, as though he had just said something very amusing.

"Is it . . . that you don't want to go into sick bay

because you're afraid someone might find out that I hurt you?" The question stung, but she asked it with such good humor that Kirk could not take offense.

He tried to shrug, forcing himself to grimace again. "I just fell on it wrong," he said lamely, and was at once embarrassed at his answer. Maybe she was right; maybe he couldn't admit that she could hurt him. His expression became so sheepish that Emma laughed, and he had to laugh, too.

"Maybe I am embarrassed . . . a little," he admitted. "Even so, I don't like making a big deal out of such a little—Ouch!" He shifted the shoulder awkwardly.

Her smile vanished. "It's not a little deal, Captain. If a separated shoulder isn't treated, you could lose the use of it. Then you'd have to get the ligaments regrown and undergo therapy for a long time. Look, if you won't go inside sick bay, then at least let me look at it in my quarters. Indulge me. I feel very guilty."

He smiled weakly. "You win, Doctor."

"Emma. Stay right there. Don't move." She wagged a commanding finger at him and disappeared into sick bay.

He waited in the corridor, feeling very conspicuous, until Emma reappeared two minutes later with a medi-kit.

"Was anyone there?"

"Just M'Benga. Don't worry, I just said that my workout partner needed a little emergency treatment. I didn't say who." Her eyes sparkled with amusement. "Funny, he laughed, too. I don't understand why people find it so difficult to believe I can be dangerous."

"Believe me," Kirk said, gritting his teeth, "I no longer find it difficult."

She led him to her cabin and, unlocking the door

with a word, gestured him inside. Kirk entered timidly, his hand on the offended shoulder, and half-expected to find McCoy lounging on the bed.

The outer office was the same as the other senior officers' cabins, but when she turned the light on in the bedroom, Kirk blinked in surprise.

"Like it?" Emma motioned him toward the bed.

The entire room—bare walls, ceiling, floor, and every piece of furniture—was stark white, reflecting the light with such glare that Kirk squinted. In her white toga, Emma blended perfectly into her surroundings as though she were an extension of them, distinguishable only by the slash of black at the waist, black hair and eyes, and the one bit of color in the room—her glowing olive skin.

"Interesting, but hardly regulation," Kirk said politely through clenched teeth.

"It's really hurting now, isn't it? Sit."

He balanced carefully on the edge of the bed. "I would think you'd get tired of not seeing any color."

"White is the presence of all colors, Captain," she murmured distractedly as she removed his toga with the skilled, economical movements of an examining physician. She stood back to study the shoulder and clicked her tongue with disapproval. "Looks like more than just a sprain here. Since you wouldn't cooperate with me and let me scan you in sick bay, I'm going to have to diagnose by touch." She paused. "If it *is* a separation, this will hurt like hell."

"I can take it," Kirk said stoically.

He did not see Emma smile behind him. She reached with slender, determined fingers and, upon finding the precise spot between the tip of the shoulder blade and the collarbone, pressed firmly.

Kirk swore explosively and almost reared up off the bed, but she restrained him.

"I thought so. First degree separation. Lucky for you, the ligaments are still in place, but we'll need to wrap it so the joint is immobilized. Even so, it's going to hurt for a couple of days." She opened the medikit.

Kirk sat on the edge of the bed, still smarting; he was not feeling particularly lucky at the moment. "For a neuropsychologist, you seem to be quite an authority on shoulders, Doctor."

"Emma," she corrected him again. "I had four years of medical school, like every other physician." He still could not see her face as she stood behind him, but he could hear by her voice that she suddenly smiled. "Besides, this isn't the first time I've had to patch together one of my workout partners."

"I'll have to remember that the next time I work out with you, Emma." She had reminded him three times now to call her by her first name, but still addressed him by his rank; it was up to Kirk to return the favor, but he could not seem to bring himself to. There was not a female on board with which he was on a first name basis; making an exception was bound to be dangerous.

Without warning, Emma emptied a hypospray into his shoulder.

"What was that for?" Kirk pulled away instinctively as he felt a rush of warmth in his shoulder; the room suddenly felt rather close.

"Cortrazide for the inflammation and an analgesic." She began to apply the aerosol bandage; it hardened instantly.

"Hey, I can't raise my arm very far," Kirk complained.

"That's because I don't want you to." Emma stood back a bit to scrutinize her work. "Not for a couple of days, anyway, so it can heal properly. Within a week, I promise I'll be injuring other parts of your anatomy."

Kirk smiled. The ache in the shoulder was receding rapidly, and he was beginning to relax in spite of himself. He looked around the room again, this time with unfeigned interest. "I think I'm beginning to like it. Bold and to the point, like its occupant."

She laughed. "So you've decided it isn't so bad? That's particularly revealing of your personality."

"Are you turning psychiatrist on me again, Doctor? Excuse me, Emma."

"Don't forget, I'm the one responsible, so it reveals more about me than you."

Kirk's anxiety had evaporated like a forgotten nightmare. "Then we must have some traits in common. Go ahead, I've been analyzed before."

"You can take it, eh?" She teased, and walked around the bed to face him with a playful expression. "It means we both like white."

"I'll bet I can guess what a psychiatrist would say, even if you won't tell me." Kirk assumed a mock clinical air. "White, hmmm . . . You prefer life to be simple, straightforward. You dislike complications."

"Who doesn't?"

"It's too bad it can't be that way," Kirk sighed.

"What?"

"Life," he intoned dramatically. "Too many shades of gray, too many compromises. It'd be simpler if everything was black . . . or white."

"Things never are," she said, taking his statement with more seriousness than he had meant it. "Sometimes, one is forced to recruit the forces of evil in order to do good." There was still the hint of a smile on her face, but something about it reminded him of Natahia, of his first meeting with the small, sad leader when she had agreed to use the Federation's weapons to save her people . . . "Especially in my business."

"A doctor?" he asked, surprised. "How does a doctor 'enlist the forces of evil'?"

She laughed at herself and stood in front of him as though she were waiting for something; with sudden embarrassment, Kirk realized that she must be waiting for him to leave. He rose unsteadily to his feet.

"Is it just me, or is it warm in here?" The lack of sleep must have finally caught up to him; he felt almost drunken as he reeled dizzily toward the door. Emma caught his elbow.

"Easy, Captain. That hypo must be relaxing you a little bit. It will help you to sleep tonight—you need rest if that shoulder is to heal, and believe me, there's no way you'd be able to find a comfortable enough position to sleep tonight without a sedative." She put an arm gently around his waist to steady him. "I'll help you to your quarters."

I don't need help, Kirk was going to say, quite absurdly, until he noticed how close she was standing to him; he breathed in her scent, and was overwhelmed.

Her eyes were open wide and glittered up at him like polished onyx. "Let me help you to your quarters, Captain," she repeated softly.

But he knew that he did not want to return to his quarters now. Buried in a different part of him, a part that seemed to be floating far away, was the memory of McCoy; Kirk's rational mind knew that his friend loved this woman, and he tried to feel guilt for wanting to touch her.

But at the moment he could not give a damn about McCoy.

"My name is Jim," he said.

"Jim," she said shyly, and loosened the arm around his waist. He turned toward her and she reached, hesitantly, for his face. He did not pull away; her hand was hot against his skin.

"Would you like to go to your quarters now, Jim?" She was so small, so dark and delicate, he could not believe that she had hurt him.

"No," he whispered, "I wouldn't." He bent down to kiss her, and let the warm, dizzying waves sweep over him.

He closed his eyes and saw nothing but white—bright, hot white.

McCoy paced aimlessly in his quarters. He had keyed up the latest neurology journals, but the dry, cumbersome wording of the texts had nearly numbed him to sleep, and sleep was the last thing he wanted at the moment.

Emma should have finished up in the gym two hours ago.

McCoy argued vehemently with himself; he was acting like a schoolboy—he should go and have dinner without her. He was old, far too old to fall into the typical lover's trap—spending all his time waiting for her, waiting for fear that she would come by his quarters and he would be gone, and miss the opportunity for a moment alone with her.

He rose, but instead of heading for the door as he had vowed to himself he would, he went to a small cupboard recessed in the wall and poured himself a shot of bourbon. He was still arguing: he was hungry, he'd been off duty almost two hours, he should get himself something to eat. And if Emma missed him—well, too bad.

He sat down at the desk with the glass and the bottle and cursed himself. Acting like a kid, too old for all this foolishness. They were adults, for God's sake; he had no right to expect her to come rushing to him the minute she finished her workout.

Still, he had hoped that she would.

He held up the bourbon so that it caught the light and shimmered golden amber in the glass. One thing he hadn't done much lately was drink. His features involuntarily crinkled at the thought; there simply hadn't been enough time for it. He and Emma had been spending every free moment together. Most nights she stayed in his quarters, and they always requested the same duty schedule. About the only time they spent apart was when she went to the gym.

Maybe that was it; they'd been spending too much time together, and she felt smothered. He needed to let her know that she could have more time to herself if she wanted—even though he hoped desperately that she did not.

He threw back his head suddenly and laughed out loud at the absurd thought. If Emma wanted time to herself, she'd be the first one to mention it; tact was definitely not on her list of virtues. She'd be the last person in the universe to let herself be smothered. . . .

And he felt anything but smothered himself. The woman was a breath of fresh air; she made him feel young, so young that he'd almost forgotten the age difference. She made it easy to love her; there was never the undercurrent of tension that had pervaded his marriage. If Emma ever had anything on her mind, she simply told him so. He was beginning to remember why people got married.

It was after almost an hour and the third generous shot of bourbon that McCoy found himself calling Emma's quarters without the memory of a conscious decision to do so.

There was no response.

He called the gym. Sulu answered, sweating, his face guard pushed up, a fencing foil still in his hand. Yes, Sulu said, Emma had left the gym, at least two hours ago with the captain, who appeared to have injured his shoulder.

There, McCoy thought, relieved and a little ashamed at himself for checking up on her. A simple explanation: she was patching Jim up in sick bay.

M'Benga answered the intercom. "Why yes, she was here . . . a couple of hours ago, and picked up a medikit. No, she didn't say where she was going . . ."

The rational part of McCoy's mind commanded him to stop, but he no longer could. He tried the captain's quarters, the rec room, and then the dining room.

His face was pale when he called Emma's quarters again, but he knew before he tried that there would be no answer.

He laid his head down on the desk.

Sulu faced his fencing partner once again, but did not push down his face mask. "We've been at it long enough, don't you think?" He was perspiring freely, his almond skin flushed.

"Tired?" came the gentle voice from under the facemask.

"Well . . ." Sulu smiled and winced at the same time. "It's been almost two hours. As much as I appreciate good parrying, I must admit that's a little longer than I'm used to."

His partner pushed up his face mask to reveal a silver complexion punctuated by a flash of white teeth. His brow was covered with a light mist, as though he had barely begun to break a sweat. Millenia ago, the planet Radu had been settled by colonists from the Klingon system. Unlike their militant cousins, however, the Radu were a gentle folk who directed their intelligence and curiosity to matters other than war.

"Don't tell me you're not tired," Sulu said. "I thought Radu was near Terran standard gravity, but you have the stamina of a Vulcan."

"Thanks," said Varth Regev. He lifted the facemask off to reveal a shock of coppery hair. "I work at it. Shall we repair to the sauna?"

The sauna was so steamy as to obscure any object more than a few feet away, but Sulu could make out Varth's stocky, muscular form; the Radun hadn't been kidding about working at it.

Varth settled himself gingerly on the hot tile bench and Sulu did the same. "What was the call about?" the Radun asked. "Someone looking for the Captain?"

"Not him this time, although that's usually the case," Sulu replied, squeezing his eyes shut and surrendering to the almost intolerable heat of the steam. "Dr. McCoy was looking for Dr. Saenz."

"Business of a medical nature, no doubt," Varth said innocently.

Eyes closed, Sulu smirked, resembling a Buddha in meditation. He did not respond.

"For such a small person," Varth continued, "she seems to have done some real damage."

"She must have had quite a bit of training," Sulu said without opening his eyes, "to do that to the captain."

"He's pretty good?"

Sulu opened one eye for emphasis and closed it again. "He usually works out with Mr. Spock—that is, he used to. And they weren't that mismatched. Of course, I understand that Dr. Saenz spent some time on Vulcan herself."

"Looks like she learned a few tricks there."

Sulu grunted assent. "From the look on the captain's face, I think the damage was serious. I doubt it's going to do much to improve his mood."

Varth's expression became doleful. "I guess it won't."

Sulu squinted at him through the steam and wiped a rivulet of condensed moisture from his forehead. "Been riding you pretty hard?"

"He doesn't like me," Varth replied matter-of-factly. "I wish I knew why, what I'd done . . ."

Sulu reached toward him with a reassuring gesture. "It's not you, Reg, not what you've done. You know you're good."

"Yes," the Radun agreed, without a trace of false modesty.

"It's just that . . . that the captain was very close to Mr. Spock. Seeing someone else take Spock's place is hard for him. But he's a fair person, Reg. He'll readjust."

"Let's hope it's soon," Varth said, sweating.

Kirk rolled slowly from the bed, mumbling incoherent curses at the insistent buzzing, and winced as the injured shoulder reminded him of its presence. He opened his eyes with a start, and relaxed again as he saw that he was in his own quarters. He shook his head and tried to remember: the injury in the gym, Emma wrapping it for him . . . he flushed because he remembered kissing her, and because he could not remember anything more. He certainly did not remember returning to his quarters, and the awful thought occurred to him that she might have carried him.

The buzzing did not stop until he stumbled to the door and opened it.

Ingrit Tomson stood, poised with mouth open, ready

to speak, but at the sight of the captain, her complexion colored to pale pink. She closed her mouth.

"Yes?" Kirk scowled. He knew he must have been something to see: bare-chested, bandaged, in his baggy white trousers, which no doubt had been interpreted as antiquated pajama bottoms. He swayed slightly in the doorway; the effect of the sedative had not yet worn off.

Tomson's surprise at the captain's awkward appearance lasted but a moment; she was as excited as Kirk had ever seen her. The mouth opened again. "Sir, I'm sorry to wake you, but you said if I ever—"

"Get to the point, Lieutenant," Kirk said crossly.

"Sir, we have a lead on a murder suspect." She actually smiled. "I preferred to contact you personally, sir. We haven't made the arrest yet, and I didn't want anyone overhearing our conversation."

"Then come in, Lieutenant."

Tomson stepped just inside the door; it closed behind her with a *swoosh*.

"A crewmember?" Kirk asked, interested but hardly sharing the enthusiasm of the security chief.

"Yes, sir. It's just circumstantial evidence, but sufficient enough in my opinion for an arrest."

"Who?" Kirk demanded.

"Lieutenant Commander Scott, sir—"

"Scotty? That's impossible, Tomson—"

"Sir, after treatment with truth serum, Ensign al-Baslama was able to clearly remember all the incidents surrounding the disappearance of the prisoner. One of the things he remembers is that not half an hour before he was fired upon, Mr. Scott came down to the brig. Al-Baslama said it struck him as very odd—Mr. Scott just stood there for several minutes staring at the prisoner, then muttered something and left."

"That's not enough to arrest a man, Lieutenant. Question him, yes—"

"Sir, that's not all. Al-Baslama was also able to recall that the force field was lowered at the exact instant he was fired upon. Star Fleet Intelligence informs me that no one has developed a shield neutralizer. So if the pirate didn't neutralize the field, and al-Baslama didn't let it down, that leaves only one way the field could have been lowered."

"Engineering," Kirk said shortly.

"Yes, sir. The emergency override controls."

"Just because Mr. Scott works in Engineering doesn't mean that he was the one who sabotaged the override—"

Tomson shook her head. "Sorry, sir. We questioned certain crewmembers in Engineering, and a Midshipman Dobson reports that at the approximate time the shields went down in the brig, Mr. Scott was servicing the manual override controls."

The muscle in Kirk's cheek began to twitch; he looked down at the floor and studied it for some time before he looked up at Tomson again.

"I'm afraid, Lieutenant," he said slowly, "that you'll have some difficulty in arresting your suspect."

Tomson looked at him quizzically.

"Mr. Scott is not on board. He's piloting a shuttlecraft to Star Base Twelve. Spock and Chapel are with him."

She paled. "Then we'd better put out a bulletin on him as soon as possible."

Kirk shook his head firmly. "No. He'll come back, Lieutenant."

Tomson gasped in disbelief. "Sir, Mr. Scott could very well be a murderer, in which case he's been given the perfect opportunity to escape. I *have* to issue a warrant—"

"Lieutenant," he said, "Mr. Scott is due to arrive back in approximately five hours. You can question him then."

"And if he doesn't return, Captain?"

"He'll return. If he's even ten minutes late, you can issue a bulletin on him and throw *me* in the brig."

"Yes, sir," Tomson said coldly. Kirk had no doubt that she fully intended to take him up on the offer.

Chapter Six

THE STAR CALLED Eridani 40 slid slowly up over Vulcan's horizon, a reddish-pink ghost of the blazing fireball it would become by midday. It eased the moonless darkness, and slowly colored the desert from black to gray to red, the sky from indigo to soft orange; the mountains in the distance remained coal black.

Nothing was so quiet, so serene as dawn over the plain. Even the hellishly hot breezes for which Vulcan's deserts were notorious would not stir until Eridani climbed higher in the sky. The still cool air carried the oddly sweet, piercing warble of silver-birds, *teresh-kah*, which sang only at dawn to greet the sun.

A lone traveler, weary from the night's journey across the desert, closed his eyes and stopped to listen to the song of the *teresh-kah*. He stood transfixed until the first warm gust swept across the plain and drowned out the ancient melody, then resumed his painfully slow pace toward his destination, the small desert township of ShiKahr.

124

To the east lay the black Arlanga Mountains, cold and forbidding in their grandeur. It was there he had tested himself, at the age of seven, in his own personal *Kahs-wan*, the ordeal of maturity. The fear of failure had led him to the mountains months before the formal ritual took place in the Sas-a-shar desert—the mountains were far more dangerous than the desert, and he knew that if he could survive them, he would easily survive the desert. Twice that year he had crossed the plain of ShiKahr on foot, once heading east to the mountains, one west to Sas-a-shar.

Now Spock crossed the plain a third time, traversing the fifteen kilometers of desert that lay between the Vulcan capital of ShanaiKahr and the city where he was born.

His hometown of ShiKahr was quite small and tourism was nonexistent; therefore, one shuttle ran in the morning to take locals into the capital, and one shuttle ran in the early evening to bring them home again. Spock arrived in ShanaiKahr shortly after the evening shuttle had left. If he had wanted to wait all night and another day in the capital, he could have caught the next shuttle going into ShiKahr.

Conveying this complex information to Chapel would have been tedious and pointless; Spock preferred to cross the desert himself in the cool night, and courtesy forbade his waking his family to have them pick him up in the skimmer. Since Chapel would have refused to allow him to do so, he let her assume that he could easily catch a shuttle so that she could dispense with her responsibility toward him. She had broken her ankle when they had crash-landed in the soft sand dunes of Star Base 12, and had refused to take anything strong for the pain, as she was obliged to keep an alert eye on Spock at all times. The ankle had begun to throb so that even with a lightweight emergency cast, she was unable to put any weight on it, and it was necessary for Spock to help her off the shuttle when they arrived on Vulcan. When he went to the nearest terminal and purchased a return ticket for the next flight back to Star Base 12, where Scott was repairing the *Galileo,* Chapel accepted without even a mild protest.

The fierce high-pitched scream of a *le matya* brought Spock's thoughts back to the desert; he continued grimly, keeping his pace steady. The *le matya* might catch his scent, in which case he would be in grave danger, but he did not flinch at the thought. He had far worse things to fear than a *le matya;* that, at least, would be a clean, quick death.

The fearsome predator had still not attacked when Spock arrived at the city border, a carefully sculpted garden springing out of the desert. He was safe; the sensors hidden in the greenery surrounding the city kept out unwanted beasts but permitted the passage of Vulcanoids, humanoids, and domesticated animals.

The dusty streets of ShiKahr were as sparse and bare as the desert itself; the hot wind stirred up dancing swirls of sand. Spock passed no one as he walked through the town, and at last he arrived at his father's house. He paused before the garden wall; the heavy gate was made from a single massive block of stone inlaid with ebony wood that had been polished to a sheen. A small metal plate hung slightly below Spock's eye level. On it was inscribed a hieroglyph, a symbol of such ancient origin that its pronunciation had been lost millennia ago by all save the clan for whose name it stood. It was not written in the modern Vulcan script, for it was not permitted for any stranger to utter the name of one's ancestors, a custom dating from before Vulcan's collective memory, from a time when one's forbears were worshipped as deities rather than merely esteemed.

Spock held his hand before the timeworn symbol; the massive gate sighed and opened before him.

The contrast to the bare sand streets outside would have startled a stranger, for the garden within the sterile stone walls was as lush and deep green as a tropical rainforest. Spock crossed the stone pathway to the front entrance of the house. He passed through the main room, not bothering to glance around him, and into the long narrow hallway that led to his bedroom. He had reached the point of exhaustion; sleep was at hand.

The sight of his old bedroom was overwhelmingly comforting; it was as it had always been, comfortably familiar, everything in its proper place.

With one notable exception.

He had removed his cloak and was nearing the bed when the figure of a young female, barely a woman, sat bolt upright in his bed, clutching the covers modestly to her bosom. Her features were Vulcan, but strangely enough she made no effort to stifle the wave of emotion that assaulted Spock: terror, followed by a mixture of anger and shame.

"Why do you trouble me here?" she hissed in English, her expression only thinly masking her turmoil. "I have promised to do as you requested."

Spock could not have responded at that moment even if he had known the answer to her question.

She studied him suspiciously for a moment before her expression became completely calm. "Who are you?" she demanded in Vulcan.

He was too taken aback to have the presence of mind not to answer her question. "Spock."

Even in the darkness, the striking elegance of her

features was visible; shining black hair fell in soft, thick folds to her waist. She blinked at him as though trying to decide if she were dreaming.

A horrible, humiliating thought struck Spock: he had entered the wrong house, and had been so stupid as to give her his name. By tomorrow evening, his awkward intrusion would be known to all in ShiKahr. Logic fled in the face of the situation, and he could think of nothing to say to the young woman save a phrase taught him by his mother, an English expression that had no counterpart in Vulcan.

"Excuse me." Spock backed out of the room swiftly, a flurry of archaic Vulcan curses chattering in the back of his mind at the cruel trick his memory had played on him. Had he mistakenly read the hieroglyph on the front door? And if his perceptions could not be trusted, how would he ever find his father's house?

He staggered, numbed by confusion, down the hall and back toward the front door, but the sight of the main room stopped him. It, too, was as unarguably familiar as his bedroom had been. In one corner sat his father's harp—in another, his mother's piano. His eyes were drawn to something above the piano: an old-fashioned family portrait, painted by a well-known Terran artist.

A woman sat, erect and gracious, her honey-colored hair piled on top of her head in the Vulcan fashion, the slightest smile playing at the corners of her mouth. Behind and to one side of her chair, not quite close enough to be touching, stiff and solemn, stood a ten-year-old boy. He was small for his age; that fact, combined with his mixed parentage, made him the favorite of bullies. Brown-black hair hung in his eyes (it always grew too fast, much to the consternation of his mother) and the ears were ridiculously large for the narrow, fine-featured face.

Amanda had been right—he had grown into them.

It had always been Spock's contention that the boy did not resemble his mother in the slightest. However, studying the portrait now, it seemed that there was something, perhaps in the eyes . . .

He sat heavily on the comfortable, overstuffed sofa. The girl-woman had been no more than an illusion, a trick of his overloaded faculties, brought on by exhaustion. Perhaps the trip had been too much for him. It occurred to him that he should return to his room, to prove to himself that the girl had been an illusion, and to sleep in his own bed, but instead he sank back into the comfortingly familiar softness of the couch.

"Spock."

He raised his eyelids at the soft, warm sound, unsure for a moment where he was.

Amanda stood with her back to the large picture window that overlooked the garden. The rising sun outlined her in a halo of dazzling white light; Spock could not see her face. He pushed against the yielding softness of the sofa, struggling to rise, but she sat down next to him.

She was older than the woman in the portrait, now; the golden hair was mostly silver, and the lines about her eyes were etched more deeply by the harshness of life on Vulcan. She reached a hand toward him in the ritual embrace: index and middle fingers extended tightly together, the thumb folded over the remaining fingers, a symbol that these two were forever tied by marriage or by blood. Amanda Grayson had for so long suppressed the urge to encircle a loved one with her arms that the impulse rarely occurred to her anymore; it had taken many years.

The small hint of a smile that curved the corners of her mouth upward was still exactly the same. Whatever anxiety she might have felt for her son was carefully shielded, a skill acquired from years of living with Sarek.

"I thought I heard someone come in last night. I thought it might be your father coming home early. Please don't tell me you walked from the capital."

Very well, thought Spock. "Father is not here?" he asked in English. He and his father always addressed her in her native tongue; she did speak Vulcan, after a fashion, as she put it—but the sibilants were impossible for her to produce, in spite of her training as a linguist.

"He's at an emergency Council meeting in the capital. I expect him back sometime tomorrow evening."

Spock's sense of relief was so deep that he was almost ashamed of it. His greatest concern upon arriving home had been the effect that his lack of mental shields would have upon Sarek; surely his father would find the chaos of Spock's mental processes offensive. About Amanda, he did not worry. Not being a telepath, she would never know of his mental infirmities, nor judge his actions against the harsh standards of logic. She would only encourage and try to understand, virtures of which Sarek seemed incapable. Perhaps she was why Spock had never minded working with humans, why he had volunteered for duty on the *Enterprise.*

"I've been in contact with Dr. McCoy," she continued gently, "and he tells me that you're taking a certain medication . . . if you could give it to me, I'll see that you receive it on the proper schedule."

Spock's head turned sharply, but not at Amanda's words.

His peripheral vision caught a glimpse of movement, a flash of white and black in the hallway. It was the apparition, the vision that had appeared in his bed the night before. He'd had no intention of mentioning it to Amanda, so convinced was he that her existence was illusory . . .

The vision stood hesitantly in the hallway, apparently afraid of intruding. She was clothed, now, in a simple white dress that fell in a straight line to her ankles, and the cascading black hair was now braided and pinned securely to the crown of her head. Although her physical features marked her as a Vulcan, there was something slightly incongruous about her demeanor—an openness, a hint of volatility—something that a human would never perceive, something that a Vulcan could not help but notice. The fleeting impression that Spock had formed of her during their brief encounter was quite accurate: she was very young, perhaps nineteen, and very beautiful.

From the warmth of Amanda's response to her, Spock assumed she was a relative of whom he had been unaware. "T'Pala," Amanda said. "Please, come in. I'd like for you to meet Spock."

There was something about Amanda's tone that made Spock distinctly uncomfortable; he knew that he had heard her use that tone before. He searched his memory.

The first time she had introduced him to his former fiancée, T'Pring. He rose stiffly.

T'Pala carried herself into the room with effortless grace and stopped below the portrait. "Your son," she said, with a solemn nod to Spock, but did not succeed in completely concealing her shy eagerness. "I recognized you from your picture. I have heard of your many accomplishments." She addressed herself to Amanda. "We have already met—but I did not extend the courtesy of introducing myself."

Amanda's eyes were questioning; Spock sensed a glimmer of amusement from T'Pala. "Last night," he said in a low voice.

Amanda must have imagined the circumstances, for she tactfully did not pursue the subject. "T'Pala is our houseguest," she said to Spock. "She's finishing up her studies at the ShanaiKahr General Academy."

"Your parents have been most kind," T'Pala said. "By offering me their home, they have made it possible for me to continue my studies without interruption."

Spock harbored no desire to pursue small talk with this young creature, but for Amanda's sake he feigned polite interest. "Your family is not living in ShiKahr, then?" Obviously not, else she would not be staying here. It was not an uncommon arrangement for students attending faraway academies to live with a family in order to save the cost of staying in the dormitory.

T'Pala lowered her eyes. "My parents are deceased. If you will excuse me, I must hurry to catch the shuttle. I have two oral exams today at the Academy."

She was gone before Spock could think of a reply.

"Well?" Amanda asked.

Spock raised an eyebrow in the expression his mother knew so well. "I scarcely know her well enough to make an assessment—"

"But?"

Spock frowned. "Her demeanor is somewhat inconsistent with her . . . physical appearance."

"I knew you'd notice. Her father was an attaché to the Terran embassy in ShanaiKahr. He married a Vulcan while there, and they returned to Earth shortly after the child was born. She grew up there."

"Half human," Spock said softly. A rarity, but more likely to occur when a member of the diplomatic service was involved, perhaps because interracial marriages required exceptional members of each species to tolerate the strain imposed by cultural differences.

"She's been with us a couple of months, since her father died. I take it you noticed she's been staying in your room." It was not in the form of a question and Spock did not feel the need to respond.

"I hope you don't mind staying in the guest room," Amanda continued. "We could have asked her to move—"

"It would have been highly improper." That was true; the comfort of houseguests took precedence over that of family, regardless of circumstances.

Amanda rose. "I doubt that the couch was very comfortable last night. Let me help you put your things in the guest room, and you can try to get some more sleep."

He let her lead him to the guest room, but he doubted that he would sleep—he was already thinking of his first encounter with Sarek . . . and of the troubling impressions he had received from the houseguest.

It was early afternoon when Spock emerged again from the guest room. Amanda was in the main room, seated on the sofa, next to her small pupil—a six-year-old Andorian child, bluish pale and atennaed. He was looking up at Amanda with childlike adoration, and speaking very quickly. Something he said must have been quite amusing, for Amanda let forth with a burst of laughter that startled and embarrassed Spock, who stood unnoticed in the hallway. He had never heard his mother make such a sound. The Andorian child, however, seemed pleased by it; he chimed in with a shy, feeble chuckle.

Amanda had been teaching at home ever since her

arrival on Vulcan. Possessing a doctorate in English literature and a master's degree in linguistics, she tutored both adults and children in English grammar and literature. It was for this precise reason that she had frequented the Vulcan embassy on Earth, where she met Sarek. On Vulcan, however, very few natives were problem students, and most of Amanda's tutorials were children of embassy workers in ShanaiKahr, some of them from Terra, sent to study their own culture and literature.

Amanda's love for her profession had led her to acquire one of the finest collections of Old Earth literature in the civilized galaxy. Spock faced the shelves of books that lined the hallway; the unmistakable smell of old paper brought back pleasant memories. He picked out a childhood favorite, a priceless volume over four hundred years old, and opened it to the frontispiece, a lithograph. The paper pages had yellowed long before the preservative with which they were now treated had been developed, and the leather cover (a barbaric, but valued material in those times) was cracked and mended in several places. Spock closed the book silently and stole to the safety of the garden, to await Sarek's return.

Amanda did not notice; she continued with her lesson, an affectionate hand laid lightly on the Andorian's shoulder.

Eridani was setting when Sarek returned home from the capital. Spock was still in the garden, watching the sunset, but he sensed his father's presence even before Sarek came out to greet him.

The meeting was uneventful; Sarek was kind, but distant. Perhaps the distance was intended to protect both of them.

"It has been too long since your mother and I last

saw you. Perhaps you will visit again under more pleasant circumstances."

"Perhaps," Spock said.

"I have arranged for a tutor . . . Tela'at Stalik will come tomorrow for the first lesson."

Spock did not ask the subject; Stalik was well known, a follower of *Kohlinahr*, the discipline of total nonemotion. He had achieved the title of *Tela'at*, Elder, and that, along with his greatly advanced age, entitled him to much respect. Sarek could have scarcely chosen a more qualified instructor to teach Spock the mind rules. Spock bowed his head to indicate his acceptance and appreciation of his father's choice.

The evening meal proceeded without too much discomfort, and afterward, as was the custom, the family sat in the main room. Spock noticed the conspicuous absence of the houseguest, but restrained his curiosity. He sat on the sofa next to Amanda and fingered Sarek's harp softly. The instrument was well over three hundred years old, older than a Vulcan lifetime, and its sound was richer and more resonant than that of Spock's harp. It had belonged to Sarek's father, and the wood from which it was hewn was no longer widely available. Spock thought of his own harp with shame, and wondered if the damage could ever be repaired.

There was the sound of a door opening and closing, and T'Pala appeared, wearing a black cape with the hood thrown back. She spoke breathlessly, as though she had been running.

"Forgive me," she said to the three of them. "The Tela'at's lesson took longer than anticipated."

Sarek studied her calmly. "Apologies serve no useful purpose. They cannot negate the fact that you are late."

T'Pala bowed her head in submission, quite clearly deflated; Spock found the scene a painfully familiar one. He shifted uncomfortably on the sofa. In all the years that Spock had lived in his father's house, he had never seen Sarek correct a guest; quite obviously, this girl was something more. There was an awkward silence.

Amanda was the first to break it. "There's still some food in the kitchen, T'Pala, if you haven't eaten yet."

"Thank you," T'Pala said. She nodded to them and went to her room; when she reemerged, she had shed the black cloak to reveal the long white dress underneath.

Sarek seated himself at the three-dimensional chessboard, and when T'Pala smoothly took the seat across from him, Spock realized that he was watching what had become an evening ritual.

At one time, he had been a participant himself.

He continued to play quietly on Sarek's harp, but he kept one eye on the game. It was immediately apparent that T'Pala was a novice, since she applied no coherent strategy, and that the purpose of this game was instructional rather than recreational.

"How did you fare on your test?" Sarek asked her.

"Well, I think." T'Pala studied the board and made a move. "Did your Council meeting go well?"

Sarek sighed. "I am having some difficulty convincing the Council of my position. I must admit that I do not understand the reasons for it. To deny protection in this case violates all precedent."

"What do you think the ultimate outcome of the vote will be?"

"I cannot predict it yet. At present, the vote is split—half favor Aritani's protection, half do not."

Spock stopped playing.

"I am especially interested in the subject," T'Pala said, "as one of my examination questions requested me to state my position on the matter and to defend it."

"And what position did you take?" Sarek smoothly captured T'Pala's bishop with a knight.

She looked at the board with dismay, displeased by her error, eager to please Sarek with her defense. "I said I was against protection in this particular case, as it violates the doctrine of noninterference, one of the key principles of the Federation. A culture must be free to determine its own path. Also, a military attack on the raiders contradicts the Vulcan principle of nonviolence. Check." She looked up at him to gauge his reaction.

Sarek was expressionless as he studied the threat posed to his king. "The noninterference directive refers to the development of a culture. If a culture unwittingly follows a path which will lead to its annihilation rather than its normal course of development, are we bound to assist that culture in committing genocide? If we have the means to protect that culture, are we not bound to do so in order that they may live in peace and continue their development? Federation history abounds with precedent favoring protection and rescue of undeveloped planets from external threats—Yonada, Betelgeuse Two, Halcyon, Capella, Soyuz Vtoroi . . . the examples are numerous. You forget, T'Pala, or you were not informed, that the reason Aritani now resists the aid of the Federation is that we were incapable of actually protecting them from the attacks, and they now consider us impotent. I believe we should comply with their original request and supply the aid they so desperately need."

T'Pala turned to look at Spock. "You were on Aritani, Spock. Do you also favor protection?"

There was a long silence. "I am not qualified to comment," he replied stonily.

"But you were there," she persisted.

"I have no memory of it."

He felt rather than saw her flush with embarrassment as she turned her eyes back to the board to find that her opponent had moved.

"Checkmate," said Sarek.

"She's very young," Amanda said after T'Pala excused herself. "She'll be nineteen next month. Her mother died when she was very young, and when her father died a few months ago, she came to stay with us. Her mother's family are distant relatives of Sarek's, and Sarek knew her father many years ago. If she's accepted into the diplomatic program, she'll continue to stay with us."

"The Vulcan Diplomatic Corps?" Spock asked. He thought he had succeeded in masking his surprise, but Sarek looked at him sharply.

"She retained her Vulcan citizenship during her long stay on Terra," his father said coldly. "Although she has acquired some Terran mannerisms as a result, she wishes to serve in the VDC. Her background makes her an excellent candidate as an attaché to the Vulcan embassy on Terra."

Spock noted that Sarek had not said T'Pala would make an excellent ambassador, merely an attaché; it was a highly sought after position available only to the most elite in the VDC. Sarek had held the post for many years, and had groomed his son carefully for it, naming him Spock, meaning the Uniter, the one who might someday unite Vulcan and Terra into one great civilization, to bring together all that was best of the two worlds.

So this girl was to be Sarek's new protégée.

"I have recommended that she be admitted into the VDC," Sarek continued, "but that is no guarantee that she will be accepted. Her grades are good, but not outstanding." He looked pointedly at Spock. "She is not as gifted as some others."

Spock remained silent.

"Of course," Sarek amended, "her strengths are in the social sciences, and she has a natural inclination toward politics. Thus, it is logical for her to pursue a diplomatic career. If her talents were elsewhere—for example, the natural sciences—perhaps another profession would be more suitable."

"Logical," Spock nodded in serene agreement.

"Of course, she has other marks against her besides her grades," Amanda said softly. "Her father was Gerald Carstairs."

Sarek fixed his disapproving gaze upon her.

"The name is unfamiliar to me," Spock said. "You said he was a friend of Father's?"

"An acquaintance," Sarek corrected. "There is no point in discussing what is no longer important, my wife."

Amanda bowed her head slightly in acquiescence. Spock knew better than to try to pursue the subject. "If you will excuse me, then," Spock said as he rose.

"Sleep well," said Amanda.

Husband and wife sat alone quietly for a moment.

"Thank you," Amanda said suddenly.

Sarek lifted an eyebrow at her as if she had just said something completely insane.

"For what you said to Spock . . . about choosing a profession. And drop that expression. You're as transparent as glass."

He let free a small, exasperated sigh, and for once

did not pretend that he had no idea what she was talking about.

McCoy responded to the buzzer in spite of his promises to himself; but it was not Emma who had pressed it, as he had hoped and feared. Kirk stood nervously in the corridor with a suspicious-looking bundle under his arm.

"Yes, Captain?" McCoy's tone was cold, and the look in his eyes could have turned the Vulcan desert to icy tundra. Kirk had already had occasion to speak to him earlier on the bridge, and McCoy had dropped more than a few hints that he was mad. Damn mad.

Now here was the captain standing in front of the door to his quarters with a peace offering—an act that served only to confirm the doctor's suspicions.

"Mind if I come in?" Kirk asked meekly.

McCoy shrugged and retreated into his study. The captain followed and set the bundle on McCoy's desk, pulling the wrapping away.

The unmarked decanter contained a clear liquid that could have been water—but it was bootleg ethanol, fresh from the *Enterprise*'s own still hidden in the depths of Engineering. White lightning, moonshine, McCoy called it. It was as close to pure ethanol as its makers could come without igniting Engineering—198 proof. One good shot and you felt no pain; two, and you'd never remember the fun you were having.

The captain, of course, was not supposed to be aware of the still's existence, as it was decidedly nonregulation. Kirk had had a hell of a time just trying to find someone who would admit its existence, much less procure some of its output for him. Former Security Chief O'Shay had been his supplier, but Tomson had seemed genuinely shocked at the captain's suggestion: she'd probably never touched the stuff and would no doubt turn in any of her subordinates who did.

Even Tersarkisov, the rowdiest engineer on board, had professed total ignorance until Kirk had convinced him that the liquor really was for the captain's personal consumption and that no court-martials would ensue.

Kirk pushed the bottle toward McCoy. "The drinks are on me."

McCoy silently produced two glasses and set them on the table. Kirk took it as a hopeful sign and filled them; usually the moonshine was mixed with something to lessen its effect and kill the taste, but this was no time for formalities. Kirk handed a glass to the sulking doctor and sat down across from him. "I think we need to talk."

"Suit yourself." McCoy played with his glass and did not look at him.

Kirk took a sip of his drink and shuddered at the taste. "Why are you angry at me, Doctor?"

"You tell me."

"Bones . . ." Kirk spread his hands helplessly.

"How's the shoulder this morning, Captain?" McCoy said suddenly.

Kirk colored slightly. "Who told you?"

"You mean, besides the fact that you're moving with all the agility and grace of a ninety-year-old arthritic?" McCoy said sarcastically. "Maybe I'm just good at putting two and two together."

"What's *that* supposed to mean?"

He could hold his rage no longer. "You can drop the innocent act, Jim! I saw her leaving your quarters early this morning."

"I see," Kirk said quietly.

"And you've got the *gall* to come here, as though

you can make everything right by bringing me a bottle—" For a moment, McCoy seemed to be deciding whether or not to smash his glass against the bulkhead.

"Doctor," Kirk said in the same calm voice, "I realize what it looks like. But I went to her quarters so she could treat the shoulder—"

"Get your story straight. She left your quarters," McCoy said from between clenched teeth.

"She gave me a sedative so I could sleep. I fell asleep in her quarters. This morning I woke up in my own. You figure it out."

McCoy folded his arms tightly and considered the Captain's words; with a sigh, he closed his eyes and tilted his head back. "You're telling me that nothing happened between you—"

"I'm not saying that I don't find her attractive. I won't lie to you, Bones. I do. And I can't remember everything that happened last night, after the medication."

McCoy flailed his arms. "Oh, that makes me feel just *great*. Thanks for the honesty, Jim. Now, am I supposed to feel better, knowing that you find her attractive and you don't remember what *happened?*"

Kirk stiffened. "If you can't trust either one of us, Doctor, you had better reexamine your personal relationships. Would you rather I lied?"

McCoy's anger flared. "I'd rather you left her the hell alone."

Kirk stood up so quickly that he spilled some of the volatile liquid down the front of his tunic and now reeked of the stuff but was too angered to care. "She's not anybody's property, Bones. You don't have the right to say that."

"So now you're concerned about her personal rights, eh, you, who treats every single female who comes aboard this ship like they're fair game—you think you have to play ladies' man with them all! Emma deserves better than that!"

"That's not true! I keep my distance from every female officer on board this ship! You should talk—going after a woman half your age. She could be your daughter!"

"She's older than Joanna," McCoy defended himself pathetically. "But it seems to me you've changed your hands-off policy toward women crewmembers. You've been flirting with Emma since she set foot on this ship."

Kirk thought for a moment and set his glass down on the desk. "Then I'll stop."

His words stole the momentum from McCoy's rage. "Well . . . what am I supposed to think, Jim?" The doctor shrugged helplessly. "You're younger than I am, handsomer—maybe you felt you needed to prove that—"

"If you don't believe me," Kirk said softly, "then ask Emma—that is, if you trust her any more than you do me."

McCoy put his head in his hands. "You don't know how I feel about her, Jim. I'm an old-fashioned Earth boy. This isn't just some convenient affair—*I love her.*"

"I know. That's why I'll stop the workouts in the gym if you like. I'll avoid all contact with her . . ."

"No, there's no point in doing that . . ." McCoy's eyes glittered with pain and alcohol. "She's attracted to you, isn't she?"

"You'll have to ask the lady that, Bones. I don't speak for her."

"I thought so." McCoy looked at a distant spot on the wall. "I guess I'll have to take this up with her."

"I guess so," said Kirk.

He left the bottle with McCoy.

Kirk was on the bridge, coming to all sorts of conclusions, none of them pleasant, about what had happened to his chief engineering officer. When the intercom finally buzzed, he nearly jumped out of his chair. He prayed it was news of Scott; he knew it was, of course, Lieutenant Tomson.

"I don't think I need to remind you of the time, sir. Shall I put the bulletin out on Mr. Scott?" Tomson had been more than patient, from her point of view—Scott was now more than two hours overdue.

"Lieutenant, I'm sure that there's a very good reason why he's been held up—"

"Even if he does have a good reason, sir, I still need to question him. And he could be trying to escape. Remember our agreement," Tomson said firmly.

Kirk listened to himself give the command as though it were someone else speaking. "I have no intention of backing down on my promise, Lieutenant. Go ahead and issue the bulletin on my authority."

He wondered if she would insist that he put himself in the brig.

Kirk stood outside the atmosphereless hangar deck and watched from behind the protective glass shield as the *Galileo* sailed through the open portal, leaving behind it the stars and the two Federation police shuttles that had escorted it back. The portal closed silently behind the small craft; Kirk heard the hiss of the airlock as pressurization began. The protective glass shield slid aside, and Kirk, Tomson, and Ensign al-Baslama walked to the door of the shuttlecraft and waited.

It seemed to Kirk like a very long time before the

door opened. Scott helped Chapel out carefully, his left arm around her waist, her right arm draped across his shoulder. She was limping painfully, and neither one seemed much amused by their present circumstances. Scott scowled up at them. "Who can help Nurse Chapel to sick bay? Her ankle's broken."

"Al-Baslamah," Kirk nodded to the security guard. The tall, formidable-looking male scooped Christine up into his muscular arms.

"Well," Chapel said, surprised but not at all struggling, "I can certainly think of worse ways to travel."

Scott waited for the guard to carry her off before he confronted the captain angrily. "Beggin' your pardon, sir, but just what the divvil is goin' on? We'd scarcely left the star base when those jokers put a tractor beam on us and told us we were bein' carried back to the ship. I told them we were headed this way anyway, but they just laughed."

Tomson stepped forward. "You're wanted in connection with the murder of the Romulan prisoner, Mr. Scott."

Scott gazed at her with disbelief, then directed a hurt look at the Captain. "Sir—is it true? Did ye give the order?"

Kirk tried to meet Scott's eyes, but did not succeed for long. He looked down. "I gave the order. Mr. Scott, you're six hours late."

"Aye, we're late, all right. We were all almost killed when the *Galileo* crashlanded on Star Base Twelve. It took me that long to repair her."

"Is everyone all right?" Kirk thought immediately of Spock.

"All but Nurse Chapel's ankle. Captain, someone deliberately tampered with the fuel indicator—"

"The way you tampered with the brig's force field using the override control in Engineering?"

Scott looked at Tomson as though she had lost her mind. "Are ye jokin', Lieutenant? The maintenance panel indicated a problem with the override controls—that's why I went to check it out—but the problem had corrected itself by the time I got there. Just exactly what are ye sayin'?"

Tomson's gaze was cool. "That you set the manual control so that it would lower the force field at the precise time you went down to the brig to murder the prisoner."

Stiff with anger and pride, Scott looked Tomson squarely in the eye and took a step toward her. "I dinna do it, Lieutenant. Go ahead and question me. I've got nothin' to hide. It so happens that right after I checked on the override controls I went back to work on the lower engineering deck, sortin' through wreckage from the pirate ship. At least three other crewmembers were workin' with me. I can give you their names."

"And would you be willing to submit to a questioning under the influence of truth drug?"

"With pleasure, Miss Tomson."

"Then come with me, Mr. Scott."

Before he followed Tomson, Scott turned to Kirk. "Ye told them about Ensign Lanz, didn't ye, Captain?" His voice was soft and wounded.

Kirk tried to speak, but the engineer would not give him a chance to reply. Scott shook his head. "I wouldna thought ye capable, sir. I wouldna thought ye capable . . ."

Head held high, shoulders back, he walked with Tomson to the brig.

Chapter Seven

SPOCK WAS UNABLE to identify what was happening to him.

His lessons with the white-haired Tela'at Stalik were at best unenlightening exercises in futility. While Stalik was accomplished in the practice of *Kohlinahr,* and in addition had reached the revered age of 265 Terran standard years, he nevertheless seemed to lack patience for Spock's slowness at relearning the mind disciplines, and did not hesitate to make his displeasure known. For Spock, the lessons were frustrating, and eventually he became convinced that Stalik was deliberately trying to be enigmatic, unclear, and to rush the lessons. Many times Spock came close to saying so, but courtesy and the esteemed position a *tela'at* held in Vulcan society forbade it.

His powers of concentration seemed to be worsening rather than improving, his memory becoming more clouded instead of clearing. His lack of progress keenly embarrassed him, and he became increasingly seclusive, eventually avoiding contact with his family as much as possible. He spent his days in lessons with

Stalik, scouring the bookshelves, and sitting alone in the garden, unable to meditate.

Spock found himself losing patience with everyone: with Stalik, with Amanda, with the overeager T'Pala. He told himself that no one noticed his increasing irritability—until one day Amanda increased his medication to two capsules a day. She had noticed his worsening condition and, without telling him, had consulted McCoy. Inexplicably furious, Spock had turned on his heel and sought the serenity of the garden to gather himself.

He stepped outside into the soothing arid heat and went to his favorite spot—a stone bench half-hidden beneath a hanging arbor of thick foliage, its blooms rustling in the hot afternoon breeze.

He stopped abruptly. T'Pala sat hidden in the shadows, eyes closed, face in the perfectly bland expression of Vulcan meditation, an expression of which Spock lately had been incapable.

He backed away quietly, not wishing to disturb her, more for his own sake than for hers. But it was too late; before he could retreat to the safety of the house, she called out to him.

He faced her reluctantly.

She spoke uncertainly, her face still hidden in the shadows. "There's something I would like to discuss with you. It's something that I would not feel at ease discussing with anyone else."

She motioned for him to sit next to her, but he remained standing. She shifted nervously.

"What do you know of my background?" T'Pala asked.

Spock's manner was brusque; he wanted only to return to the serenity of the guest room and Amanda's books. "I know that you are half-human, and that you grew up on Terra. Nothing more."

She nodded to indicate that his information was correct. "As I say, this is a subject too sensitive to discuss with anyone else. I . . . I wanted to tell you that I admire your emotional control. I wanted to ask you how you accomplished it."

If she had not seemed so ingenuously earnest, he would have thought she had chosen this particularly inopportune moment to make fun of him. He decided that she was sincere. "I was raised on Vulcan. I spent years learning emotional discipline and the Vulcan mind control techniques."

"I did not," T'Pala replied sadly. "My mother was Vulcan, but she died when I was three. I learned of Vulcan culture and language at school and from my father. There was no one who could teach me all the ancient disciplines." She leaned forward and he caught sight of her face, intense, almost . . . begging. "Would you be willing to help me?"

He almost left, sure now that she was making fun of him, but something in her voice made him remain. Perhaps she did not know . . . perhaps his parents had not told her of his condition . . . perhaps even after her question to him about Aritani, she had not thought it proper to ask. "You receive lessons from the Tela'at Stalik, do you not?"

"Yes, but my progress is very slow. It could take years . . ."

"He is far better qualified to teach Vulcan discipline than I. I . . ." he almost faltered, then continued evenly, "I have lost the mind rules. I was injured in an accident on Aritani."

"I know," she answered.

His temper flared. "Then why do you make such a ridiculous request?"

"It's not ridiculous," she responded swiftly. "You've lost the mind rules, yet your control is better than mine. Being half-human, as I am, you must be relying on human methods of control, yet after years of living on Vulcan, you know how to *act* like a Vulcan, something I don't know. If you could just show me how . . ."

"For what purpose?"

"To be accepted. I am a Vulcan citizen. I want to be worthy of my heritage. And I want to join the Vulcan Diplomatic Corps."

"I see," Spock said stiffly. "Why not the Terran diplomatic service?"

The insult failed to register. "I'm no longer a citizen of Terra."

"And you believe that learning how to behave as a Vulcan will increase your chances of entering the VDC?"

She frowned. "You make it sound as though I'm doing this for entirely selfish reasons."

"You may reach your own conclusions." He spoke vehemently. "If you feel yourself to be a Vulcan, T'Pala, then you must embrace the Vulcan path completely. You cannot choose those aspects of Vulcan life which appeal to you. Learning emotional control may indeed take years, but if you truly desire it, it must come from inner discipline, not from outer playacting. Any Vulcan you meet will know the difference. To follow the path merely for furthering your own political ambitions would be no less than an obscenity."

T'Pala jumped to her feet, her chin quivering. "I wish to follow the Vulcan path, and my reasons are valid. And you sound like all the others, insisting that the Vulcan path is the only way, and there is but one way to follow it. I see no logic in your blind loyalty."

"Vulcan loyalty is not blind," Spock replied hotly. "Quite the opposite. But I have not come to debate that with you. As to your question of whether I can help you enter the VDC, I cannot. What vestige of control I now possess is the direct result of years of habit."

"I was not asking you to help me get into the VDC," she said. "I have very deep personal reasons for wanting to join, reasons which I do not care to discuss with anyone, not even you. But I resent your implication that my reasons are not honorable."

"You will get in. My father has recommended you." He did not say it kindly.

"Even that may not be enough."

"Because you are half-human?"

Her lips twisted bitterly. "That, among other reasons."

"If you believe that your human behavior patterns have cost you admission into the Corps, then clearly, my help is of no use to you. I believe that on Terra you have an expression: too little, too late."

Her face hardened and became perfectly expressionless. "Then you will not help me."

"That is correct," he answered coldly, and went into the house.

Emma was waiting for McCoy when he got off duty. She stood outside the door to his cabin and smiled at his as though nothing had changed, as though he had not pointedly avoided her for the past two days.

He moved past her without acknowledgment, but she followed him inside.

"I think we need to talk, Leonard. You're angry at me."

He went to the cabinet and poured himself three fingers of moonshine. "Funny, a lot of people seem to be saying that to me these days," he muttered.

"What?"

"Nothing. I merely said, how observant of you to notice. Drink?"

"No. Please tell me why you're so angry."

"It hasn't seemed to bother you for the past couple of days. In fact, I was beginning to think you hadn't noticed at all. Why don't you see if you can figure it out all by yourself? Cheers." McCoy held up his glass for an instant and looked at Emma through the volatile liquid before taking the largest gulp physically possible.

"Please don't play games with me."

"I'm afraid you have it backwards, my dear. I'm not the one who's playing the games. Why do I always have to tell everyone on this ship things they already know?"

"But I *don't* know." Her exasperation seemed genuine enough. "All I know is that you've been avoiding me for the past two days. You wouldn't even speak to me in sick bay. At first I thought you were depressed or in a bad mood, but I can see now it's more than that."

"Well," he said softly. "At least you're capable of making *some* deductions." He hated himself for the sarcasm in his voice, but most of all he hated her—for the position she had put him in, for the innocence she feigned so well—hated her, because he still loved her and would believe absolutely anything she told him, even if she told him Jim had lied and that he, McCoy, had jumped to conclusions, had been a fool, a jealous old fool. . . .

But she did not. Emma planted herself firmly in the same chair Jim had sat in the night before and held him with those clear, guileless eyes. "I'm not leaving until you tell me what I've done to offend you."

McCoy sank shakily into the chair opposite her and

tried to guess what her reaction to his accusation would be. Denial, most likely, proving her to be a liar, she who prided herself so on her honesty. He let go a sigh that seemed to come straight from his heart. "The captain told me that he spent the night in your cabin night before last."

"Yes," she said, waiting.

"Are you telling me that nothing happened between you?"

He watched the subtle changes in her facial muscles as she finally understood his implication. There was surprise first—the lifted brow, widened eyes, lips slightly parted—but following quickly came something very much like fury. The lips closed and tightened, the jaw tensed; she contained her anger, but her eyes blazed.

"For God's sake, Emma," McCoy said plaintively, "do you really expect me to react casually to that? Do you really expect me not to be jealous?"

Emma took a deep breath and sat back in the chair. The anger glimmered for a moment more, then was extinguished as rapidly as it had first appeared. "No," she said calmly. "No, I don't expect you not to be jealous." She knitted her hands together in her lap and looked down at them.

"But my reaction is two questions for you. First—is that what you think of me, Leonard?"

"Emma, are you so naive to think that if a man sleeps over in your cabin, it's absurd for anyone to think he might have made love with you?"

"If you're suspicious, then your first reaction should be to come to me and ask me what happened, not to pout for two days, and not to jump to whatever you may think is a logical conclusion."

"All right," McCoy conceded icily. "What's the second question?"

"What the hell business is it of yours anyway? We haven't come to any sort of understanding about other relationships."

McCoy rose and turned away from her, clasping his hands behind him as he stared into the darkness of the inner room. "Maybe it's none of my business at all," he said, the anger in his voice replaced by sadness. "I know I have no right to be jealous. But I am. I'm jealous because I felt our relationship was special. I'm jealous because I have feelings for you that I haven't felt in a very long time, and I don't want anyone to take you away from me."

"No one's going to take me away. If I leave, it will be because it's time for me to leave." Emma rose from her chair and placed a hand lightly on McCoy's back, but he did not turn around. "I asked you if that was what you thought of me because I thought you understood something about me—I am a loyal person. I would never do something to hurt you, Leonard, not unless it absolutely couldn't be helped. Even if I were physically attracted to Jim Kirk, I would not act on it."

McCoy turned halfway toward her in the darkness. "*Are* you attracted to him, Emma?"

Her gaze was steady and sought no pardon. "If I said I didn't find him attractive, I would be a liar."

He turned away instinctively, to hide his hurt, but she placed a hand on his face and drew it gently toward her. "But I love *you*. I gave him a hypo and it put him to sleep before I could get him out of my cabin. That's all there was to it."

"All?" McCoy's eyes searched hers so hopefully that she felt pity for him. She took a deep breath.

"No, not all. He got a little relaxed . . . and he kissed me. That was all."

McCoy sighed with relief. So she was telling the

truth, she and Jim . . . "As you pointed out, we don't have an understanding about other relationships. Would you like to?"

She smiled at the realization that he believed her. "Of what sort?"

"How does marriage strike you?"

Her smile vanished, replaced by something very close to panic. "Leonard . . . no, that wouldn't be possible."

"Why not? I admit it's an old-fashioned idea, but still a popular one—"

"It's not that I think it's a bad idea—I love you very much—but you will remain on the *Enterprise* and I will be reassigned somewhere else."

"Well then, just request a permanent assignment here. You don't have to be reassigned—"

"I do. It's the nature of my job."

"What the devil are you talking about? Medical personnel can request permanent assignments, especially married medical personnel." His tone became heated again.

"Please try to understand—that's the agreement I have with Star Fleet."

"Well you could change the agreement, then. Certainly someone—" he almost said, the captain "—can pull some strings so you could be assigned here. If you'd just rather not marry me, please say so."

"It's not that." She closed her eyes at the hopelessness of explaining it to him. "Please, there's no point in talking about it any more. I'll have to be reassigned somewhere else soon, and that's the way it is."

He panicked. "How soon?"

"I wish I knew," she said, with a misery that broke his heart. "I'd prefer to spend what time I have with you, if you'll let me. I do care about you."

He pulled her close to him and kissed the top of her

head. "I'm going to do everything in my power to keep you on this ship. In the meantime, I'd like to ask one favor."

"Anything," she murmured.

A smile played at the corners of his mouth. "Call me next time you're going to be two days late for dinner."

"Your concentration is imperative, Spock," Tela'at Stalik admonished sternly, "if you are to make any progress."

Spock directed his gaze away from the window and back toward the flame statue. Outside, a light rain fell upon the water-starved desert, one of those rare gray days on Vulcan when the sun did not scorch the sky orange.

Spock repressed a sigh and attempted once again to concentrate. He sat cross-legged beside the Tela'at as both regarded the flame statue and Stalik explained the process of meditation for the twentieth time. Spock's mental agitation was increasing daily, along with his forgetfulness. The lessons with Stalik had become cruel parodies of the lessons Spock had taken as a child; but then, he had retained the information, and had understood. Now it seemed impossible.

As Stalik droned on in monotone, Spock became drowsy staring at the flickering flame. With each passing second, his irritation at Stalik increased—the lessons all seemed interminably long, and he wanted more than anything for Stalik to finish and leave.

"Spock," Stalik snapped.

Spock started; he hadn't heard a word Stalik had been saying.

The Tela'at's regal serenity seemed incongruous with his words. "You are a dreadful student, Spock. After weeks of daily lessons, you have not mastered even the first level of meditation. I am beginning to form the opinion that you will never do so."

The muscles in Spock's body tensed, although his expression did not change and his eyes remained fixed on the flame. "Perhaps you are right, Tela'at." He turned his eyes on his teacher. "Then why do you continue to instruct me?"

Stalik's tone, unlike his words, was not insulting. "It is difficult to believe that an adult Vulcan could not master such elementary concepts."

The temptation was great to defend himself by explaining the extent of his difficulties, but Spock held his peace; he would not further shame himself by excusing his weaknesses. Instead he said, "Why does the Tela'at waste his time with me?"

"Out of respect for your father." Stalik's response was calculated to inspire remorse, but in Spock's case it merely served as fuel for his anger.

For the father, not the son. "If the Tela'at does not expect me to progress, is not such a waste of his time illogical?"

Spock knew full well that his question contained the ultimate insult to one who had passed through the rigors of *Kohlinahr*—the intimation of illogical, ill-considered action. Stalik had no trouble interpreting Spock's intent: he rose stiffly to his feet.

"This will be the end of my instruction, Spock," he said. "You are correct. There is no logic in continuing the lessons."

Spock remained seated before the statue; he did not watch as the Tela'at left.

But Amanda had seen Stalik leave, and went to tap lightly on Spock's door. She was not at all prepared for the angry stranger who answered.

"Spock—is everything all right? Stalik was scarcely here ten minutes . . ."

Spock stared stonily down at her. "I insulted the Tela'at. I indicated that further lessons were illogical."

"Illogical? Spock, I don't understand."

"The lessons were a waste of time, Mother. I do not wish to discuss it further." He began to retreat back inside the room.

She caught him gently by the elbow. "What do you want me to tell your father, then? How can I tell him that?"

The mention of Sarek seemed to infuriate Spock; he practically shouted at her. "That is none of my concern. You may tell him whatever you wish."

She drew back and dropped the elbow, mouth open. "Spock, what's wrong?"

"You know. Must you shame me into saying it?"

"Please . . . I don't understand."

He turned his face away from her, miserable. "The mind rules. I cannot relearn them. I can no longer function as a Vulcan—I apparently cannot even control my temper as well as a human. And my memory is getting worse."

"Spock." Amanda's voice was soothing. "You'll learn, I promise you . . . it's just that it will take more time. You were used to learning so quickly. You must be patient. It will all come back . . ."

"No." Spock fought despair with anger. *"No.* Mother, can't you see . . . I'm *not* improving slowly. Each day, I'm getting worse, forgetting more and more . . ."

"Then let me call Dr. McCoy. Perhaps we should increase the medication—"

"The medication hasn't helped," he said dully. "I am going to get worse, and that is why I shall leave here as quickly as possible, before I bring further shame to my family."

"But where will you go?"

"A star base hospital. Perhaps Star Base Twelve."

Hot tears gathered behind Amanda's eyes; she wanted to stamp her foot, to scream, but she had lived with Vulcans for too long. "No," she commanded with a mother's determination. "You will *not* go there. You will stay here with us, where you belong."

He shook his head. "I don't belong here, Mother. You and father have been shamed enough, especially after the trouble I have caused with the Tela'at."

"I don't give a damn about Stalik," Amanda said, losing her own temper at last. "I don't care if he tells everybody in ShiKahr. And don't you ever, ever say that we're ashamed of you. How could you even think such a thing?"

His jaw twitched in a scarcely visible spasm. "Are you forgetting, Mother, that I am a telepath?"

Amanda quickly clapped a hand over her open mouth, but did not succeed in stifling the first sob. Perhaps she wept from surprise as much as from pain—Spock had never said anything cruel to her before, nor accused her of anything untrue. Now he was doing both. She disappeared to the safety of her room before she embarrassed them both any further.

Spock stood frozen with horror at what he had just done. Amanda was probably the last person in the universe whom he would choose to cause pain. But even though Amanda was hidden in her room on the other side of the house, Spock could detect the faint sound of her weeping. A human would not have heard it.

. . . An ugly, muffled sound. Spock had heard it only once before, when he was four years old, standing outside the door to Amanda's room; it had taken him some time to realize that his mother was responsible for the wrenching, faraway sound. Spock, the child, had been terrified. Sarek had come out of the room, and for an instant the noise had stopped. "Go and comfort your mother," his father had said, in a voice gentler than Spock had ever heard before. "You are her only child."

He had not understood, but he had gone inside.

He could not go to her now.

Instead, he went to the cabinet in the kitchen where Amanda kept the medication and poured the capsules into his hand. They really were rather pretty—an intensely brilliant shade of purple—and quite useless. Spock's hand closed over them in a tight fist.

Perhaps . . . not totally useless. . . .

Chapter Eight

Captain's Log, Stardate 7006.4:

Under orders of Star Fleet Command, the *Enterprise* has left Aritani in order to deliver delegates to an emergency meeting of the Federation Council which is being held on the planet Vulcan. The *Fidelity,* a patrol vessel currently assigned to the area, will take the *Enterprise*'s place as watchdog, although I frankly doubt that the presence of any ship will serve as a deterrent to the raiders. The meeting's purpose is to determine whether the Federation should continue its involvement with Aritani given the growers' refusal to accept further Federation protection. While a case can be made for abiding by the Aritanians' wishes, the fact that the planet's mineral wealth makes it an attractive target for exploitation by unfriendly powers has led the Federation to consider continuing protection. Intelligence sources indicate the Romulan government may already be eyeing the planet for use as a mining colony.

The murder of the Romulan prisoner is still unsolved. The murder charges pending against Lieutenant Commander Montgomery Scott have been dropped on the ground of insufficient evidence; three witnesses verified his presence on the engineering deck at the time of the murder. Lieutenant Tomson informs me that she has uncovered no further evidence in the case.

He awoke with a gasp, heart pounding so hard he could scarcely catch his breath. He looked about to reassure himself that he was in the garden, under the hanging arbor, and that he had been dreaming—a nightmare of something intensely purple, something that filled him with a sense of terror.

Spock straightened and intentionally slowed his breathing. He had dreamed of the pills, no doubt, because he had held them in his hand and studied them for some time, contemplating what might happen if he swallowed them all. Some lingering shred of logic had saved him, had reminded him that he was uncertain of the effects of an overdose, had dictated that the intentional ending of his life could not be the result of an emotional decision. He had thrown them with disgust into the garbage slot on the kitchen wall, knowing that they would immediately be incinerated.

The hanging vines shielded Spock's eyes from the intense light of the midday sun; the gray misting rain of the day before had at last been burned away. Spock had been sitting in the garden for a full day. He rose and stretched stiffly, his tunic still damp from the rain and smelling slightly mildewed, and went to his room.

The flame in the belly of the statue was still burning, as he and Stalik had left it the day before. As he stood with his eyes fixed on the pulsating red light, Stalik's instructions came to his mind with sudden clarity.

Spock sat in the cross-legged position before it, his muscles complaining with their need to be stretched, but he ignored the discomfort and kept his eyes on the flame.

Logic. One must formulate the question first, before one can arrive at the answer. And Spock had questions; he would begin to sift them now, one by one. Today he would answer at least one of them.

Stalik had said that there were always answers.

It was late afternoon when Spock emerged from his room into the hallway.

The Andorian child had just completed his lesson; it must have been his last, for Amanda was presenting him with a gift: one of the rare paper books, this one bound in red cloth. It was typical of her, loaning—sometimes giving—the priceless volumes to those she felt would profit from them most. Spock squinted, but he could not make out the title.

The Andorian, child though he was, seemed to appreciate the worth of the gift and the intent of the giver, for he reverently set the book aside and with youthful impulse hugged his teacher.

Spock knew he should allow them some privacy, but the enormity of his curiosity compelled him to stay. He wanted to know how his mother would respond.

Amanda was almost knocked off balance by the child's momentum, but her expression quickly became one of pleasure; her arms enfolded the child and drew him to her with honest affection.

Spock drew back so that they would not see him as they walked to the door. When the Andorian had departed, Spock walked up silently behind Amanda.

She almost ran into him when she turned around and drew back, startled. "Spock, you look terrible. Were you out in the garden all night? In the rain?"

She did not mention the hurt he had caused her the day before; there was no recrimination in her face, only concern. Spock permitted himself a moment's envy for the Andorian boy.

"Mother, I wish to apologize for the unkind and untrue remark I made yesterday—"

"Don't." She dismissed his offense with a wave of her hand. Both she and Spock knew that Vulcans did not apologize.

"Let me continue. For whatever reason, I was not in control of my temper earlier, and my behavior toward you and toward Tela'at Stalik was inexcusable. I regret it deeply. If I could reclaim the remark—"

"You weren't yourself. I can't hold anything you might have said against you."

"My thought patterns were most confused and illogical. However, I seem to have regained control of them. I shall go to Stalik's house to apologize and ask him to return, although I doubt he will do so."

Amanda's face was hopeful. "Then you think it *is* useful to continue the lessons. And you'll stay with us."

"For the moment, yes."

She studied his face. "You *are* yourself again, aren't you? I'm glad. We've been so worried. But I must ask you—your medication isn't where I left it. Did you take it?"

Spock nodded.

"Good," she said, relieved. "I trust you to take it, then. I'm just very grateful for the sudden improvement . . . perhaps the effects are cumulative.

Spock's expression was bland, even agreeable; there was no reason to alarm her by revealing the fate of the neodopazine. If his condition worsened, he would contact McCoy himself.

But his mother's statement about the effects of the

drug aroused a strange emotion in him, one that for some odd reason was connected in his subconscious with his accident. . . . He tried to identify it before it passed as quickly as it had descended.

Fear . . . a feeling of imminent danger.

That night it visited him again as he dreamed of purple . . . not the porcelain capsules this time, but steep purple mountains.

Kirk sat miserably in his command chair, fingering the stiff collar of the dress uniform. It was no secret to the crew that their captain had been in a less than perfect mood for the last few weeks. Maybe his dress uniform was getting too tight and making him cranky, Sulu suggested in a low voice to Chekhov. The helmsman's eyes darted sideways at the captain, who was distracted by a yeoman's report requiring his signature. The low rumble of laughter quickly faded to silence as Kirk glared up from the yeoman's clipboard, sensing that he was somehow responsible for the merriment.

"Coming into orbit around Tellar, Captain," Sulu said glibly.

"Visual of the Tellarite delegation," Kirk said without enthusiasm.

Uhura's fingers were poised over her console; she'd been waiting for the command. "On visual, Captain."

Stocky, bristle-haired, heavy-browed, the Tellarite ambassador was impossible to describe in Terran terms as anything other than porcine; certainly, his manners served little to disabuse anyone of the comparison. He glared at Kirk with small, bilious eyes set over a nasal appendage best described as a snout.

Kirk affected a weak smile of dubious sincerity. "This is Captain James T. Kirk of the starship *Enterprise*. Is your party ready to beam aboard?"

"Ambassador Zev. It's about time," the Tellarite boomed in a low, hoarse voice, quite unlike the squeal one expected from looking at him. "We've been waiting almost an hour!"

Kirk's lips tightened. It was a lie, and Ambassador Zev knew it. The *Enterprise* had arrived at the promised moment. But a Tellarite never passed up the opportunity for an argument—tell one that the Terran sky was blue, and they would insist it was as orange as Vulcan's, and then throw in a few insults at your mother for good measure. It was a characteristic of Tellarite culture for which Kirk was in no mood.

"Please stand by to beam up." Kirk cut off the communication abruptly and wondered whose bright idea it was to let Tellar into the Federation. Zev's piggish snout was the last object to fade from the viewscreen. "Mr. Varth."

The first officer, his expression gracious and alert, turned from Spock's console to face the captain. Like Kirk, he wore his full-dress uniform, but his was science officer's blue, a color that complemented his copper hair. "Sir," he replied in his soft tenor voice.

"Accompany me to the transporter room."

"Yes, sir."

Kirk left, taking his foul mood with him, while Varth followed at a polite distance.

Sulu took the con and when the doors to the lift had closed, sighed.

"What's been eating *him?*" Uhura asked in a low voice.

Sulu just shook his head.

Kirk maintained a sullen silence until the lift deposited them on the level of the transporter room. "Ever dealt with Tellarites before, Mr. Varth?" he asked with the supremely confident voice of experience.

"Yes, sir," Varth replied eagerly. "I roomed with one at the Academy."

Kirk looked at him sharply, wanting to ask what the hell one had been doing at the Academy, but he bit his tongue and held the lecture on how not to lose one's temper with Tellarites.

Scott and McCoy were already waiting in the transporter room, both in their dress uniforms; they had been talking but when the captain entered, an awkward silence descended. Kirk was certain Scott still thought he had mentioned Ensign Lanz to Tomson, thus precipitating Scott's arrest; he had no idea if McCoy still blamed him for the incident with Emma.

McCoy cleared his throat and tugged at the collar of his uniform. "How many more of these delegations do we have to pick up? This thing is killing me. They can transport a man's atoms through space and back, but they can't dress him up and let him be comfortable at the same time."

"This is the last delegation," Kirk said.

"Thank God," Scott sighed. "I'll be glad when we're finished with all this pomp and circumstance." He turned to the young Radun and with a paternal air, said, "Now tell me, Mr. Varth, have ye ever had the misfortune to have dealings with Tellarites before?"

"Yes," Kirk said shortly, before Varth could open his mouth. "He has."

Varth nodded politely in Kirk's direction and waited to be sure the captain was finished speaking. "I was friends with a Tellarite back at the Academy."

"Friends? With a Tellarite?" Scott's eyes widened with horror at the thought. "I dinna think that's possible. Ye must have some special diplomatic gift to make friends with those piggish little—"

"Mr. Scott," Kirk warned.

"—beasties," Scott finished. "Are ye sure your people are related to the Klingons? I can't think of a more unlikely combination, a Klingon and a Tellarite."

Varth smiled. "Raduns have a special knack for getting along with almost anyone. I've never met someone I couldn't be friends with." He looked hesitantly at the captain.

Kirk scowled. "I suppose we have no choice but to beam them aboard, Mr. Scott."

"Aye," Scott sighed, "I suppose not." He went behind the transporter control console.

Three squat forms shimmered and materialized into reality on the transporter pads. The tallest one spoke.

"I am Ambassador Zev." It sounded more like a hysterical accusation than an introduction.

"And I am, of course, Captain Kirk. This is my first officer, Mr. Varth, Chief Engineer Scott, and Chief Medical Officer McCoy."

Zev flared his already wide nostrils. "Is this why you made us wait so long before you beamed us up? So that you could assemble half your crew in this useless display of pomp?"

Kirk smiled at the thought of the immense pleasure involved in poking Zev in his oversized snout. "This is hardly half the crew, Ambassador. There are over four hundred personnel aboard this ship. It is our custom to honor important diplomats such as yourself by having our senior officers greet you—"

"A ridiculous waste of time!" Zev waved a stubby arm imperiously. "Take us to our quarters now."

"Sir," Varth said in a low voice to Kirk, "if I may—"

"He's all yours," Kirk said, his smile faded.

"What do you mean, we made you wait so long?" Varth shouted so loud that McCoy jumped. "That's an outright lie! You know we were right on time. And speaking of useless displays of pomp, I notice you came with an entourage yourself. They're here just for show, as we are."

Kirk, Scott and McCoy stared at the first officer as if he had gone mad, but Varth ignored them, glaring defiantly at the Tellarites.

Zev made a rasping sound that Kirk was finally able to identify as laughter. "I don't need to explain my attachés to you, son of a Klingon."

"And we don't have to explain ourselves to you."

"Maybe not," Zev said with gusto. "But quit wasting my time with all this talk. Take us to our quarters. And I hope that they're suitable. You humans always put us in rooms which suit your ridiculously oversized bodies—"

"It's not our fault you're so short," Varth sneered.

"Mr. Varth—" Kirk broke in, "I'm sorry to interrupt the mutual admiration society, but if you would take them to their quarters . . ."

"Certainly, sir," the Radun replied politely. He gestured to the Tellarites to follow.

Zev chuckled as he and his diminutive entourage waddled past Kirk. "Captain, I was with former Ambassador Gav's delegation when he was on your ship several years before, and I must say that I find your new first officer a vast improvement over the old one. This one, at least, has a little personality."

Kirk did not smile at the remark.

The Tellarites fell in behind Varth like baby ducks behind their mother; as the door slid closed behind them, they could hear Varth in the corridor: "I always thought that the terms *Tellarite* and *diplomat* were mutually exclusive."

"Did you ever see anything like that before?" McCoy said with awe.

"I'd 'a thought he'd hit Mr. Varth for saying things

like that, but it didn't seem to make him any madder. I think he liked it," Scott puzzled.

McCoy nodded. "That Varth really knows what he's doing."

"Maybe," Kirk said without conviction.

McCoy turned on him. "Give the man a little credit, for God's sake, Captain. It's not his fault he's not Spock." He brushed past Kirk. "Come on, Scotty. This is the last of the diplomats, and I've got some white lightning in my quarters."

"Could I talk to you for a moment first, Mr. Scott?"

Scott stopped. "I'll be there in a minute," he told McCoy.

Kirk waited for McCoy to leave before he began to speak.

Scott stopped him. "Captain, I think I know what you want to talk about . . . and it's all right. You were just tryin' to do your duty."

"Scotty . . . I want you to know that I didn't tell anyone about Ensign Lanz. I never for a moment thought you could have done it. Tomson wanted to put a bulletin out on you immediately, but I wouldn't, not until you were late. I'm sorry, Scotty."

Scott lowered his eyes. "I appreciate what ye tried to do for me, sir. And I'm sorry for what I said. No hard feelings?"

"No hard feelings."

He smiled and straightened his shoulders. "Then, sir, why don't ye join me and the doctor for a little tipple? Ye look like you could use some cheerin' up . . ."

"Thanks. Maybe later, Scotty."

But Kirk had no intention of going to the doctor's quarters. He seriously doubted he would be welcome there for quite some time.

* * *

It was not the most comfortable situation James Kirk had ever been in, but then it was not the most uncomfortable either. The reception for the delegates was in full swing in the rec lounge, and from the looks of things, at least half the crew was present. Kirk headed toward his first officer, who was having an earnest discussion with the Radun ambassador; Varth had been seriously embarrassed to learn that the Radun delegation opposed protection for Aritani. It looked as if Varth was engaging in a little diplomacy himself.

On the other side of the room the Saurian ambassador was calling and waving to Kirk so loudly that Kirk could no longer pretend he did not notice. Reluctantly, Kirk went to join his group.

Next to the Saurian stood Emma Saenz and Leonard McCoy, both wearing identical medical dress uniforms of pale blue, although Kirk could not help thinking that Emma did hers infinitely more justice. The Saurian and Emma were grinning broadly, oblivious to anyone's discomfort; Kirk and McCoy nodded, unsmiling, at each other.

Kirk addressed himself to the Saurian; he had to raise his voice to be heard above the rumble of the crowd. "By the sound of things, Ambassador Taureng, everyone here has already enjoyed a substantial amount of your contribution to our reception."

"Glad to be of service, Captain," Taureng boomed gleefully, obviously having also indulged in a fair portion of his planet's most lucrative export. He was nearly seven feet tall, black-skinned, and exuding charm, a welcome contrast to the pygmyish Tellarite who stood nearby, arguing quite obnoxiously with the ambassador from Cygnus V. "Permit me to get you a glass."

Kirk started to protest about the impropriety of

ambassadors waiting on the hired help, but Taureng did not seem to hear; after all, his own glass was again empty and needed filling.

Jim turned back awkwardly to face Emma and McCoy; the doctor was studying his Saurian brandy with furious intensity, apparently in an attempt to appreciate the visual and olfactory attributes of the fiery amber liquid. Emma leaned forward. She seemed to be the only sober person in the room.

"How divided are these delegates on the Aritanian question, Captain?" she asked, nodding at the group next to them, which consisted of Ambassador Zev, the Cygnusian with whom he was arguing, and an Andorian who was quietly watching the exchange.

"As far as I can tell," Kirk said, loud enough for Emma and McCoy to hear, but not so loud that he could be heard over the growl of the Tellarite or the silken response of the Cygnusian, "about half the diplomats favor protection. The Tellarites and the Raduns are against it. The Andorians haven't committed themselves, and the Cygnusians are one of the strongest supporters—that's why the Tellarite's arguing with her."

The native of Cygnus V sat on a large sofa next to the Andorian ambassador. Indeed, she found it quite taxing to stand for long periods of time, since Cygnus V's gravity was some ten percent less than Terran standard, but there had been no time to arrange more comfortable travel accommodations and still arrive on Vulcan in time for the vote. McCoy was giving her injections to ease the strain, but even the slightest movement was tiring. Next to the Andorian, she looked like a graceful giantess; she was taller than a Saurian, and even seated, was taller than the Tellarite who stood before her. Her skin was translucent white, and her frail bones were so thin and elongated that a human child could snap them easily. In fact, she avoided any quick movements and often went to the antigrav compartment in the gym, so that she could move about and exercise without fear of breaking a fragile limb. She responded to the shouted accusations of the Tellarite with a voice that was breathless and feathery.

"Don't you realize," Zev yelled, "that you are violating one of the Federation's most revered precepts? We have no right to interfere when they've made it clear they want no help. I can't believe the Federation is even calling this conference!"

The Cygnusian craned her long neck forward and directed a sharply angled chin at the Tellarite. "That is a common misconception among those who do not truly understand Federation Code."

Zev sputtered. "What kind of insult—"

"The noninterference directive states that no representative of the Federation may interfere with the sociological or technological development of a culture, either by hindering or helping it. By giving Aritani a second chance to accept our help, we are in no way interfering with their cultural development. Quite the opposite—we are protecting them from interference, from those who would hinder their development. We are upholding the noninterference directive, not violating it."

"But we are defying their own government's decision," Zev roared.

"We do not defy it." The Cygnusian shook her elongated head slowly, carefully. "We are giving them the opportunity to reconsider their position. They would have no such chance if we permitted the pirates to destroy them."

"They have the right to choose genocide, if they want to. The whole point of this so-called second chance is that the Federation can't bear to see all those fuel sources go to the Romulans."

"Romulans?" Emma whispered in Kirk's ear.

"The latest rumor."

"If the Romulans take the planet, then the Aritanians have certainly chosen genocide," said the Cygnusian, "for the Romulans would destroy the inhabitants and strip what they wanted from the planet without concern for its ecosystem. They would effectively destroy it. That is their way."

"I still say that's the Aritanians' decision to make," Zev persisted.

She frowned. "Perhaps, Zev, you don't realize that when the Aritanians told us to leave, they felt we couldn't help them. If we could show them that we *can* stop the attacks, they might change their minds."

"And how, pray tell, will we do that now?"

"I'll leave that up to Federation Intelligence." She sipped her brandy delicately.

"There's no way we can protect them against a shield neutralizer!"

The Cygnusian dismissed his remark with a tinkling laugh; frustrated, Zev turned his attention to the Andorian. "I still say we mustn't interfere! What do you say, Thelev?"

The Andorian was as delicate and wrinkled as an old woman; he pursed his lips at the Tellarite. "I can say nothing at this point, Zev. Surely even you can respect the fact that my government has ordered me to hold my tongue until I cast the vote at the conference on Vulcan."

"I can respect the fact that your government is just too namby-pamby to make up its mind until it hears what the other delegates think!"

"Tellarites are most unpleasant when they are

drunk," the gentle Thelev lisped to the Cygnusian, completely ignoring Zev's sputters.

"I agree, although I must add that they are almost as unpleasant when sober," she replied sweetly, angling her head from side to side. "This one, though, makes me a little homesick."

"How so?"

"He reminds me of a Cygnusian *drelu.*"

Zev bellowed loudly and jumped toward the Cygnusian's tender neck with both arms outstretched. Emma was closest and got there first, pinning the Tellarite's pudgy arms with ease. Zev struggled and roared with anger.

"How dare you let this woman touch me, Captain! If I am injured, my government will exact revenge—"

Taureng reappeared in the midst of the commotion with two glasses and a decanter. "What in the names of the gods—"

Kirk glared angrily at Zev, who was struggling pathetically to break free from Emma's grasp. "Ambassador Zev, you will have to leave this reception if you can't keep from fighting with the other delegates."

"First get this she-devil off me!"

Varth appeared at Kirk's side. "I think I can help, Captain."

Kirk was grateful for once to see his first officer. He motioned graciously toward the Tellarite. "Be my guest, Mister Varth."

Emma released her grip, and Zev padded out of the room with Varth on his heels, berating him.

Zev stopped in the entranceway and called to the Cygnusian. "You haven't heard the last of this! I will have my revenge!"

The Cygnusian laughed sweetly and waved.

"I don't understand," Emma said. "What's a *drelu*?"

The Cygnusian giggled. "A *drelu* is a scavenger animal. It subsists on the excrement of other animals."

Kirk addressed himself with relief to the glass of brandy the Saurian proffered him. "I brought a bottle of my own private stock," said Taureng. "One hundred twenty Saurian years in the cask. You won't believe the difference between this and what the others are drinking."

"*Drelu*, huh?" McCoy murmured thoughtfully. "I'll have to remember that one."

"Thank God Varth was here to take Zev off our hands," Emma sighed. "Is it always this difficult, dealing with diplomats?"

The question was addressed to Kirk, but Taureng answered first. "Only when the diplomats involved are Tellarites."

Kirk nursed his brandy for a good while before he spoke.

"Let's hope," he said, "that this is as difficult as it gets."

It wasn't. Kirk was awakened in the middle of the night by a call from Tomson. They had found the Cygnusian ambassador stuffed into a stairwell, the bones in her delicate body snapped like matchsticks.

Chapter Nine

T'PALA SAT UNDER the arbor in the darkness of the garden. She did not speak or stir as Spock approached.

He was glad that his mental shields now afforded him some protection against the anguish that she could not hide, even in the moonless night.

"My parents are concerned," Spock said, drawing his cloak closer against the chill of the night air. "You absented the evening meal and have spoken to no one all day. We did not know if you had returned from ShanaiKahr. Are you unwell?"

She turned her face away. "You know what I went to the capital to find out today. Are you incapable of making deductions?"

"You were not accepted into the diplomatic program."

T'Pala faced him in the blackness, eyes glittering. For a moment Spock feared she had been crying, but her cheeks were dry. "I was not."

Spock thought for a moment before he spoke. "You are very young, T'Pala. It might be that after another year of study, the regents would find you mature enough to enter the program."

She shook her head bitterly. "Maturity has nothing to do with the reason I was not accepted. It has to do with something you can't possibly understand."

"I can't if you don't tell me the reason," Spock countered gently.

She struggled to say it. "My background—"

"T'Pala," he said, "I believe I understand perfectly."

"Then surely you know the prejudice I face here," she said, unable to completely master her anger. "Even if they had accepted me, I'm not sure that I would be happy here. I don't belong. You were wise to leave."

Spock tried to say something, but she stopped him. "But you—you were raised on Vulcan. I was not. I did not acquire all the disciplines as a child. I even speak Vulcan like a Terran."

"T'Pala, I cannot accept that those were the things that prevented your admittance."

"I know. I know that you were accepted and turned it down—"

Spock looked at her sharply.

"—so I know that being half-human, although it did present some difficulty, did not keep me out. It was more than that." She looked down at her hands, folded together in her lap, and sighed. "I wish Sarek were my father."

Spock stiffened. "The reason for my acceptance was not the fact that Sarek was my father. And he did endorse you to the committee."

She looked up at him, quick to explain. "I didn't

mean that it was. I meant that I did not wish to be the daughter of Gerald Carstairs. Even Sarek's endorsement of me could not change that fact."

Spock lifted an eyebrow questioningly.

"No one told you?"

"I have heard the name. Is the fact somehow significant?"

"Significant enough to require our family to leave Terra, to make no Vulcan male want to bond with me—"

"I can think of nothing that would cause you to be an unsuitable mate."

She looked at him gratefully and closed her eyes. "My father had access to certain classified research information because of the nature of his work. The Vulcans accused him of selling that information to the Romulans."

"Did he?"

"The Vulcans never pressed charges, but they made him leave. Of course, that was the end of his diplomatic career. When he died last year, I returned to Vulcan. I feared that I would not be accepted because of what my father did. Now my fear has been realized."

Spock sat next to her on the stone bench to emphasize the sincerity of what he said. "T'Pala, I still maintain that although Vulcans, like all sentient beings, are not totally immune to prejudice, the committee would not reject you on the basis that Gerald Carstairs was your father."

She pulled away from him, back into the shadows. "Think what you like, it makes no difference. I will not shame myself by offering my loyalty to those who reject it. I shall be leaving soon."

"Do not leave," Spock said. "Go to the admissions

committee, and ask them why you were not accepted. They will tell you. Perhaps it is a flaw that can be improved."

But she left him in the garden and would not listen.

It was not a good night. Kirk spent the first half of it questioning the Tellarite delegation and Thelev, the Andorian, who had been the last one to see the Cygnusian alive. Kirk had managed to exact a small measure of revenge: he confined the Tellarites, under Zev's very loud protest, to their quarters. Maybe that would keep them out of trouble for a while—but he doubted it.

Kirk had just lain down on his bunk and closed his eyes when the intercom whistled; he swore loudly as he hit the control.

At least it was Uhura on the bridge, and not Tomson telling him another diplomat had bit the dust.

She smiled at him apologetically. "Sorry to bother, Captain, but I assumed you would still be up after all the excitement. . . ."

Kirk grunted. "What's the problem, Lieutenant?"

"Since the murder of the ambassador, sir, I've been monitoring all channels—alert standby procedure. I just happened to listen in on a very low frequency band, and . . . well, it's hard to explain, but I picked up something that could either be a shadow or a carefully hidden signal. I'm not really sure, but it's definitely some kind of disturbance. Maybe I'm being overcautious . . ."

"I hardly think that's possible, Lieutenant, considering our cargo." Kirk remembered the last time he'd had a shipful of diplomats—and wound up being tailed by an Orion spy ship. "What's the source?"

"This ship, sir." She did not hide her surprise. "Dr. McCoy's quarters."

At first Kirk thought he had heard her wrong. "Did you say *McCoy*'s quarters?"

"Yes, sir. No mistake."

"I'll check it out, Uhura. Thank you for notifying me."

"Thank you, sir."

Kirk adjusted the sonic pick to the correct frequency and stepped back as the door to McCoy's cabin opened.

Inside, the only light in the cabin came from the small lamp on the desk, where Emma sat looking up at him in silent amazement. Kirk was not surprised to find her there, but he had not expected to see what she held cupped in her hand.

Sickened, he pointed his phaser at her. "I'll take that."

She handed the transmitter to him without a word.

"Bones?" Kirk called hoarsely.

No answer came from the darkened bedroom.

He pushed the phaser at her, forcing back the panic that rose in his chest. "By God, if you've done anything to him—"

"I gave him something to put him to sleep. You won't be able to wake him up," Emma said. Her voice betrayed no guilt, no hostility, no anger; it was flat and calm. "What were your people doing monitoring this frequency?"

Kirk's voice shook with rage; he fought to steady it, to be as cool as she. "What the hell were you doing with this on my ship?"

"I need it for my work," she said urgently, and stood up. Kirk waved the phaser at her.

"Sit down."

Emma sat down. "Captain, before you call Security—"

"Be quiet." He could not bear to listen to her speak, not with that honest, unafraid expression—she was going to say something sincere, and Kirk did not trust himself to disbelieve her. He found it hard enough to believe what he had just seen.

"Go ahead and fire, but I'm not going to shut up. Please call Admiral Komack first, and tell him what's happened. Please. Before you call Security."

Keeping his phaser leveled at her, Kirk went to the intercom.

"I'm on your side," Emma said.

Perhaps because he wanted to believe, he did not call Security. "Uhura, I'm sending a message to Admiral Komack from McCoy's quarters. It will be top priority. When the reply comes through, I want you to relay it here the instant it comes in."

"Thank you," Emma said.

Kirk settled into the chair across from her and pointed the phaser at her chest. "At this distance, we should get a reply before McCoy wakes up. I've got plenty of time to wait."

SAENZ, EMMA MARIA. SECURITY CLEARANCE CONFIDENTIAL. POSSESSION OF TRANSMITTER CLEARED ON MY AUTHORITY. ADMIRAL KOMACK, OUT.

Kirk put down the phaser and closed his eyes with grateful relief. Emma was slumped forward in the chair with her head on the desk; he reached forward and put a hand on her shoulder. When she raised her head to look at him, he smiled at her.

"Komack?" she yawned.

Kirk nodded. "Sorry. I didn't know."

She sat up straight in the chair and stretched her

arms above her head. "Thank you for not calling Security. No one must know, not even Leonard." She looked at him with somber eyes. "My life depends on it."

"No one will know." Kirk rose to leave, but something made him hesitate.

"Emma . . . about what happened between us . . ."

She raised an eyebrow in an expression of curiosity that strikingly resembled Spock's. "Nothing happened between us, Captain."

"Uh, huh," he said slowly. "Of course. Nothing happened." He moved toward the door and stopped. "And as far as I'm concerned, nothing ever will."

"If that's the way you want it."

"That's the way I want it." He felt slightly exasperated with her; she was not helping him out of this very gracefully; she almost seemed to be having fun with him, the way Spock sometimes used to pretend not to understand Terran figurative speech.

Until she leaned forward and quite seriously said, "I don't want to do anything that would hurt either one of you. I care very much about you both."

When Kirk saw the look in her eyes, he left hurriedly before he kissed her again.

"What the hell—" Kirk was nearly thrown from the command console as the ship lurched forward.

"Captain—" Sulu called urgently, "we've lost warp drive."

"Manual override, Mr. Sulu."

"Not responding, sir."

"Captain!"

The agitation in Uhura's voice made Kirk swivel around to face her.

"Engineering reports an explosion, sir . . . in the main engine room."

"Get me Scott."

"Captain—" Kirk could hear coughing and confusion in the background "—this is Scott." The engineer was struggling to speak.

"What's going on down there, Scotty? Any casualties?"

"No, sir, but somebody's blasted the warp drive. We can't see right now for the smoke to judge the extent of the damage, but I think manual override was also affected. No danger of coolant leakage, and the anti-matter pods are undamaged. Nothing permanent—but whoever set that blast knew right where to put it to slow us down." He broke off, overcome by a spasm of coughing.

Kirk waited for him to finish. "Estimated repair time?"

"All the damage reports aren't in yet, but my guess is at least a solar day's work."

"Get your men to sick bay, Mr. Scott. Sounds like you're all suffering from smoke inhalation. And that includes you."

"Aye, sir."

"As soon as McCoy gives you a clean bill of health, I want a full report on the damage."

He had scarcely made up his mind to call Security next when Tomson came on the intercom.

"Lieutenant Tomson, I was just calling you. As soon as the smoke is cleared out of Engineering, I want you to get some people down there to investigate. Scott says the explosion was no accident."

"An explosion in Engineering, too, sir?"

"What do you mean, too, Lieutenant?" Kirk sat forward with an angry, sick certainty in the pit of his stomach.

The explosion in Taureng's room had sent the Saurian hurtling outside into the corridor, where he impacted with the bulkhead. His aide, who was closer to the site of the blast, was killed instantly. The ambassador had been taken to surgery, condition critical.

Kirk snapped off the intercom, for the second time faced with the unpleasant task of informing a government that their delegation had been the target of a murderer aboard his ship.

"Someone on this ship," he said to no one in particular on the bridge, "does not want us to get to Vulcan."

Captain's Log, Stardate 7006.9:

Lieutenant Tomson informs me that the blasts set in Engineering and in Ambassador Taureng's quarters were set by someone who is not only an explosives expert (since no clue, not even a trace of the material used, was ever found) but who is intimately familiar with the ship's layout.

Security has done a thorough check and found that none of the personnel on board have any training in the use of explosives. Tomson therefore suggests only one possible conclusion.

One of my crewmembers is working for the other side.

Emma Saenz and Kirk faced each other on the padded floor of the gym.

"How's the shoulder?"

Kirk shrugged to show the extent of the improvement. "Hasn't bothered me at all today. Although I must say," he added lightly, "it certainly caused enough trouble at first."

Emma cast a knowing smile at him as they bowed ceremonially.

Instead of the slow-paced dance around her to size her up, Kirk lunged immediately, grasping at his opponent.

Emma moved directly into the attack, into his arms, with enough force to throw him off balance.

It was exactly what he'd hoped. He pulled her down to the floor with him, and rolled swiftly so that she was pinned beneath him. Emma fought, and almost succeeded in breaking away, but this time brute strength triumphed over cleverness. It was one of the few times she had to concede.

"You learn fast," she gasped up at him.

"I have an excellent teacher. You're not the only one good at fooling people."

She learned fast, too. His initial surprise attack had taught her to anticipate similar tricks from him; the rest of the match was a draw.

They were on their way to the sauna when Kirk stopped. There might be others in the sauna, and he wanted only Emma to hear what he had to say. He turned to her, and she looked up at him expectantly; she was still glowing from the workout, and the flush of color in her cheeks and lips had made her truly beautiful. So fragile, and so strong . . .

Kirk instinctively stiffened and assumed a more formal air. "Doctor, I need your help."

"Of course," she said softly. "Name it."

He swallowed. "I must find the person who planted the explosives on my ship. I assume it would also be the same person who killed the Romulan and the Cygnusian ambassador."

She took an indignant step back as though he had insulted her. "Aren't you capable of making any deductions, Captain?" Her hands flew to her hips. "Did you think Komack sent me here just to take care of Spock?"

"No . . ."

"Anything that happens to those delegates is more my failure than yours. Rest assured, I'm working on it."

If there were any words that could make him feel better about the current situation, Emma had just said them. He sighed and relaxed his posture. "Any leads yet?"

"I'd rather not discuss it. For this part of my job, I take orders only from Komack."

He flinched internally at that, but aloud said, "I understand. But certainly you can understand that I wanted to find out what was going on."

"Certainly you realize that you have a spy on board," she said. Then as an afterthought she added in a voice so low he could scarcely hear, "All right, two."

He nodded, sick at the thought.

"When I find out who it is, you'll know," she said, and went to change before he could ask her any more questions.

Lavender deepening to purple deepening to darkest violet, fading to gray and then black—moving up and down, undulating, rolling, rolling into hills, into mountains. Gray, black mountains, and he was rolling down them, gathering speed, faster and faster until he spun like a top and the dizziness made him cry out for it to stop. . . .

Spock sat up with a start. The dream came often now, repeating itself, but each time changing ever so slightly. Soon, he told himself, soon the image of the mountains would no longer be shrouded in mystery.

He glanced up at the chronometer on the ceiling and rose to dress himself for the evening meal. His body was no longer as thin and fragile as it had been; for the past week, he had indulged Amanda's desire to fatten him up. He had even begun taking afternoon naps. He needed the strength now, for he had a purpose: to return as quickly as possible to the *Enterprise*.

Spock was confident that he was once again fit for duty. His memory had completely returned, with the exception of the incident on Aritani, and as the dreams grew more vivid, he knew that memory would soon return as well. Even the mind rules were now his; indeed, that very morning he had received his last instruction from the Tela'at.

"I marvel at the change, Spock," Stalik had told him. "In all my years, I have never seen anyone master the rules more quickly. This is the final lesson. And this time, it is because you no longer have need of my instruction."

Spock had bowed low to him. "I have indeed been fortunate to have the Tela'at as a teacher. Your willingness to return after my indiscreet behavior speaks highly of your character. I will not forget this time what I have learned." He raised his hand in the Vulcan greeting. "Live long and prosper, Tela'at Stalik."

Stalik returned the salute with fingers that trembled with age. "I have done both, Spock. May you also do likewise."

Spock helped his teacher to the door and watched as the Tela'at disappeared down the dusty path. Stalik had reached an age attained by few Vulcans; surely he would soon die, and the wealth of knowledge he had accumulated during his lifetime would be lost, except for that which he had imparted to his students. Spock had not been merely polite when he had said he was fortunate to have Stalik as a teacher.

He was still thinking of Stalik as he finished dressing and walked from his room into the hallway. A flash of black and white startled him.

"T'Pala." He spoke her name almost without meaning to; he had not seen her since their meeting in the garden.

With the exception of her pale face, T'Pala was completely enshrouded by her black cloak. She jumped back nervously, as though she had meant to slip into her room undetected.

"T'Pala," Spock repeated. "My parents have been most concerned about you. They did not know whether to be alarmed by your disappearance. Will you be joining us for the evening meal?"

Her eyes, though defiant, could not meet his. "No. I am preparing to leave Vulcan."

Spock considered this silently for a moment. "Where will you go?"

"Terra, I suppose. I haven't decided yet. But there is nothing for me here."

"Did you speak to the admission committee about their decision—"

"There is no point," she said vehemently, cutting him off. "The Vulcan path is not for me. The Vulcans feel no loyalty toward me, therefore, it is illogical for me to feel loyalty toward them."

"T'Pala—"

She held up her hand to silence him. "I will be gone before you rise tomorrow. You will not see me again."

Spock sighed; there was clearly no point in pursuing the discussion. She had made her decision, just as he had once made a decision many, many years ago, to leave—and even Amanda had been unable to dissuade him. "I, too, will be leaving Vulcan shortly," Spock said.

T'Pala's expression changed abruptly; she looked at him with concern. "Are you certain you are well enough?"

Spock nodded. "My father informs me that the

Enterprise will arrive with the delegates to the Aritanian conference in approximately thirty-four-point-seven standard hours."

T'Pala's eyes had become unreadable. "So the medication is working?"

Spock paused. "Actually, I am no longer taking it—"

She could not restrain herself and interrupted him. "Spock, do you think that is wise? Have you consulted with the doctors about this?"

He continued calmly. "—nevertheless, I seem to be improving. The medication was apparently quite useless."

She persisted. "Not all medications work immediately. Sometimes it takes time for a medication to accumulate to a therapeutic level; and if that is the case, the positive effects may soon begin to wear off. Promise me you will consult the physicians."

She seemed so genuinely distressed that Spock saw no reason to refuse. "Very well. Perhaps it would be wise to consult Dr. McCoy. You are certain you will not join us for the evening meal?" Perhaps Sarek would find some way to make her reconsider her decision.

T'Pala shook her head and backed toward the door to her room.

"In that case," Spock said in Vulcan, "live long, and prosper, T'Pala."

"Good-bye," she whispered in English.

He dreamed again that night of purple, and of the deepest shades of red, blue and orange. The colors shimmered, melted together, and then slowly sorted themselves into their proper places. Spock could see the purple mountains, the deep blue sky, the scarlet sun, which was setting and fading the sky to gray. He looked about, absorbed by the planet's beauty and the heady fragrance of blooming flowers . . .

"Smell that," Jim Kirk said. Spock was glad to see him again, and called the captain's name, but Jim did not turn around, did not seem to hear him at all. He stood on the plateau and breathed in the scent of the wildflowers.

Spock looked and saw Montgomery Scott, and Leonard McCoy; the four of them were together, walking in a very beautiful garden—very beautiful, and very dangerous. Spock decided to warn them, but the words that came out were not the ones he intended.

"Are you having trouble with your eyes, Mr. Scott?" He wanted to tell them to leave, to return to the ship, but once again, he could not control his speech; the old frustration washed over him.

Scott did not appreciate what Spock said; it was a beautiful place, he argued, beautiful, and Spock had to agree. A beautiful place, Aritani.

Aritani.

The word filled him with joy—at last, he could speak of Aritani, and know where it was that he had been.

His joy turned quickly to terror as he realized that his friends had disappeared, and that he was alone in the near-total darkness. He had nothing to fear, he reminded himself. His eyes would adjust quickly to the darkness, his hearing would warn him . . . The sun had disappeared and taken with it the brilliant colors, leaving behind only black and gray. The tricorder led him across the plateau to its edge, to the side of the charcoal-colored mountain; his night vision guided him safely, his footing was sure.

He would not fall.

Spock crouched by the side of the mountain, and in the glow of the transporter beam, he saw and knew that he had been seen. He also knew he had a choice to make: a sure, quick death, or an uncertain fate three hundred feet below.

He jumped.

Spock woke with the sudden start of one who dreams he is falling. Shaking, he rose from his bed.

He remembered now what he had wanted to tell the captain, and was determined to contact the *Enterprise* before they tried again to kill him. He went to the subspace radio provided in the room for offworld guests; the *Enterprise* should be close enough by now for almost immediate reception.

Spock had no trouble remembering the proper frequency. "*Enterprise*, come in. This is Commander Spock on the planet Vulcan. *Enterprise*, do you read?"

There was no time to listen for a response—a sound came from the living room, the sound of a struggle, and of his father's voice, muffled, calling his name—a plea for help, or perhaps a warning—

Spock followed the sound into the main room and saw the glint of hard polished metal in the darkness, and two bodies of apparently evenly matched strength struggling; one was hidden in the loose folds of a desert softsuit.

The other was his father.

Spock rushed to his aid, but not before the assassin's dagger slashed out. Sarek slumped backward into Spock's arms, and as Spock's hands closed on his father's chest, he felt something hot, and wet.

He left Sarek on the floor as the assassin lunged at him with the dagger. Spock recognized the weapon; it had adorned the wall of his old room, the room that was T'Pala's now. He leaned back to avoid the swipe of the blade, and at the same time grasped the assailant's wrist. The assailant fought Spock's hold with

Vulcan strength, pulling back until he freed himself, but he was forced to drop the dagger.

Both lunged for it; the assassin reached it first and managed to nick Spock's wrist with it before he could leap back. Spock cursed himself for his clumsiness— the assassin had taken perfect advantage of the situation, for the small nick had perforated a vein, which was bleeding profusely. Spock would now have to disarm his opponent quickly before the loss of blood affected his coordination.

He sprang at the intruder, tangling his legs to try to force him down, but to no avail. The intruder forced Spock back, back until he stumbled over the unconscious form of Sarek, and fell.

Dizzy, his strength fading, Spock struggled against his attacker as he held Spock's wrist firmly and with medical precision began to cut. Spock looked on with helpless fury—once again, they would try to make it look like a ritual suicide. His vision began to dim and he ceased struggling; it was a useless waste of his ebbing energy.

Suddenly, the attacker was engulfed by radiant light that intensified until his entire form glowed with energy and dissolved into the darkness. The dagger clattered helplessly to the floor.

In his place stood T'Pala. She clutched a phaser in her right hand, her cheeks streaming with tears, but her face calm, composed—Vulcan.

She knelt down beside Spock and spoke in a voice that was measured, steady. "I have summoned aid."

Spock tried to turn his head to determine Sarek's condition, but movement was impossible. He heard his own labored breathing as though it were very far away.

T'Pala, too, seemed to be moving farther and farther away; he strained to hear what she was saying.

"Forgive me. They said I would never be accepted here. They promised me a glorious career in the service of the Praetor, whether I worked for them here in the Vulcan Diplomatic Corps or elsewhere. I would not commit their violence for them, but I told them when you stopped taking the neodopazine, and I told them about your dreams. Don't take it any more—you will understand when you read the article by Silak.

"Then they asked me to neutralize the security scanner and the alarm, and I agreed. But when I saw the assassin wield his dagger . . ."

She bowed her head. "I knew I could never follow their path. I was foolish. Now I have made a complete commitment to the path I was meant to follow."

T'Pala fingered the phaser and cradled it next to her bosom. Spock struggled to speak, but could not.

T'Pala spoke to him in Vulcan. "I have brought further shame to my mother's family, and to my father's as well. Logically, there is only one course to take.

"Live long, and prosper, Spock."

For a millisecond, Spock's eyes were dazzled by the form of T'Pala, blazing more brilliantly than the Vulcan sun.

And then there was darkness.

Chapter Ten

Captain's Log, Stardate 7007.3:
Commendations to Mr. Scott, who worked around the clock to repair the warp drive as quickly as possible. As it is, the damage will cost us less than twenty-four hours' delay. We anticipate arriving at our destination in approximately—"

The intercom whistled and Kirk turned off the recorder. "Kirk here."

"Tomson here, sir."

"Good news this time, I hope?"

Tomson flushed at the slight hint of sarcasm she thought she detected in the captain's tone—she was hardly pleased herself at the total lack of evidence Security had turned up in their investigation. "I'm not sure if it's good or bad, sir. But it's something you'd definitely better take a look at."

"What is it, Lieutenant?"

She hesitated. "I think it'd be better if we discussed it in Security, sir."

"On my way." Kirk snapped off the intercom. "Mr. Varth, you have the con."

Tomson held up the small black object for Kirk to see.

"What is it?" Kirk asked. Its smooth, polished surface gave no clue as to its function; in fact, it looked capable of doing precisely nothing.

"We don't exactly know yet, Captain. It seems to be some type of subspace radio device, although it isn't receiving a signal and we can't figure out how to transmit on it. Whatever it is, it's definitely not Star Fleet issue."

"Ah," said Kirk. "I think I know where you found this, Tomson . . ."

Her brows knitted together in puzzlement. "You do, sir?"

"Yes, and I'd appreciate it if you'd just forget about finding it." He was going to have to remind Emma to be more careful.

"If you want me to, Captain." Tomson was confused. "Then I suppose you'll want me to cancel the surveillance on Varth—"

"Varth?" He looked at her, thunderstruck. "Wait a minute, where *did* you find this thing?"

"Varth's quarters, sir. We were conducting a very thorough search of the ship, sir, and we found it among the personal effects in his closet—"

"You've been searching crewmembers' cabins without my permission, Lieutenant?"

She colored scarlet. "It's the closest thing to a lead we've found, sir. I'll discontinue the search—"

"By all means, Tomson. In the meantime—" Kirk

said gruffly, "—I'll take this." He picked up the device.

"Sir, that's the only evidence we've uncovered—" Tomson began in dismay.

Kirk ignored her. "And have a couple of people escort Mr. Varth to the brig for questioning. You'll find him in command of this ship."

Emma Saenz was in sick bay, running scans on a crewman. Kirk took her by the arm and led her, protesting, into the laboratory. She was incensed.

"You'd better have a damn good excuse, Captain, for interrupting me when I'm with a patient—"

"Later," said Kirk. He held the device in front of Emma's nose. She reached for it, but he pulled it away.

"Where'd you get that?"

"First tell me what it does."

"It probably deflects subspace radio waves. It could also be a transmitter."

"What good is deflecting radio waves?"

"A lot of good, if you want to keep someone from receiving a message that could blow your cover. Now tell me where you found it."

"Varth's quarters," Kirk replied softly.

She did not seem very surprised. "Yes . . . it makes sense. Radu opposes protection for Aritani. It might back the murders of the Cygnusian and the Saurian."

"Come on, Doctor. The Raduns are dyed-in-the-wool Federation. Varth's family has served in Star Fleet for generations . . ."

She was skeptical. "It makes no difference, Captain. There are a lot of people in this business who would think nothing of betraying all that. Now, if you'll excuse me, I have to tend a patient."

* * *

By the time Kirk finally made it back to the bridge, Uhura was breathless. "Sir, I've been trying to locate you—"

"I was questioning Varth in the brig." Kirk tried to ignore the look of questioning disbelief on Sulu's face. "What is it, Uhura?"

"It's Mr. Spock, sir. He just contacted the ship—"

Kirk fought to contain his excitement. "Are we close enough to Vulcan for visual contact, Lieutenant?"

"Yes, sir, but Mr. Spock is no longer transmitting."

"He's not? Was there a message?"

"No message. It was very strange—he had just established contact when the transmission . . . stopped."

"Interference?" Kirk immediately thought of the device found in Varth's cabin.

"No, sir. The channel's still open, as though he simply walked away from the transmitter."

"Have you tried hailing him again?"

"Several times, Captain. No response." Her dark eyes shone with concern.

Kirk acknowledged that concern and shared it with the lightest touch of his hand on her shoulder. "Keep the channel open, Lieutenant, and keep trying until you get in touch with *someone*. Just find him."

She smiled gratefully. "Aye, sir."

"Captain?"

Kirk turned to look at Sulu. "Yes?"

"Sir, you said that Mr. Varth was in the brig. May I ask what the charges were?"

"Any particular reason you're interested, Mr. Sulu?"

Sulu swallowed. "We're friends, sir."

The expression on the captain's face was absolutely

enigmatic. "Mr. Varth is now confined to quarters under guard. I may or may not decide to release him shortly. And no, you may not ask what the charges are."

"Yes, sir." Stone-faced, Sulu swiveled in his chair to once again face the viewscreen. The captain had to have his reasons—Sulu himself had told Varth that Kirk was a fair person, that the captain would not persecute a person, regardless of how much he disliked him. . . .

But he was left with a very uncomfortable feeling.

"Top priority message from Admiral Komack, Captain," Uhura said. "Scrambled and coded."

"Relay it to my quarters," Kirk said. "I'll take it there."

When he returned to the bridge, it was with a rather smug-looking first officer. But the instant he stepped from the turbolift, Kirk knew that something was wrong. All eyes were fastened on his; Uhura's eyes were full of sympathy.

Varth immediately went to his station, but Kirk remained standing in front of Uhura.

"You've located Mr. Spock, haven't you, Lieutenant?" he asked softly. *Dear God, don't let her tell me he's dead . . .*

"Yes, sir." Her voice was barely audible. "I kept the hailing frequency open and finally a Vulcan Security officer responded. He said that Mr. Spock is in ShanaiKahr Hospital."

"What happened?"

"I contacted the hospital. They say Spock is in serious condition, but is expected to recover." Uhura paused, unable for a moment to continue or to meet the captain's gaze.

"Uhura," Kirk pleaded.

She drew a breath and looked up at him. "They also

199

say that circumstances indicate he attacked his father and then attempted suicide."

Emma Saenz sat on the stool and shook her head sadly. "I was afraid something like this would happen," she said, in a voice that conveyed no recrimination, only regret.

McCoy's jaw was stubbornly set. "Whatever Spock has been charged with, I'm sure he's innocent. I'm going to try to see him."

"No!" Emma's fist struck the lab counter with such force that both Kirk and McCoy jumped. "Spock won't want to see you now. The shame would be too great for him. I know from experience—"

"Doctor Saenz," Kirk said in an aggrieved tone, "we are all well aware by this time of your experience with Vulcans."

"You may know Vulcans, Emma," McCoy said with the old fire, "but I know *Spock*, and have for many years, and right now I happen to think that Spock needs our help."

Emma shook her head vehemently.

"I know Spock better than anyone here," Kirk said, "and I know that he could never hurt anyone. That's why I'm going down there to do what I can to clear him of the charges."

Emma sprang from her seat, her body tensed with anger. "I fail to see, gentlemen, why no one here seems to give a damn about my medical opinion. Why did you request a medical specialist, Doctor, if you had no intention of listening to her?"

"Take it easy." McCoy motioned for her to sit back down. "I *have* listened to your medical opinion. I gave Spock the neodopazine on your recommendation and I sent him to his quarters earlier than I would have liked to, again on your recommendation. But here I draw the line. Spock is our friend, and we know him better than you do."

She sat back down and folded her arms tightly. "How can I make you understand that damage to the brain can change a person, can even make a person like Spock violent, regardless of how well you think you know him? If you are his friends, don't make it any more difficult for him than it has to be. Just let him go."

Kirk stiffened. "What do you mean, let him go?"

"Spock is not responding to the medication. He's dangerous to himself, and to others. I'm going to recommend he be sent to Ebla Two."

McCoy was livid. "You'll never get me to sign the papers to send Spock to an asylum for the criminally insane!"

"You haven't seen him in over a month," Kirk pointed out, leaning over her. "Aren't you even interested in looking at him before you diagnose him as incurable and ship him off?"

"I've been in contact with his family," Emma said coldly. "As you may recall, I suspected Spock might become violent before McCoy sent him to Vulcan, and he went there under my protest.

"Gentlemen, if you go to him now, you will accomplish two things—you will shame Spock, and you will break your own hearts, seeing him in such a condition."

Kirk and McCoy looked at each other in silence for a moment, each one contemplating the possibility that Emma might be right.

"We're still going," Jim told her.

McCoy entered Emma's quarters without knocking, and got the briefest impression of a Vulcan face before she could snap the viewscreen off.

"Checking up on Spock, are you?" He asked it gently, almost teasingly; he had seen her bursts of temper before, but they usually blew over quickly. This was the first time she had ever remained angry about something, and he was not quite sure how to approach her. "How is he?"

She did not answer. She did not look up from the viewscreen.

McCoy shifted uneasily. "I just came to say that we're in orbit around Vulcan and we're beaming down. You're welcome to come with us if you change your mind."

She turned in the chair to face him, and he could see that her eyes were troubled, clouded, an expression far different from their usual clarity. "I won't change my mind."

"Look, Emma, I didn't mean to insult your medical judgment. It's just that we have to try to help Spock if we can. Please try to understand."

"I think I do." She looked blankly at the viewscreen in front of her, but it was clear to McCoy that she was thinking, thinking very hard about something. She continued to stare at the screen as she spoke thoughtfully.

"You three . . . you care about each other very much, don't you?"

"Which three?" McCoy was not following her.

"You, Spock, the captain. Spock is very important to both of you."

"I told you that the day I met you."

She smiled an odd, tight little smile. "Yes, you did, didn't you? I suppose that was before I cared about . . . anyone here. . . ."

McCoy walked over to the chair and put his hand on her shoulder. "Come with us," he said gently. "Spock might need you."

She rose from the chair, but the woman who stood before him seemed nothing like the Emma he knew. She was still smiling tightly, but her lower lip trembled almost imperceptibly. With a sudden urgent tenderness, McCoy realized that she was trying not to cry, and he took her in his arms.

She pulled away apologetically, speaking with an irony that he did not understand. "Of all people, Spock needs me least. Besides, I couldn't go with you if I wanted to."

"Why not?"

"I'm leaving, Leonard. I've been reassigned. When you get back, I won't be here."

This time, she let him hold her.

"I am required to search you for weapons." The Vulcan guard pointed his hand-held scanner at Kirk.

Kirk scowled. Vulcan Security had already verified his and McCoy's identities; he had not expected to be submitted to a body search.

"I will take your communicator," the guard said.

"Now wait a minute—" Kirk said hotly.

The guard waited a minute, staring down humorlessly at Kirk from his six-foot-five-inch height, every inch of it lean muscle mass.

"Never mind." Kirk handed him the communicator, but not without a twinge of exasperation. While he knew that the Vulcans could not risk Spock's sudden transportation from his hospital room to the *Enterprise*, he resented the implication that they did not trust a starship captain to refrain from doing so.

Although they were probably right not to.

McCoy submitted to the scan without so much as an insult, handing over his communicator before it was even asked for. Kirk could not help feeling disappointed; he had counted on the doctor's outspoken disregard for all things Vulcan to add a bit of humor to this otherwise unbearably somber occasion. But McCoy had not spoken since they beamed down; something was troubling him, something other than the prospect of seeing Spock.

The guard was apparently satisfied with the results of the scan, for he led them to the door of Spock's room. Beyond the shimmering force field, Spock lay pale and barely breathing. Tubes of dark green led from his arm to above the bed. Another Vulcan, apparently the attending physician, was watching Spock's vital signs on the monitor with keen interest.

"Your conversation will be monitored," the guard said. He moved a massive arm and the field evaporated just long enough for Kirk and McCoy to cross the threshhold.

The Vulcan doctor did not bother to turn around when they entered; she seemed to be timing something critical.

"How does he look to you, Bones?" Kirk whispered.

"Pretty good, except he's lost a lot of blood." McCoy cleared his throat and addressed the Vulcan. "Excuse me, ma'am . . ."

The Vulcan turned her head just enough to fix him with a cold look.

McCoy turned on the charm. "We're friends of Mr. Spock, ma'am, and we're very concerned. That security guard out there won't tell us a thing about how he got here. Can you tell us how it happened?"

She looked back at the monitor. "The patient's wrists were slit. He suffered critical blood loss. He will recover."

"Why was he arrested?" Kirk asked.

In spite of remaining totally expressionless, the Vulcan physician managed somehow to convey the fact that she found the presence of both men to be terribly annoying. "From the circumstantial evidence that was found, it appears that the patient first attacked his father with an *ahn-vahr* and then turned the weapon on himself."

"*Ahn*-what?"

"A ceremonial dagger. In ancient times, it was used in a ritual form of suicide when the victim believed he had brought shame to his family. Vulcan Security is waiting for the patient's father to regain consciousness to verify if this was what actually happened before the suspect is actually placed under arrest."

"Then Sarek is expected to recover?" Kirk asked.

She raised her left eyebrow in an expression that made Kirk very homesick for his first officer. "I believe that can easily be inferred from what I just said."

She bent down suddenly to look at Spock, then peered up again at the monitor. As if by magic, the indicator needles rose slightly. It was what she had been waiting for; she turned her back to the two humans, and hoisting a long, thin arm back, swung it forward with a force that would have knocked a human to the floor.

It hit Spock squarely on the jaw.

Kirk lunged at her with a short cry, but McCoy grabbed his arms and held him.

"Jim, you fool! That's the nicest thing I've seen anyone do in a long time."

Kirk looked at the doctor as though he had gone mad.

"Jim," said McCoy, grinning from ear to ear, "she's bringing him out of the Vulcan healing mode."

The physician drew her arm back to administer a second blow, but Spock's hand reached out and firmly grabbed her wrist. "That will be sufficient."

She nodded silently at Spock, and giving the humans a final glance that indicated what simpletons she considered them to be, she signaled the guard to let her exit.

Spock propped himself up to a sitting position.

"Spock!" McCoy could contain himself no longer. "You know the mind rules!"

A familiar eyebrow rose. "Obviously, Doctor McCoy."

The two humans looked at each other and laughed with delight. "You've got a hell of a nerve," said McCoy, "getting logical on me at a time like this. Admit it, you overgrown elf, you're glad to see us."

There was a brightness in Spock's eyes that belied his cool manner. "I believe that 'getting logical' was what you sent me here for, Doctor, although I do not deny that I am, as you put it, 'glad' to see you." His expression became more serious. "Captain, I have something rather urgent to tell you . . ."

"Yes, Uhura said you were signaling the ship when you were cut off."

"As you can see, I was . . . interrupted."

"What happened?"

"I went to the aid of my father, who was being attacked." He searched their faces. "Do you know his condition?"

"He'll be all right," McCoy volunteered.

Kirk nodded. "They're waiting for him to regain consciousness so he can tell them what happened."

Spock frowned slightly. *"I'm* conscious. *I* am able to supply the information."

Kirk and McCoy exchanged embarrassed glances. "I think they'd rather hear it from Sarek. You're being held on suspicion of attempted murder," Kirk said gently. "It looked like you attacked your father and then tried to kill yourself."

"T'Pala," Spock whispered. A shadow crossed his face, and disappeared as quickly as it had come.

"Who?" Kirk asked.

"No one. How convenient. I assure you that is not the case."

"I believe you, Spock," McCoy volunteered gallantly.

"I appreciate your vote of confidence, Dr. McCoy. I only wish Vulcan Security were as easily convinced."

"It's a lucky thing both of you survived the attack," Kirk said. "Whoever tried to kill you seemed to botch the job. Did you see who it was?"

"I did not know the individual, but I do not doubt that he was a Romulan. Vulcans do not, as a rule, engage in murder. And the fact that my father and I survived at all was due to something other than luck. We were rescued by a friend."

"Someone else was there? Where is he? He could clear you."

Spock studied a point in the far distance. "She was killed in the incident—vaporized. She and the attacker."

"Oh. I'm sorry."

Spock was silent for a short time before continuing. "The message I have for you, Captain, is one that I have wanted to remember for some time, but was unable to."

"Which is?"

"After I left you, Dr. McCoy and Mr. Scott with the Aritanian representative, I followed my tricorder signal out to the edge of the plateau, near the mountain. It seems, Captain, that the mountains are quite rich in uritanium—"

"We already know that, Spock."

"Of course. That, however, is not my message. As I was scanning the mountains, two surface fighters materialized almost directly in front of me. They were so close that I could clearly see the pilots inside, even in the darkness. They were Romulans."

"But where could they have beamed down from?" Kirk asked. "There weren't any ships in the area—if they had beamed down from a cloaked vessel, they would have had to let down their cloak to beam the fighters down, and we would have detected them."

"Captain," said Spock, "you are assuming that they beamed *down*. At the same time the ships materialized, my tricorder detected a slight power surge—merely a glimmer—from beneath the planet surface. Although the cloaking device currently in use by the Federation does not permit the simultaneous use of transporters, there have been reports that the Romulans are working on a design which currently affords a rather imperfect degree of protection during transporter use. If the *Enterprise* scanned the surface, it would probably interpret the mild power surge as a minor seismic disturbance."

"What are you getting at, Spock?" asked McCoy.

"I submit, Doctor, that the ships were not beaming down—rather, they were beaming *up*."

"That would explain it!" Kirk was exultant. "Spock, we erected the protective shield, but the pirates apparently penetrated it."

"There was no need for them to penetrate the shield. They were already beneath it, able to come and go as they pleased to the surface."

"So it wasn't an accident," McCoy said grimly. "They pushed you off the edge for what you saw."

"Not at all, Doctor. I jumped."

"You *what?*"

"It was a choice between rolling off the edge of the plateau or facing the pirates' burning phasers."

"You made the right decision." Kirk shuddered, remembering the smell of singed flesh.

McCoy changed the subject. "I must say, Spock, that your recovery is quite impressive. I'm going to recommend neodopazine to all my cortex-damaged Vulcan patients from now on."

"Doctor," Spock asked hesitantly, "just how familiar are you with the effects of neodopazine on Vulcans?"

McCoy shrugged. "Hardly at all. It's very new, so I've never used it myself. Dr. Saenz has, though, and she recommended it very highly."

"Is there a reader in this room?" Spock craned his neck.

"Over here. What do you want to know?"

"A . . . friend suggested I look at a recent article by Silak. I wonder if you could key it up for me."

"Sure." McCoy entered the name, got the cross index, and retrieved the article. "It's recent, all right, published less than two weeks ago . . ." His face registered surprise, and then he smiled. "Well, how about that—a study by Silak, Wreen . . . and Saenz."

"Emma?" Kirk asked.

"One and the same. She wasn't kidding about having worked with the drug. I thought she said it hadn't been tested on Vulcans, though . . ." McCoy furrowed his brow as he scanned the article.

"Read the conclusion," Spock suggested.

McCoy moved his finger down the reader to the conclusion of the article and stiffened.

"What is it, Bones?"

He read aloud, unable to believe what he saw on the terminal before him. "Our study indicates that the use of neodopazine on Vulcans is definitely contraindicated . . ." He skipped over a sentence, ". . . notable side effects include paranoia, loss of concentration, impairment of memory, mental confusion, irritability, and depression . . . The effects of neodopazine can be more devastating than the traumatic brain damage it is used to treat." His voice broke off as he looked at the captain.

"But why?" Kirk could not understand. "Why would she knowingly use it to treat Spock?"

Spock's tone was gentle but resolute. "Gentlemen, several attempts have been made to stop me from divulging the information I have just given you. To list a few: the so-called suicide attempt while I was on the *Enterprise,* the sabotage of the fuel indicator on the *Galileo,* Dr. Saenz's use of neodopazine to prolong my amnesia and to trigger psychological disturbances which conveniently provided an explanation for my last so-called suicide attempt and attempted murder of my father, who I should like to point out is one of the most outspoken proponents of protection for Aritani. It would have been a convenient way for the Romulans to be rid of both of us."

"He's not the only diplomat the Romulans have tried to kill," Kirk said darkly.

McCoy was still in shock, but anger began to creep into his voice. "Are you trying to tell me that Emma is the one who's been trying to kill you?"

"She is definitely a suspect, Doctor."

"You're wrong," McCoy lashed out. "You don't know Emma—she's not capable of murder. And she's a very loyal person who would never sell out to the Romulans."

Spock was unmoved by McCoy's vehement denial; he folded his arms calmly. "It's not always possible to predict people or circumstances. Perhaps there might be some situation in which Dr. Saenz would find it logical to join forces with the Romulans. However, I do not expect you to take my word alone. I suggest you consult Dr. Saenz on the matter."

"That's exactly what I intend to do," McCoy said hotly, "because I don't believe you."

"Doctor, you read the article yourself. Aren't you the least bit curious to hear her explanation?"

"Yes, but I'm sure it's not that she's a Romulan spy."

"She couldn't be," Kirk said slowly. "She works for Admiral Komack."

McCoy and Spock regarded him with disbelief.

"It's true," Kirk insisted. "I heard it from Komack himself."

Spock sighed. "Then I suggest, Captain, that you notify the Admiral of the possibility that he has a double agent working for him. In the meantime, I also suggest you try to locate Dr. Saenz before she has a chance to escape."

"You don't really think she'd try to—" Kirk began.

"Captain, if she is working for the Romulans, then she knows that my memory is close to returning and that I quit taking the neodopazine a week ago. I am sure she did everything in her power to discourage both of you from coming here, for she cannot risk my discovering the effects of the medication she prescribed and divulging that information to you."

"She said she was leaving," McCoy mumbled inaudibly.

"What?" Kirk asked.

"She said I wouldn't see her when I got back, because she was being reassigned." McCoy looked at the captain helplessly, his anger replaced by numbness. "But I still can't—"

"Captain," Spock interrupted, "in that case, haste

is essential. It may already be too late to find her."

"Let me go," McCoy said swiftly. "I could stop her."

Spock lifted a skeptical brow. "Doctor, if it is true that the lady is a Romulan spy, I doubt that even your powers of persuasion—"

"Go ahead," Kirk told him. "I'll call Security."

"If you call Security now," Spock pointed out, "she will certainly know that she is being pursued, assuming she is monitoring ship-to-surface communication."

Kirk's expression was somber. "Take a phaser with you, Bones. That's an order."

"Yes, yes, of course, Captain," McCoy lied. "And I'll give Scotty a good excuse for beaming up, in case she's listening."

"All I want you to do, Doctor, is to distract her for a few minutes, so I can notify Security without her being aware of it. After you beam up, I'll give you ten minutes to find her before I call them."

"Right, Captain." McCoy anxiously signaled the guard to let him out.

When he had gone, Spock looked at his captain with eyes Kirk tried to avoid. "Captain, I hope that you have not made a mistake in sending Dr. McCoy to find her."

"Don't you trust McCoy to turn her in?"

"I trust the good doctor, but I dare not presume what his relationship with Dr. Saenz is—"

"He loves her."

"I thought as much. Even so, I trust Dr. McCoy. Dr. Saenz, however, is another matter. She has killed, Captain, and I do not trust her even in this circumstance not to kill again."

Emma was waiting by the transporter console when McCoy stepped from the platform. *My God*, he thought, *it's true; she was listening when I asked to beam aboard.*

But she looked at him, puzzled, and frowned. "What are you doing here?"

McCoy sighed with silent relief. "I was hoping to catch you—before you left, that is. I need to talk to you . . ." He shot a glance at Lyle, who stood behind the transporter control, awkwardly pretending not to listen.

She shook her head. "This is a mistake, Leonard. There's nothing you can say that will convince me to stay. Please, I'll miss my shuttle—"

"Emma, *please.*"

The desperation in his words must have convinced her, for she turned to Lyle. "This won't take long."

McCoy led her down the hall to a nearby conference room and they went inside.

"All right, Leonard, what's this all about?"

"Emma, there's something I have to ask you . . . there's something I must know before you leave." He took her gently by the shoulders.

"We've been through this before, Leonard—"

"I'm not talking about marriage. This is something else entirely. Please, answer me honestly."

Her eyes narrowed. "Do you expect me to do otherwise?"

McCoy took a deep breath and searched her eyes; they were as clear and genuine as they had always been. Right now they regarded him with honest puzzlement. "In this case, maybe. But I want you to know that if you answer me truthfully, regardless of what the answer is, I won't try to stop you from leaving. That's a promise."

"Fair enough," she said. "What's the question?"

"The neodopazine. Emma, why?"

"I can't tell you that, Leonard. Ask me anything

else." She began to pull away, but he tightened his grip on her.

"I'm the chief medical officer on board this ship. You work for me, remember? I'm asking you a question. Why can't you tell me?"

"I don't answer to you in this instance. I don't have to explain my actions to you." She pulled harder to break free.

A sudden rage kindled within him, and he squeezed her arms so tightly that she cried out in surprise. "You were sent here to kill Spock, weren't you? And you had to get on good terms with the chief medical officer, so that you could manipulate him to do what you wanted with Spock. That's it, isn't it?" He shook her. *"Isn't it?"*

She pushed free with a gasp. When McCoy approached her again, he saw the small phaser directed at his chest.

Her eyes flashed with the heat of her own anger. "I don't have to tell you anything, Leonard. I'm not responsible to you or to anyone else on board this ship. Who I am or what I am is not important. I have a job to do, and no one, not even you, will interfere with it."

"You used me," McCoy whispered miserably.

"I don't have to tell you anything, but I will tell you this: I love whom I please, not whom I am ordered to. Understand?"

"No," said McCoy.

For a moment, he thought she looked at him with something very much like affection.

"Fool," she murmured. "I have risked myself for your friend because you loved him. Now everything may be lost. What more do you want from me?"

McCoy did not have a chance to answer; she aimed the phaser at him and fired.

Chapter Eleven

EMMA SAENZ SMILED sweetly at Ensign Lyle. "Sorry to keep you waiting, Mr. Lyle. A last minute medical problem . . ."

Somewhat abashed, Lyle returned the smile. He was not the sort to stick his nose into other people's business, making it a point to ignore any rumors circulated about senior officers, but it would have been impossible not to have heard the gossip about the heated affair between the chief medical officer and the new specialist.

He was convinced now that it was more than just gossip. "No problem at all, Doctor."

She stepped onto the transporter pad and positioned a small suitcase by her feet. "Ready to beam down, Mr. Lyle."

What followed next took place so quickly that Lyle was never quite sure what happened.

The door opened and Second Lieutenant Reems of Security stood in the doorway, phaser drawn. When he saw Dr. Saenz on the platform, he aimed his weapon at her and started to speak.

He did not have time to say anything. Emma, still calm and smiling, produced a phaser of her own and fired it at Reems. It surprised Lyle; he shouted at her and she turned smoothly toward him and fired again.

Emma ran over to the transporter console and pushed the slumped form of Lyle aside so that she could reach the automatic control. He slid to the floor with a heavy thud.

"Stop. That's as far as you're going."

Emma stopped and looked over her shoulder. Ingrit Tomson stood over Reems in the doorway, her phaser pointed at Emma's back. "Drop it."

Emma laid her phaser carefully on the console.

Tomson motioned toward the door. "Now move." Obediently, Emma approached Tomson, but as she came upon the body of Reems lying in the doorway, she stumbled.

Tomson moved in closer with the phaser, and Emma succeeded in knocking it across the room. Tomson watched it sail past with a look of dull surprise.

"Now let's see how far I get," Emma said.

They faced each other for battle; Tomson, tall and pale, towered over Emma's dark intensity. "I'm almost twice your size," Tomson sneered. "You couldn't hurt me if you wanted to."

Emma's voice was soft and low. "Want to make a bet?"

Kirk strode up and down the hospital corridor, swearing at his communicator and ignoring the disapproving stares of the Vulcans who passed.

"What the hell is going on up there, Mr. Scott?"

"Mr. Lyle was unconscious, Captain, but we've got someone in the transporter room now, and—"

"Unconscious? How long? Never mind, don't answer that. Have Uhura notify Vulcan Security Central *immediately* and tell them that Emma Saenz is probably on the planet surface."

"Aye, sir."

"Have you found McCoy?"

"Not yet, sir."

"Let me talk to Tomson."

Scott hesitated. "I'm afraid she's incapacitated, sir."

"What happened?"

"She and Reems and Lyle were all found unconscious in the transporter room. Stunned, it looks like. They should be coming to shortly."

"Then tell Tomson's second-in-command—"

"That would be Reems, sir."

Kirk gritted his teeth. "Dammit, find someone in Security who was *not* incapacitated by Dr. Saenz and tell them to cancel the search for Saenz. I want them to find McCoy."

"Anything else, Captain?"

"Yes. Get me the hell out of here."

Emma wouldn't hurt McCoy, Kirk kept repeating to himself as the hospital hallway shimmered into nothingness. She wouldn't hurt him, especially if she had been merciful enough to only stun Tomson and Lyle. Still, for a split second he imagined himself ordering Security to scan the internal atmosphere of the *Enterprise* for any free-floating molecules of what remained of his friend. . . .

Kirk stepped off the transporter platform to find Tomson, Reems and Lyle sitting on the floor being examined by a medic. He scowled down at them.

"I take it that you all encountered Emma Saenz. Are you going to tell me that the three of you couldn't stop her?"

Lyle rubbed his head and grimaced. "She stunned Reems and me before either of us knew that she had a phaser, Captain."

Of the three, Tomson seemed to be in the worst shape; she stared down at the floor disconsolately, unable to meet Kirk's gaze. "I disarmed her, sir, but she managed to knock my phaser away." Tomson tried to touch her left shoulder, but the pain made her stop and suck in air between her teeth. "In hand-to-hand combat, she's excellent. I think my shoulder's separated."

Kirk's expression became wry; at first Tomson thought the captain simply found it amusing that she could be done in by someone of Saenz's height; but then he said, "Believe me, I understand, Lieutenant. My shoulder and I have also had firsthand experience with Dr. Saenz's combat abilities."

Tomson leaned painfully against the bulkhead. "Thank you, sir."

Kirk straightened and went over to the intercom. "Kirk to Security."

"Security. Kazan here."

"Any word on McCoy?"

"No, sir. We're still looking."

Kirk hit the intercom in frustration, and went in search of McCoy himself. He had not gotten far down the corridor, however, when the door to one of the conference rooms opened and McCoy leaned out, staggering.

Kirk managed to catch him before he fell and supported him against the wall in a half-sitting position. "Bones, thank God . . . are you all right?"

McCoy moaned and cradled his head in his hands. "She's gone, Jim. God, what a first-class headache . . ."

"Did she stun you?"

"With more than just the phaser. Spock was right, Jim . . . dear God, he was right. Did you catch her?"

"Not yet. We think she's on Vulcan." Kirk paused. "I'm sorry, Bones."

"That makes two of us." McCoy closed his eyes and let his head roll back against the bulkhead. "But the damn thing is . . ." his voice faced.

"The . . . what?" Kirk leaned forward to hear.

"I can't say I'm sorry she hasn't been caught."

That makes two of us, Kirk wanted to say, but instead he put his arm under the doctor's shoulders and helped him to sick bay.

The room was a hybrid of the best of Vulcan and Earth, much like the solemn, slightly forlorn child who stared down at Kirk from the portrait above the piano. The Vulcan influence was clearly the stronger, reflected in the stark, powerful lines of the architecture, the furniture, and the artifacts that decorated the walls—the *ahn-vahr,* sabers, and weapons whose function Kirk dared not guess, the reminders of long-forsaken wars. While the Terran influence was subtler, it was unmistakable: the piano, the portrait of mother and son, and—most of all—the books, shelves upon shelves of old paper books that lined the far wall of the main room and extended into the hallway, and with them that distinct aroma that reminded Kirk of the last pleasurable time that he had been in the rare book section of a library.

Kirk was drawn to the shelves immediately, and knelt down to peer at the authors' names on the bindings. The collection was marvelously eclectic: Roth, Twain, Zelazny, Dickens, Dostoevsky, Wisen, McIntyre, Oates . . . and that was simply part of the small corner representing the nineteenth and twentieth centuries. His fingers hovered above the volumes until they found what they wanted, and withdrew it from the shelf.

Behind him, McCoy cleared his throat nervously.

Kirk looked up over his shoulder at him. The doctor was still pale, so pale that the chronic dark circles under his eyes stood out with greater than usual emphasis; McCoy was troubled by more than just the aftereffects of a phaser stun.

"Come take a look at this, Bones. This is without a doubt the most incredible collection of rare books you'll ever see outside of an archive."

"Uh, huh." McCoy's voice was flat and faraway, politely bored. "What's that you're looking at?"

"An old favorite of mine when I was a kid. Horatio Hornblower."

McCoy squinted. "Who?"

Kirk reshelved the book and stood up quickly as Sarek entered the room. "Tell you later."

Sarek seemed none the worse for the assassin's attack; in fact, he looked to be in far better shape than McCoy. Spock flanked him, dressed once again in his blue science officer's uniform. Shoulder to shoulder, the resemblance between father and son was unmistakable—Spock was a taller, leaner version of his father. But there was a slight difference in the face, some feature that Spock no doubt owed to Amanda's side of the family, although Kirk could not determine exactly what it was. . . .

Sarek gestured for them to sit. "Captain Kirk, I appreciate your promptness in responding to my invitation. However, I must admit that my motive includes more than simple hospitality."

Kirk sat on the couch next to McCoy; Spock sat across from them, in the chair next to Sarek. Kirk could not shake the feeling that he was sitting in on a

Vulcan Council meeting. "Would I be correct in assuming that this has something to do with Aritani, Ambassador?"

"You would. As you know, the delegates meet tomorrow for the vote. In spite of the Romulans' efforts, it appears that the vote will be in favor of sending a delegation."

"I'm glad to hear it," said Kirk. "However, I am concerned about the safety of the other diplomats after the attack on you. And perhaps Spock told you that two ambassadors were attacked on board the *Enterprise*. One was killed."

Sarek nodded. "Vulcan Security has been alerted. The ambassadors are under its protection."

"But they have as yet found no trace of Dr. Saenz," Spock added. "Apparently she managed to leave ShanaiKahr, and no doubt the planet, without detection."

"How can we be so sure that the Romulan government is involved?" McCoy asked suddenly. "All we've seen so far are pirates who happen to be Romulan."

Sarek looked coolly at him. "True. But pirates generally do not engage in concerted intrigue. Intelligence reports have indicated the involvement of the Praetor. Also, my attacker was definitely a Romulan."

"You're certain he was not a Vulcan?"

"Beside the obvious fact that Vulcans do not commit murder, the position of the stab wound he inflicted—one centimeter above my heart—indicates he was definitely a Romulan."

"The Romulan heart," Spock said, "sits two centimeters higher than the Vulcan."

"You don't need to give me an anatomy lesson," McCoy said huffily. "I remember."

Spock ignored him and quietly addressed the captain. "The family friend who was killed in the attack informed me shortly before her death that the Romulans had approached her and offered her 'a glorious career in the service of the Praetor,' as she put it, should she agree to kill Sarek and myself."

Kirk leaned forward. "What did she tell them?"

Spock's eyes became hooded. "She refused, of course. She was a Vulcan."

"To use one of your expressions, Captain," Sarek said, "the arm of the Romulans is very long. The young woman in question was studying to enter the Vulcan diplomatic service. The Romulans obviously wanted an informant within the VDC. They are quite skilled at espionage, and I fear their influence reaches as far as the Federation Council.

"But back to the matter at hand. The delegation sent to Aritani would consist of the Terran ambassador and myself. However, no matter how skilled either of us are at diplomacy, asking the Aritanians to consider joining the Federation under the present circumstances would be absurd, since there would be absolutely no benefit to them from so doing. The Federation must first prove to the Aritanians that it is capable of stopping the Romulans. Before we can do that, of course, we will need transportation to Aritani—"

"The *Enterprise,* naturally," Kirk said.

"Naturally, Captain. Star Fleet has already agreed that your vessel is the logical choice, but that is not the only thing I wish to discuss with you. We need more than transportation to Aritani—we need a plan for stopping the Romulans. Spock and I have such a plan."

Kirk suddenly felt uncomfortable. "Do you think it's wise to discuss that here? If the Romulans were able to enter your home and attack you, then certainly—"

"You hardly need worry about the possibility of our conversation being monitored here, Captain."

Spock explained. "Because of the sensitive nature of information discussed in the home of an ambassador, this house is equipped with a transmission scrambling device. Only authorized transmissions are not scrambled. Even if the Romulans had succeeded in planting a transmitter here, they would not understand the messages they received."

"All right, then. My ship is at your disposal. Now tell me your plan."

Sarek did not smile, but his eyes brightened. "It requires your assistance, Captain, and yours, too, Doctor, if you are willing. . . ."

"Scotty, how's the cloaking device working?"

"Like a charm, sir, but it's drainin' the bejesus out o' my poor engines. God help us all if we have to make it out of here at warp speed anytime soon."

"Just keep the cloaking device working, Scotty, and I personally promise you we won't need the warp drive *or* divine intervention. Kirk out."

Kirk looked up to see Aritani on the bridge viewscreen, a swirling globe of blue and purple, dotted with occasional wisps of white. He stared for a moment, mesmerized.

Sulu broke the spell. "Standard orbit, Captain?"

"Very good, Lieutenant." Kirk glanced over at his first officer.

Spock was watching it, too.

"Beautiful, isn't it, Spock?"

The Vulcan's eyes met Kirk's; he nodded softly, then bent over his scanner. "Significant pirate activity on the surface below, Captain." He straightened and faced Kirk. "They are no longer bothering to cloak their vessels."

"Since the *Fidelity* has left, they think nobody's watching." Kirk snapped a toggle on the arm of his chair as the intercom whistled.

McCoy's voice was filled with a sense of urgency. "Captain, I've got an emergency down here. I need you in sick bay immediately."

Uhura and Sulu could not help turning to look at the captain. Why in the galaxy should the doctor be calling the captain about a medical emergency?

It seemed to make perfect sense to Kirk. "I'll be right there, Doctor." He jerked his head at Spock, who moved smoothly to take his captain's place in the command chair.

As the doors to the turbolift opened, Kirk narrowly missed colliding with Varth, who stepped off the turbolift as the captain stepped on. Sulu was watching as Kirk smiled and winked at the Radun; he turned back to the navigation console and pinched himself to be sure he wasn't dreaming.

It was not time for a shift change, and Sulu knew for a fact that Kirk had not summoned Varth to the bridge, but the Radun went directly to Spock's station as though drawn there by some sort of telepathic instinct. Sulu was dying to ask him how he knew he was needed on the bridge, but dared not as long as Spock was there.

Sulu was therefore not that surprised when McCoy called Spock less than an hour later.

"Dare I presume, Doctor McCoy," Spock asked him, "that this is in regards to another medical emergency?"

"Spock, get your Vulcan posterior down here *now*."

Spock raised his eyebrows mildly and terminated the communication. "Mr. Varth," he said, "you are in command."

Sulu waited until the Vulcan left the bridge and Varth had settled down in the captain's chair.

He turned halfway toward Varth. "All right. What's going on?"

Varth regarded him coldly. "Is there a problem, Lieutenant Sulu?"

"You know what I mean, sir." He hadn't talked to Varth since the Radun's brief but unexplained stay in the brig. "Something's up—between you and the captain and Mr. Spock." He decided not to ask why Varth and the captain were suddenly buddy-buddy—not here, on the bridge, since Varth was, after all, a senior officer; but Sulu was far too curious not to mention the recent events on the bridge. "It's very unusual for Dr. McCoy to call the captain and Mr. Spock to sick bay like that."

"Yes, it is," Varth agreed. "Anything else, Mister?"

"No, sir." Sulu sighed and turned back to his panel, resigned. Varth was letting him know that he had overstepped his bounds; maybe they would explain it to him when it was all over.

He could not see Varth grinning behind him.

Spock hovered outside the door to sick bay. "How is he, Doctor?"

McCoy gestured him inside. "Why don't you come judge for yourself, Mr. Spock? Your opinion just might be useful for once."

Kirk sat on the bed, studying his reflection in a hand mirror. When Spock came in, he swung his legs over the side and attempted to stand up.

"Not so fast," said McCoy, pushing him back into a sitting position. "Give the anesthesia a few more seconds to wear off." He stepped back and viewed his handiwork with almost paternal pride. "Well, Spock, what do you think?"

Spock leaned closer to Kirk and, putting his hand to his chin, grunted and slowly circled the bed as he studied the new alterations to his captain. He stopped and remained silent until McCoy could stand it no longer.

"Well?"

"Adequate," Spock replied.

"Adequate?" McCoy was highly insulted. "That's not adequate, that's a masterpiece."

Kirk smiled, then winced suddenly and gingerly touched his fingers to the new tips on his ears. "Hey, Bones, they pull when I smile. Shouldn't you fix that?"

"Where you're going," McCoy said tartly, "you won't *need* to smile."

Kirk looked up at Spock and almost smiled again, but caught himself in time. "Is *that* why you Vulcans avoid smiling, Spock? Because it pulls your ears?"

Spock was not the least bit intrigued by the thought. "I really wouldn't know, Captain."

McCoy was still smarting from Spock's remark. "Spock, how can you call this adequate? Last time I did this, it was good enough to fool the Romulans, and I think I did an even better job this time."

"I did not say that your work would not fool the Romulans, Doctor, I merely stated that it was adequate for its purpose. That is what you wanted to know, isn't it?"

"Yes, but—"

"However, as far as aesthetics are concerned, I must admit that there is something rather . . . that is to say, the captain does not seem well suited . . ."

"I make a lousy Vulcanoid." Kirk pushed the fretting McCoy aside and finally stood up. "Is that what you're saying, Spock?"

"A colorful term, but rather accurate. Perhaps it's your coloring . . ." Spock suggested.

McCoy sniffed. "That can be fixed with a little makeup. But I think those ears are some of my finest work."

"I must agree," Spock said. "They are, therefore, adequate . . ."

"Why, what's *that* supposed to mean—" McCoy began hotly.

"It doesn't matter." Kirk waved his hand to signal an end to the discussion. "All that matters is, they fooled the Romulans once, and they'll certainly fool them again."

Scott and McCoy were waiting when Kirk arrived in the transporter room, and neither one looked particularly pleased. McCoy stood scowling with his arms folded resolutely; Kirk knew the lecture would be forthcoming shortly.

"Where's Spock?" he asked, hoping to forestall McCoy.

"Probably trying to find a costume that coordinates with yours," the doctor replied. "I must say, you look rather dashing."

"What, this old thing?" Kirk spread his arms and looked down at his costume; the computer had designed it along the same lines as the one the Romulan prisoner had worn. "I thought the color of the vest was a little loud."

"It's perfect," McCoy answered. "Brings out the green in your complexion."

Kirk grimaced wryly and turned to Scott. "Scotty, Varth will be calling any minute with those coordinates."

"Aye, sir," Scott sighed, shaking his head.

"All right, Scotty, out with it."

"Well . . . Captain, I wish I felt a little better about this. I can't help rememberin' what happened to that last poor divvil we beamed up from his ship—"

"Amen," McCoy nodded. "I had to do the autopsy, Jim."

Kirk assumed his best authoritarian air. "Gentlemen, there is nothing more to discuss. That pirate moved his ship on purpose from its projected course. It won't happen this time."

"You mean, you *hope* it won't happen this time," McCoy muttered.

Scott did not seem at all reassured. "It's a very delicate operation, puttin' two men into fast-moving surface vessels."

Kirk put a confident hand on the engineer's shoulder. "And I trust you to do it, Mr. Scott. You're the best. Subject closed."

The door opened and Spock entered, dressed in pirate clothes.

"Spock, you certainly look convincing."

"Thank you, Doctor McCoy."

"But I don't understand why you wouldn't let me pierce one ear. Then you'd *really* look authentic."

Spock was not amused. "It is enough that the captain was forced to submit to your scalpel, Doctor."

"Which reminds me, what did Sarek think about the captain's new ears?"

"He said nothing to me about them."

"Nothing?" McCoy was obviously deflated.

Spock kept his expression bland. "My father is a diplomat, Doctor. He avoids comment if he fears it will offend others."

McCoy was about to respond acidly to Spock's remark when a beep emanated from the transporter console. "Ye'd best get on the pads, gentlemen,"

Scott said. "This is goin' to take a fine bit of timin'."

Kirk felt a sudden rush of exhilaration. "Ready, Spock?"

"Ready, Captain."

"For God's sake," McCoy said, "be careful down there."

The last thing Kirk saw as he was caught in the transporter beam was the look of worry on McCoy's face.

The ship felt as light as a feather, with controls as sensitive as a highstrung thoroughbred. Varth had been right—these were not the antique jerry-rigged fighters used by pirate bands, but the newest, sleekest surface fighters outfitted with every device possible, compliments no doubt of the Romulan Empire. The ship seated one, and it hugged Kirk's body so that he could move his arms freely, but not stretch his legs. He studied the control panel and found the radio next to the control for firing the burning phaser.

"Remus, do you read?"

"Affirmative, Romulus. We are not far from the beamdown site. If you would follow me, please."

They flew together in close formation, Spock's vessel leading. Kirk looked out and could see that the land below was scarred and blackened where the pirates had discharged their phasers, and that the dark brown soil was turned up in the areas where mining had begun on the surface. The sight was sickening, even more so because he could recognize the area from the configuration of the plateaus—it was the place where Natahia's fields and hut had once stood, but its beauty had been completely stripped away.

Then he saw it.

A plateau edged by a jagged mountain, and the next plateau down a clean four-hundred-foot drop, softened by tangling red and blue vines—the place where they had found Spock.

Kirk looked gratefully at the reassuring presence in the other vessel.

Spock hovered near the edge of the plateau for an instant, then smoothly set his vessel down. Kirk brought his alongside. He knew that Spock would now contact the pirates in flawless Romulan with the beam-down code supplied by Varth. Within seconds, the interior of the fighter began to blink and glimmer until it disappeared, taking Kirk along with it.

Kirk opened his eyes to absolute darkness, and for an instant felt panic—they had beamed down into solid rock; in less than a second their molecules would be crushed out of existence by the tons of sheer pressure exerted on their bodies. . . .

But death did not come. Kirk's lungs filled easily with recirculated air, thin but breathable, and his eyes adjusted slowly to the blackness. "Remus?"

"Here." Spock swung gracefully from the belly of the fighter as though he had been doing it all his life. When his feet touched the floor, the cavern filled with harsh pinkish light. Kirk fumbled with the tophatch and crawled out stiffly.

The hangar had been carved from rock, and held at least another hundred of the gleaming silver fighters. Kirk and Spock walked past them, their steps echoing against the cold stone floor.

A small exit in the far corner of the hangar led them to an equally small passageway. Had Kirk ever entertained doubts that the Praetor was involved, they were now completely erased, for the guard who sat staring at a monitor wore the uniform of a Romulan centurion. He looked up just long enough to frown at Kirk and Spock before turning back to the screen.

They continued down the narrow stone corridor.

"That was too easy." Kirk's hand unconsciously groped for the communicator hidden under his long tunic.

"Easier than anticipated," Spock agreed. "Perhaps the beamdown code is the only security measure required to achieve this level of access. Or perhaps the Federation has friends here."

"Or maybe someone ought to put that centurion on report."

"Spoken like a true disciplinarian, sir."

Kirk glanced at Spock sharply, but there was no time to answer. They had come to the end of the passage; in front of them, a massive stone wall shuddered and rose.

The surfaces of the vast interior were not stone, but slick white metal, and the wide corridors broken by hundreds of entranceways seemed to stretch into infinity. Dozens of Romulans—some in military uniforms, others dressed as pirates—strode through the corridors, far too involved in the performance of their duties to be concerned about the two pirates who hung back by the entrance, watching.

"Remind you of someplace you've been before?" Kirk whispered with awe.

"Indeed . . . the interior of a Romulan battleship. If Varth is correct, those should be the officers' quarters. I believe we should proceed in . . . that direction." Spock inclined his head.

"Lead the way, Remus. You're the one who memorized the map."

Kirk was becoming more exhilarated by the success of their masquerade as each moment that they remained unnoticed passed. They had taken the turbolift down two levels and were proceeding along the corridor that Spock assured him would take them to the cloaking device—and Kirk was just beginning to feel secure—when Spock suddenly stopped.

The corridor in front of them forked in two directions.

"What is it, Spock?"

"Sir, the plan of the base that I studied did not include . . . that." Spock pointed to the corridor that branched off to the left. It was blocked by a rather large centurion and a force field. "The plan showed only one path to the cloaking device, the hallway which is now unguarded."

"Which way do you think we should go."

Spock looked at him directly. "Which one would you put a cloaking device behind, sir?"

Kirk sighed. "I was afraid you'd say that."

They directed their steps toward the force field. "As we approach the centurion, Captain," Spock said in a low voice, "I would appreciate it if you would—"

"—shut up?"

Spock nodded.

"*No lo contendere*, Remus. My Romulan is a little rusty."

Square of jaw and build, the centurion regarded them with small, untrusting eyes. Clearly, this one would not be as careless as his comrade. Spock gave the Romulan salute as he approached, bringing one fist to his chest, and then extending the arm.

He spoke rapidly to the centurion in what Kirk perceived to be an extremely convincing imitation of Romulan military style. "Centurion, let us pass."

The Romulan shook his head and produced a hand-held scanner. "You know the rules. Scan first."

"Of course," Spock agreed, and stood still as the centurion scanned him. The device beeped.

"How stupid of me," Spock said. "My communications device, of course." He handed it to the Romulan, who did a double take.

"Where'd you get this?"

"One of the corpses on the planet surface. A souvenir. Here, let me show you." He bent over to assist the centurion, who was trying unsuccessfully to open a hailing frequency. "The frequency band is here." Spock reached over the Romulan's shoulder to point.

He finished by easing the Romulan to the floor with a strategically placed hand on his trapezius.

"That was great, Spock," Kirk said approvingly. "But how did you explain the communicator?"

"It's hardly important, Captain . . ."

"Well, whatever you told him, he bought it. I never knew you were such a skillful liar, Mr. Spock. Good work."

Spock dragged the centurion to one side and propped him gently against the bulkhead while Kirk found the control to deactivate the force field. "This is hardly the time for either insults or compliments, Captain. I suggest we continue our search as quickly as possible."

"I couldn't agree with you more."

Spock read the inscription on the bulkhead above the force field. "This is designated as a weapons area."

"But Varth said that the Romulans hadn't completed the base—that they didn't have attack capacity yet."

Spock's tone was grim. "Apparently Varth's information is somewhat outdated. If it is true that the Romulans have completed construction of their weapons—"

Kirk finished for him. "Then we'll have to find a way to stop them down here. The *Enterprise* can't obliterate the planet surface with photon torpedoes in an attempt to destroy an underground base."

"Agreed, sir. Therefore, it is logical that I remain behind and—"

Kirk held up his hand. "We'll discuss it when it happens, Spock. In any case you won't be staying behind."

"Sir—"

"End of discussion, Mister." Kirk looked down the seemingly endless row of doors. "I'll take the ones on the left, you take the ones on the right, and whoever locates the cloaking device or the main weapons room, contacts the other."

"Yes, sir."

Kirk could not find the cloaking device, but he located the weapons room on the third try. Clearly, Varth was right: the Romulans wanted far more than Aritani. One wall was lined with defense computers; the console was manned for what Kirk assumed were photon torpedoes and phasers capable of blowing a starship from its orbit.

He was reaching for his communicator when the door slid open. He dropped his hand quickly.

Kirk recognized the uniform of a Romulan subcommander and saluted quickly, but the small female did not return the courtesy. Next to her stood a discouraging-looking centurion who held a phaser that was not quite pointed at Kirk; but it was neither the phaser nor the subcommander's failure to salute that made Kirk distinctly uncomfortable.

"Subcommander Tanirius," she said, with a voice as cold as her opaque black eyes.

The upswept eyebrows and delicately pointed ears added an exotic beauty to features Kirk had once thought of as almost plain. They suited her, as nature had intended, but the cloaked eyes and cold manner hid what had been most beautiful about her—her openness, her warmth.

Emma, Kirk mouthed, but he did not say it aloud.

She appeared not to notice. "A centurion was injured outside the high security area. I would like to see your clearance."

"I don't have it with me."

She motioned to the centurion, who directed the phaser at Kirk's head. "Then you will come with me for questioning."

"It doesn't look as though I have a choice."

She did not smile. "You don't."

Chapter Twelve

TANIRIUS ENTERED THE detention cell alone, holding a phaser tightly at chest level. When the door closed behind her, she lowered her arm and hung the phaser on her belt. She looked up at Kirk again, and face, voice, and posture underwent a subtle transformation from cool to warm, from Romulan to human.

She gestured at Kirk's ears.

"Dr. McCoy's work?"

Kirk did not try to disguise the hatred in his voice. "And yours, Subcommander?"

He half expected her to tell him to call her Emma, but she did not. Her eyes smiled with controlled amusement. "These are mine. Tell Leonard he did a good job."

"I don't see how I can do that, Subcommander." The muscle in Kirk's jaw twitched. "It's my understanding that I will shortly be executed for espionage. That is what you Romulans do to spies, isn't it?"

She answered by holding something out to him—his communicator, but he stood back from her, stiff with anger, and would not touch it. "Things are not always as they appear, Captain. I told you that I was on your side."

"You'd like me to open up a channel to the *Enterprise* here, wouldn't you?" He smiled bitterly. "So you could trace the transmission and destroy her with your new weapons. I was gullible to fall for your charms the first time, but you can't expect me to do it again."

She moved toward him, her face taut and desperate, Emma and not-Emma. "They are not monitoring us now. I will try to explain, but there is not much time. I ask only that you listen."

Kirk leaned against the bare wall and folded his arms. "Go ahead. The longer you talk, the longer I live. But don't expect me to believe anything you say."

"Very well." She lifted her head proudly. "I am a Romulan, Captain Kirk, but I do not serve the Praetor."

"A pirate, then—"

"Let me speak!" Her urgency forced him to silence; he closed his mouth and listened. "Not a pirate. I will not tell you by what name we call ourselves, lest the secret somehow reach the Praetor's ears. We are a group more than two hundred years old, who despise the atrocities of both the pirates and our Praetor. Our hope is to throw off the yoke of our military government and coexist peacefully with the Federation. Like our Vulcan brothers, we are weary of constant warring and its toll upon our population. We seek peace.

"Many of us have risen to high positions within the military. We profess allegiance to the Praetor, but serve our group as best we can within our position. I was chosen as a young girl to serve in Intelligence. They sent me away to Earth, to receive medical training and to infiltrate Star Fleet Intelligence. Their plan worked so well that, as you saw, I was trusted by and took my orders directly from Admiral Komack. And the Praetor, of course.

"But my true aim was to serve my brothers and sisters in the underground . . . by destroying this military outpost. The government has been working on this project for years, Captain, and now it has the capability to dissolve the *Enterprise* and any other Federation vessel to atoms and spread the Praetor's tyranny to every populated planet in this sector. That has always been its purpose."

"You speak of peace," Kirk said hotly, "but you tried to kill Spock—not once, but several times, just as you killed the Cygnusian and the pirate, and tried to kill the Saurian ambassador. What kind of people talk of peace while using murder to achieve their goals?"

He stopped at the sight of the pain on her face.

"An unhappy people, Captain," Tanirius answered. "Do you think I welcome the Praetor's assignments? But if I do not carry any of them out, I endanger my position and the help I can give my people. I am forced to do what I despise."

"You gave Spock the neodopazine—you lied to McCoy, convinced him it would help—"

"It did. It bought Spock time. The Empire wanted him killed immediately. I was here, at the base, when they sent me to the *Enterprise*. I wanted to remain, to find a way to stop construction of the base, but I had the medical credentials, the appropriate cover. When I realized what Spock meant to Leonard . . . and to you . . ." she lowered her eyes, "I did what I could. The medication was the only way to appease the Empire. If Spock were incapacitated, could not remember what he had seen, then that was as good as death." She looked up again. "Do you think I enjoyed what I had to do?"

"Enlisting the forces of evil," Kirk said slowly, remembering, ". . . in order to do good." He shook his head. "If it *is* true, then why didn't you stay on the *Enterprise* . . . explain who and what you are—"

"No. No one could know. The Romulans had to believe I came back because I had been uncovered, not because I feared they had completed their base and would soon make their move. If they had thought otherwise—"

"Then it was you." Kirk understood suddenly. "You were the one who gave Varth the beamdown code—"

"And the description of the fighter controls and the layout of the base. I left the scrambling device in his cabin so that I could tell the Romulans I framed a Star Fleet Intelligence officer. Once the vote on Vulcan had been taken, Varth would have told you of the military base, but Spock recovered his memory sooner than we anticipated—"

"But Varth didn't tell us you would be here."

"The arm of the Romulans is very long," she said, and Kirk started. She smiled, but her expression darkened as she continued. "If you had known, and been caught and questioned—if there had been any hint of complicity with Star Fleet on my part, I would have been killed immediately. We couldn't risk it."

"What of McCoy?" Kirk asked softly. "Were you merely following orders with him?"

She winced visibly and turned away. "Would you believe me, Captain, if I said I was not? And that I was not following orders when I tried to seduce you, as well?"

Kirk remained silent.

Tanirius reached for her phaser and motioned with it toward the door. "Enough. Whether you believe me or not doesn't matter. I'm still going to help you."

"Where are you taking me?"

"To the cloaking device."

"It doesn't look like I have a choice."

Tanirius grinned, and looked so much like Emma that Kirk drew in his breath. "You don't."

Spock stood next to the cloaking device and was preparing to signal the *Enterprise* when the door opened; he froze at the sight of the phaser Tanirius held at the captain's back. Kirk could not see Tanirius's face, but the look on the Vulcan's was one of cold recognition.

Tanirius put the phaser on the console and moved to Kirk's side. Spock still did not move.

"She tells an interesting story, Mr. Spock. She keeps insisting she's on our side."

Spock was unconvinced. "Captain, I respectfully submit that the subcommander not be trusted, considering her actions . . ."

"Gentlemen," Tanirius said, "the time for explanations has passed. I would like to warn Mr. Spock that the instant he removes the cloaking device from the console, an alarm will sound."

"I see. And what do you propose we do?" Spock asked with as much sarcasm as Kirk had ever heard him muster.

Kirk made a sudden move to grab Tanirius; surprised, she moved instinctively to defend herself. The phaser was already in Spock's hand when she turned toward him.

"Then shoot me, Spock," she said quietly. "But then one of you will have to stay behind to see the base destroyed. Which one of you knows how to do it?"

Spock was silent.

"Your cloaking device is inferior to ours," Tanirius said. "You'll have to lower it in order to beam up. And when you do, the sensors on this base will locate your ship and lock in the automatic phasers. Blanket beams, wide range—and they won't stop firing until they're manually overridden or the sensors pick up debris."

She handed Kirk his communicator. "Go."

He caught her arm. "You could come with us—"

She shook her head. "Someone has to stay and stop the phasers before the *Enterprise* is destroyed—and it's time I completed my mission and destroyed this base."

Kirk fought to keep the concern from showing in his voice. "With you on it?"

She almost smiled. "That is most certainly not my intention." She went to the door and paused. "One thing—"

Kirk looked at her.

She bit her lip. "Tell Leonard I love him."

And she was gone.

"Captain," Spock said as Kirk flipped open his communicator, "I am not at all sure it's wise to trust her."

Kirk looked pointedly at the cloaking device and back at his first officer. "Would you prefer I go back to the detention cell, Mr. Spock?"

They materialized on the transporter platform just in time for the first blast, which swept them off the platform and against the console. Tanirius had been telling the truth about the phasers, at least.

Kirk dragged himself to the nearest intercom and called Engineering. "Scotty, get the deflector shields up!"

"I'll do what I can, Captain, but they won't hold long," Scott lamented. "That bleedin' cloakin' device has just about taken all our power. There's barely anythin' left for the shields."

"Any chance you could get us out of here?"

"A wee bit of impulse power is all we've got left, sir, but nothin' fast enough to pull us out of range of those phasers before the shields buckle."

"Sorry, Scotty. I guess I was wrong when I said we wouldn't be needing the warp drive—or divine intervention. Just get those deflectors up. Kirk out."

The fact that Kirk and Spock appeared on the bridge in full pirate regalia, including Kirk's new ears, failed to produce even mildly curious stares from the bridge crew; under conditions other than red alert, there might have been more time for double takes. McCoy moved to the side of Kirk's chair.

"I take it the ears fooled 'em."

Kirk knew there was no time for polite exchanges. "Bones, I saw her."

"Wha—"

"Emma. She helped us escape. She might be on our side—Mr. Varth!"

Varth had already vacated the con to assist Spock in scanning the newly revealed Romulan base. "Sir," the Radun said excitedly, "beside the network of mining tunnels beneath the main continent, the military base itself houses more than five hundred personnel."

"There isn't time, Varth. I have to know about her—"

Varth straightened from the scanner abruptly. "Tanirius."

"Then what she said was true?"

"I'm fairly sure we can trust her to help us, sir."

"*Fairly* sure?"

"Nothing's sure, Captain, until those phaser blasts stop."

As if on cue, there was the rumbling thunder of an explosion as the bridge pitched forward and crewmen went flying. Kirk slid from the con and bounced off the back of Sulu's chair; the helmsman's forehead struck the navigation console with a resounding thud.

The room slowly righted itself to the background chatter of damage reports coming from Uhura's station. Scott's voice came from the arm of Kirk's chair; it had taken on the darkness of a Gaelic prophet of doom.

"That's it for the shields, Captain. We nae kinna stand another direct hit."

Kirk knew the answer to his question before he asked it. "Can you get us out of here, Scotty?"

"All we've got is impulse power, sir. We can't outrun those phasers."

"In other words," Kirk said grimly, "we're sitting ducks."

Spock looked up from his scanner. "I fail to see how our situation is comparable to that of an aquatic waterfowl—"

"Oh, shut up," said McCoy.

Spock raised a surprised eyebrow and returned to his scanner.

Kirk paid them no attention. "Divert all power to the deflectors, Mr. Scott."

"The cloakin' device too, sir?"

"And all the impulse power you've got."

"*Sir.*" Scott was deeply offended by the thought of his engines motionless, powerless.

"Do it, Scotty. *Now.*"

"The blasts are occurring at approximately one

minute intervals," Spock offered helpfully. "I estimate the next one will arrive in twenty seconds."

"She'll stop it, Jim," McCoy said. "I know she'll do everything she can to stop it."

"Let's hope you're right, Bones."

"Fifteen seconds," said Spock.

"She's really a Romulan," Kirk said.

"I'll be damned," McCoy whispered. "That explains something . . . the levirol."

"The what?"

"Eleven seconds," Spock chanted.

"Levirol. It's a drug that elevates blood pressure and slows the pulse. Emma was taking it . . . no wonder our sensors never showed an extra Romulan on board ship."

"She wanted me to give you a message." Kirk lowered his voice so that only McCoy could hear. "She says she loves you."

"Six seconds."

"Dammit, Spock," McCoy yelled, "if we must all be blown to kingdom come in the next few seconds, I do not want your countdown to be the last thing I hear."

Spock regarded the doctor with mild surprise.

"He's right, Spock," Kirk said quietly; but internally, he continued the countdown. Four seconds . . .

Scott came back on the intercom. "I'm sorry, Captain . . . I can't raise enough power to get the deflectors back up."

There was no point in bracing for the explosion. They would be vaporized by a direct hit, or in the case of an indirect hit, struck by flying debris as the bridge shattered, or asphyxiated when the inner hull tore. But Kirk braced for the shock in spite of himself, and prayed that Tanirius had made it to the weapons room before she changed her mind . . .

Spock rose so suddenly from his scanner that Kirk almost jumped out of his chair. "Explosion, Captain, beneath the planet surface. I believe in the area of . . ." he squinted back at the viewer, ". . . the weapons room. The Romulans have lost attack capability."

McCoy grabbed the captain's wrist, his face splitting with a grin. "She did it, Jim! She did it!"

Kirk released his breath slowly and smiled weakly up at McCoy as he reached toward the intercom. "Scotty."

"Aye, Captain?"

"Forget those deflector shields. Just give us enough impulse power to nudge her back into orbit."

"With pleasure, sir."

"Standard orbit, Mr. Sulu. Uhura, open a hailing frequency to the Romulans. I want to speak to whoever's in charge."

"Captain," Spock interrupted, "six fighter vessels beaming up from the hangar area to the surface—"

"Let them go for now."

"Captain," said Uhura, "I have the Romulan subcommander."

Kirk caught his breath silently. "Put her on the screen, Lieutenant."

The Romulan male was young for his rank, the equivalent of a starship captain. Tears streamed down his soot-smudged face, more from the sting of the thick smoke than from grief or pain. From behind him came the death-cries of his fellows; he glared at Kirk with undisguised hatred.

"Captain," Spock said.

"Not now, Spock."

Spock persisted. "An explosion, sir, in the hangar area. The vessels that remained have been destroyed."

Kirk studied the face on the screen for a moment

before speaking. "This is Captain James T. Kirk of the *Enterprise*. Are you the commander of the base?"

"Subcommander Tardus. My superiors are dead. I now command."

"Subcommander, we know that you have lost your cloaking device, your weapons and your vessels. I suggest you cooperate with us."

The young Romulan regarded him haughtily. "In what manner, Captain?"

"We will assist your surviving personnel to evacuate."

"To become your prisoners," Tardus said with utter disgust.

"To be processed and then released to your government."

Tardus struggled unsuccessfully to suppress a cough. "To be used as prisoners to bargain with the Empire. This is totally unacceptable to us, Captain. Surely you know that we will never surrender ourselves." A painful spasm of coughing overtook him; afterwards, he glared at Kirk through dull eyes. "This is the work of Federation spies, but we shall take them with us. You shall learn no more about our installation, Captain Kirk."

"We already know everything about your installation," Kirk said quickly. "No purpose would be served by your death—"

"Captain," Uhura's voice was gentle, "he's no longer transmitting."

The flash that lit up the bridge was blinding, forcing those present to shield their eyes until the screen faded to blackness. Slowly, the familiar sight of Aritani reappeared.

"The entire operation has been destroyed," Spock reported from his viewer, "with the exception of a few mining tunnels. Shock waves on the surface reaching six-point-three on the Richter scale." He looked steadily at Kirk. "No survivors beneath the surface, Captain."

Kirk's gaze was fierce and directed straight ahead at the quietly rotating planet. He could not meet McCoy's eyes; he knew the horror in them matched his own.

The grass no longer grew as high as Kirk's hip; in most places the soil had been bared by the pirates' phasers, leaving black, evil-smelling scars. The neat rows of golden vines had disappeared entirely from the landscape, burned from existence, but the grass persisted. Already it crept back in timid blue-green clumps to cover the blackened earth.

Kirk called out.

There was a rustling sound near the side of the mountain, and the sound of small footsteps. Natahia appeared from behind the charred stump of what was once a great tree. Around her stood three male growers who carried handmade spears.

"The pirates are gone," Kirk called. "The earthquake resulted from the destruction of their ships and weapons."

They stopped several feet from Kirk. Natahia's beautiful blue robe was torn and heavy with mud; her streaming hair was wild and unkempt. But her manner was as regal as it had always been.

She eyed Kirk distrustfully. "Six of my people died in that earthquake."

"I'm sorry," Kirk said gently. "But there will be no more earthquakes, and no more attacks on your people. Our enemies were using your planet as a military base. Their weapons were hidden beneath the ground. They wanted control of Aritani because of its minerals and so that they could control other nearby planets from it as well. When we discovered their base, they killed themselves and destroyed the base rather than be taken prisoner."

Natahia closed her eyes. "So we stand at last on the bones of our enemies. And what does the Federation want with us now?"

"We only want to offer our assistance to help you rebuild what the pirates have destroyed."

"We require no assistance in rebuilding our huts—"

"I was speaking of the land, Natahia. To restore it to what it was."

Her eyes widened slightly. The growers with her whispered among themselves with hopeful excitement, but she silenced them with a quick motion of her hand. "You have methods for doing so?"

"Yes. We can make your land fertile again. We can help you to produce crops quickly so that your people can be fed."

Natahia's voice suddenly sounded very old and feeble. "We have been eating the small animals and birds—it was repugnant, but necessary for survival."

"Our offer is unconditional. However, the offer to join the Federation remains open."

Natahia bowed her head for a moment; when she raised it again, her eyes had lost some of their proudness. "I have learned many things since the pirates forced us to flee to the caves in the mountains. If we had not banded together, we would certainly have starved. We have learned to be dependent."

"And is it such a bad thing?" Kirk asked.

"I cannot say that it is always bad, nor can I say that it is always good, for it often forces one to compromise one's belief. I would call it a necessary evil."

Kirk looked down at the scarred earth and thought of those who lay beneath it. "Sometimes, Natahia, we must do things we despise, in order to achieve a greater good."

"I must agree with you, Captain Kirk. I speak now for all the growers who have survived. We do not value technology or the weapons it has produced, but we do value our way of life, so much so that we will not permit other invaders to destroy it again. And so we shall compromise our beliefs to some extent in order to preserve them. We welcome the assistance of the Federation and wish to ally ourselves with it."

Captain's Log, Stardate 7008.4:

The *Enterprise* is leaving Aritani with two extra passengers: the Aritanian delegation to the Federation. Following the delivery of all diplomats to their appropriate destinations, we will proceed to Star Base Two for some long overdue shore leave.

Kirk turned off the recorder and turned to look at McCoy. The doctor stood watching Aritani turn slowly on the viewscreen.

"Slow day at the office, Bones?"

"Not much to do in sick bay these days," McCoy replied, keeping his eyes on the screen.

"A lovely place, wasn't it?" Kirk said softly.

"What? Oh . . . yes, I suppose it was."

Kirk gave up his attempt at conversation. McCoy had for once come to the bridge for something else . . . *she* was there, somewhere far below the surface, and this was the only way he had to say good-bye.

When Spock stepped off the turbolift, the captain and the doctor were too entranced by the viewscreen to notice. He walked over to Kirk's side and cleared his throat delicately.

Kirk glanced up. "What is it, Spock?"

"The Aritanian delegation has been properly welcomed aboard and escorted to their quarters, Captain."

"Good." Kirk sat up straight in his chair. "I have the feeling that this time the return trip from Aritani will be a little less eventful."

"I sincerely hope so, Captain." Spock turned to regard McCoy's faraway stare. "You have been uncharacteristically reticent as of late, Doctor."

Kirk winced. Surely Spock was aware of McCoy's feelings for Emma, and was capable of greater tact . . .

McCoy tore his gaze from the screen at last. "I suppose I have, Spock," he said with unusual seriousness.

"I think Spock misses his daily argument," Kirk said in an attempt to lighten the situation.

Spock did not acknowledge the captain's remark. "I can surmise the cause of your depression, Doctor, and while I am not insensitive to it, I feel that condolences are somewhat premature."

McCoy suddenly became alert. "What are you talking about, Spock?"

"Six fighter vessels are still unaccounted for, Doctor. I submit that Tanirius, or Dr. Saenz if you wish, was on one of them."

"How would you know?" McCoy struggled angrily against hope.

"It is a perfectly logical assumption, Doctor. The most likely candidates to evacuate the hangar in the seconds preceding its destruction would be those who knew it was going to explode."

McCoy sounded bitterly tired. "Or maybe just rats deserting what they figured was a sinking ship after the weapons room was destroyed. Do you think I haven't thought about it, Spock? But she would have let me know she was alive—"

Spock seemed to think for a moment before he

spoke again. "I rather doubt that they were rats, as you call them, Doctor, considering the fact that shortly before he left for his new assignment, Mr. Varth informed me that precisely six Federation sympathizers were working at the Romulan installation, including Tanirius."

A small spark of hope entered McCoy and slowly warmed. "Is that true, Spock?"

Spock gave a slight nod.

"But why wouldn't she tell me—why would she leave me to think that she was dead?"

"Perhaps it is necessary for her to be presumed dead, to protect her from the wrath of the Praetor."

The spark dimmed. "Then even if she *is* alive . . . she couldn't risk seeing me again."

"Not as Tanirius," said Spock, "or as Emma Saenz, but perhaps . . ."

McCoy actually smiled weakly at the Vulcan. "It'll never happen, Spock, but it's nice to think about." He squared his shoulders. "Guess I'd better get back to sick bay."

"I thought you didn't have any work," Kirk protested.

"Did I say that? I can't imagine what I must have been thinking of . . ." McCoy walked with a slightly brisker step to the turbolift and did not look back at the viewscreen again.

Kirk waited for the lift to close before turning to face his first officer. "Thank you."

Spock frowned in puzzlement. "For what, Captain?"

"For letting McCoy think she might still be alive. We Earthers have a word for it—compassion."

"Call it what you will," Spock replied stiffly, "considering the doctor's current mental state, I thought he should be made aware of the possibility—"

"Then what you said about Varth and the six sympathizers—that was true?"

Without changing his expression, Spock managed to convey the fact that he had been highly insulted. "I would not intentionally attempt to mislead the good doctor . . ."

Kirk sighed. "And every woman he meets, he'll be wondering if it could be her. You know, Emma Saenz was under orders to kill you, Spock, but she didn't, because she came to realize how much McCoy cared about you. And after what you just did for McCoy, I might almost be tempted to think that the affection was mutual."

Spock rose to his full height. "Captain, I scarcely think that the bridge is an appropriate place for such insulting accusations." He moved with cool dignity back to his station.

Kirk smiled and leaned forward to address the helmsman. "Take us out of orbit, Mr. Sulu."

And the blue orb on the screen grew smaller and smaller, until at last it faded from view.

COMPLETELY NEW

STAR TREK®

NOVELS

___MY ENEMY, MY ALLY
by Diane Duane
55446/$3.50

___THE FINAL REFLECTION
by John M. Ford
62230/$3.50

___CORONA
by Greg Bear
47390/$2.95

___THE TRELLISANE
CONFRONTATION
by David Dvorkin
46543/$2.95

___THE ABODE OF LIFE
by Lee Correy
47719/$2.95

___BLACK FIRE
by Sonni Cooper
61758/$3.50

___THE CONVENANT OF THE
CROWN
by Howard Weinstein
49297/$2.95

___THE ENTROPY EFFECT
by Vonda N. McIntyre
62229/$3.50

___THE TEARS OF THE SINGERS
by Melinda Snodgrass
50284/$3.50

___ISHMAEL
by Barbara Hambly
55427/$3.50

___UHURA'S SONG
by Janet Kagan
54730/$3.50

___THE KLINGON GAMBIT
by Robert E. Vardeman
62231/$3.50

___ THE PROMETHEUS DESIGN
by Sondra Marshak & Myrna
Culbreath
49299/$2.95

___ TRIANGLE
by Sondra Marshak & Myrna
Culbreath
49298/$2.95

___ WEB OF THE ROMULANS
by M.S. Murdock
60549/$3.50

___ YESTERDAY'S SON
by A.C. Crispin
60550/$3.50

___ MUTINY ON THE ENTERPRISE
by Robert E. Vardeman
60551/$3.50

___ THE WOUNDED SKY
by Diane Duane
60061/$3.50

___ THE VULCAN ACADEMY
MURDERS
by Jean Lorrah
50054/$3.50

___ KILLING TIME
by Della Vanttise
52488/$3.50

___ SHADOW LORD
by Laurence Yep
47392/$3.50

___ DWELLERS IN THE CRUCIBLE
by Margaret Wander Bonanno
60373/$3.50

___ PAWNS AND SYMBOLS
by Majliss Larson
55425/$3.50

___ MINDSHADOW
by J.M. Dillard
60756/$3.50

POCKET BOOKS, Department STN
1230 Avenue of the Americas, New York, N.Y. 10020

Please send me the books I have checked above. I am enclosing $_____
(please add 75¢ to cover postage and handling for each order. N.Y.S. and N.Y.C.
residents please add appropriate sales tax). Send check or money order—no cash
or C.O.D.'s please. Allow up to six weeks for delivery. For purchases over $10.00, you
may use VISA: card number, expiration date and customer signature must be
included.

NAME _____

ADDRESS _____

CITY _____ STATE/ZIP _____

753